Adria

BAD FOR LOVE

by

Adriane Leigh

BAD FOR LOVE

Adriane Leigh

"The whole time I was reading **Whiskey Girl** I felt like I was reading beautiful poetry. Fallon and Augusta's story will prove to you that **soulmates do exist** and that second chances are worth fighting for. **I loved this book so much!**" - **Aurora Rose Reynolds New York Times Bestselling Author**
★★★★★

"A **raw**, gritty second chance romance threaded with a country music theme about **first-time love**, second chances, regrets, **heartbreak** and a love that never ceased to burn despite everything that stood in its way. Adriane Leigh delivered a **beautiful slow burn** second chance romance that truly **made us feel** with twists that made our hearts plummet and soar." - **TotallyBooked Blog**
★★★★★

"With prose that is **beautiful and confident**, affecting without being maudlin--Whiskey Girl squeezed my heart while continuously bringing tears of joy to my eyes, and I had to take a very long, deep breath in the end to fully absorb all the emotions it left in me. I was **totally captivated** from the first page and it left me in **absolute awe of this author's talent**--every moment between these characters leapt from the page with **profound emotion**. This was undoubtedly one of the most moving books I've read in a long time." - **Natasha is a Book Junkie**
★★★★★

"An **unforgettable, epic love story** about two lost souls. Filled with raw emotion, this lyrical, all-the-feels masterpiece may catapult Adriane Leigh into the league of Colleen Hoover, Brittainy Cherry, and L.J. Shen. -- **Nelle L'Amour, New York Times Bestselling author of THAT MAN**
★★★★★

"6+ cliff diving, whiskey shot, hung over for days stars! Leigh reached out and grabbed me from the very first line, and never let go. The writing was **beautiful and captivating**, the characters were perfectly imperfect, and the story... well, it was **flawless**. Fallon and Augusta Belle's story is one that will be with me forever--it was **heart breaking, intense, swoon worthy, and raw**--

BAD FOR LOVE

everything I love in a story." - **AR Myles, Amazon Bestselling Author**

Adriane Leigh

He's bad news wrapped in a beautiful package.

The way his eyes flick up and down my form whenever I enter the room leaves little to the imagination. He's the definition of bad boy and my heart's worst nightmare, and he's made himself clear: he wants me. But not even his devilish grin can change the fact that I've already said yes once before to a man who brought me back to life when we were just kids.

But a lonely heart is a runaway train, and circumstances can turn from sweet to rotten overnight as rivalries and revenge light like kindling, and the flames are about to destroy more than just broken hearts.

Love pressed them hard,
as thirst presses the dying stag to the
stream.
Love dropped upon them from high
heaven,
as a hawk slipped after long hunger falls
right upon the bird.
And love will not be hidden.

~ *The Romance of Tristan and Isolde*

ONE

Georgia

"TOOK YOU LONG enough. How many potty breaks did you take?" My charming best friend leaned against his car door with a grin. He looked like a natural on the beach with flip-flops, cargos, and a bright green polo shirt. His bronzed skin and perfectly styled, sandy blond hair a clear indication that he took care to look good.

I took a few steps toward him and stopped, gazing up at the sprawling beach house. My eyes locked on the white shutters, the multiple decks, the wooden staircases, and weathered shingles—it took my breath away all over again. I closed my eyes and inhaled the salty sea breeze caressing my face and whirling my dark hair. The call of gulls that swooped overhead, a far cry from the sounds of the city that I'd just left.

"Earth to Georgia," Silas called, throwing an empty Styrofoam coffee cup at my head.

"I stopped for coffee a while ago and called

Drew."

"How's that hussy doing?" Silas mumbled as he pulled a duffel bag out of the back seat of his car.

"You can ask her tomorrow," I grinned.

"What? Fuck!" Silas swore as he knocked his head on the doorframe of his car. I hadn't told him that I was going to invite Drew.

"She's bringing her new man candy."

"Of course she is."

I laughed and faked a punch on his bicep before heading back to my car and getting my own bag. "Ready, sport?"

"Enough with the macho names," he grumbled, in a sour mood no doubt because Drew would be up in his business for the rest of the summer.

"Fine, cupcake. Let's go in," I teased as he followed me up the first set of steps to the front door.

The beach house was built on wood pilings that elevated the first floor nearly twenty feet above the sand. The ground level on the beach was semi-enclosed and served as storage space. The house was less than a hundred yards off the water and surrounded by rolling dunes and swaying grass. When the realtor walked us through the house, she assured us that the water rarely made it up this far on the beach, but the house would be protected if it did. Hurricanes were another issue entirely and she'd suggested I have a hurricane safety inspection done to make sure the house could withstand hurricane-force winds.

I unlocked the front door and we stepped into an open space that featured a spacious living room with French doors that looked out over another grand deck and the ocean. Water and waves dominated my vision. To the left was a large kitchen and to the right were the guest bath and a hallway leading to two bedrooms. Beyond the kitchen, another hallway led to three bedrooms and the stairway to the second floor. Each first-floor bedroom had an en suite bathroom, which made arrangements for this summer much more comfortable. Drew and I were certainly capable of logging time in the bathroom, but Silas was on a whole other level—he could spend hours in front of a mirror spiking his hair with half a dozen different products.

A large island divided the kitchen and living room, and the house was completely white walls and worn wood floors. The realtor had suggested I refinish the floors, but I adored their charm. Whoever had designed the house was inspired by the simple beauty of the beach. I had fallen in love at first sight.

Walking across the room, I threw open the French doors and felt the warm wind wash over my skin. I wanted these doors open the entire summer to let the ocean breeze waft in and keep the dust bunnies and stale air at bay.

"I'm going to throw this stuff in my room."

Silas headed down a hallway.

"The corner room is mine, Silas," I called after him. He shot me a dirty look. It was the largest room on this floor with the best views. "Advantage of being the owner," I grinned.

The house had two floors, but the three bedrooms on the second floor were in rough shape and I'd need to call a carpenter in to replace flooring and update the plumbing.

While the bedrooms on the main floor were livable, they could use a fresh coat of paint and some modern updates, just one of the summer jobs I'd roped Drew into helping me with. While Silas said he would help, I knew his version of help was more like overseeing while sipping a drink with a little umbrella in his hand. He was good for opinions though–he had plenty of those.

I continued to walk around the living room, opening all the windows before lifting the sheet off the ratty, old couch. There was some wicker furniture tucked in a corner that was in need of a paint job, but I liked it and planned on leaving it.

"I'm starving. Let's order something." Silas ambled back into the kitchen. "Stop working, we just got here."

"That's why we're here, Silas. Let's get our stuff hauled in and then we'll talk dinner."

"Fine, Mom." Silas always complained that I was too responsible, but on the flip side he was entirely too irresponsible, making us a perfect fit.

Later that night we sat on the couch eating pizza and drinking beer.

"I'm dying without TV, love." Silas took another slice out of the box between us. I smiled at his pet name for me. He'd begun to call me that shortly after we met our freshmen year at Duke. I'd assumed he called everyone that, but I soon found out I was the only one who'd earned that affectionate epithet. It made me feel safe and protected, loved. Silas soon after became a part of me. He was there whenever the pain became too much to bear, listened with open ears, sat with me quietly when I needed silence, and started calling me "love," something that had helped warm my frozen heart.

"I'll work on it tomorrow, but you should know that I believe you have an entertainment addiction." I crooked a grin at him.

"I fully admit to that. If there were a twelve-step program I'd be there."

"I bet." I rolled my eyes. "You okay with Drew being here this summer?"

"Do I have a choice?" He scowled through a bite of pizza.

"No. Maybe you could come to an understanding," I trailed off.

"Doubtful. When will she be here exactly?" He traipsed to the kitchen and grabbed us both another beer. The boy was absolutely delectable. If he didn't like other boys, I would, without a doubt, have been in trouble. I'd have fallen for his mischievous grin and sexy dimples, and he would have broken my naïve heart.

"Thanks." I took the beer. "I talked to her

earlier—she and *Gavin* will be here tomorrow afternoon." I emphasized his name.

"Gavin, huh? Sounds like a tool."

I shook my head at Silas. "Well, apparently he's a hot tool, with a big tool." Silas and I erupted into a fit of giggles.

"Can't wait." His brown eyes sparked with amusement. "Did you talk to Kyle?"

"Yeah." I took another sip.

"And how is he?" Silas watched me with a thoughtful expression.

"He's…okay."

"Still not happy about this summer's arrangements?" Silas asked.

"Not particularly," I picked the pepperoni off my pizza.

"Are you guys going to be okay?"

"Sure. He'll get over it."

"What if he doesn't?" Silas continued to watch me. I was fast becoming uncomfortable with his scrutiny.

"He will. It's just for the summer."

"And what about next summer?"

"I don't know, Silas. I don't want to talk about it. I'm here and he's there. That's it. That's what it is." I jumped off the couch and headed for the kitchen to dispose of my paper plate. Kyle was an up and coming attorney in D.C. working seventy plus hours a week. That left me alone a lot. Or in recent months, Silas and I snuggled up on the couch instead, watching movies together long past our bedtime.

"I didn't mean to upset you, love." He wrapped his arms around my waist and set his chin on my shoulder.

"I know. I just don't want to talk about it. We'll be fine. We've always been fine." I plastered a half-hearted smile on my face. "I'm exhausted."

"Okay." Silas regarded me with somber eyes. "If you need anything, just holler. I'll come running like the valiant knight in shining armor that I am."

"Brandishing your blow dryer?" I chortled.

"Absolutely." He grinned before gathering our empty beer bottles. I slid the pizza box into the empty fridge and then flicked off the light before we headed down the hall to our respective bedrooms. Silas paused outside his door.

"Are you really going to be okay, love?"

Silas knew sleeping in a new place often triggered nightmares. "Yes."

I was never good at lying.

"Come on." He wrapped his arm around mine and headed for my bedroom where we curled up together as I tried to swallow the burning lump of tears that fought for release.

TWO

Georgia

"HONEY, I'M HOME!" Drew's voice sang as she opened the front door the following afternoon. Earlier that morning I'd scrubbed out the fridge, then gone to the grocery store to stock up on food and drinks. I'd also bought cheap utensils and dishes and was now arranging the kitchen. Silas had just finished washing the main floor windows and was sweeping when my dark-haired pixie of a best friend arrived.

I set down the glasses in my hands, skidded to the front door, and wrapped Drew in my arms.

"God, G, I've missed you so much." She held me tightly as we rocked back and forth. Tears sprang to my eyes as I inhaled her familiar perfume.

"Me too. I'm so glad you came. Your hair is shorter." I held her at arm's length and took in her layered brown bob. "I love it."

Drew was obstinate, opinionated, and self-centered, but she, much like Silas, had the ability to set me straight. She told it like it was unapologetically. She and Silas were also the two most hilarious people I'd ever met, so unlike me I couldn't help but be drawn to them.

"Drew," Silas said behind me with a curt nod. I rolled my eyes.

"Silas." She rolled her bright blue eyes before a smile broke out across her face. For all their bickering I think they really enjoyed each other.

"Great house. Give me a tour?" Drew looped her arm in mine and we headed down the closest hallway.

"I'll take you to your room first." She dropped a bag off in the bedroom I was giving her before we made our way through the sprawling house. At each room we talked paint colors and design schemes. My degree was in hospitality with a focus on interior design–I was in my element. After the tour we made our way back to the kitchen and found Silas making margaritas.

"It's a proper girls' night already," Drew said as Silas poured the frothy drink into glasses. "Thanks for letting Gavin come, Georgia. I know it's weird since you haven't met him, but he's great. You'll love him."

"Can't wait to meet him." I sipped the cold drink.

"Tristan's great too, and off-the-charts hot." She rested her hip against the counter and took a drink.

"Who's Tristan?" I asked.

"Is he single? How old?" Silas buzzed, suddenly all ears.

"Twenty-seven, single, and *straight*." Drew shot Silas a warning look.

"Perfect, and not a problem." Silas winked at her.

"Tristan is Gavin's best friend. They're in business together and working on a project they need to log hours on this summer. Plus he's going through this thing—so I told him that you wouldn't mind if he tagged along."

"Drew." I frowned.

"What kind of thing?" Silas cocked an eyebrow.

"Lady trouble. He just needs to get away for a while, put his past in the past kind of thing. You're not mad are you, Georgia?" Drew pouted.

"Kind of weird that I don't even know him..."

"Do you think I would invite a lunatic? Gavin's known him since they were kids."

"Technically I don't even know Gavin," I reminded her. She only pouted in response.

"He's great. They both are, plus the more muscle we have here this summer the less we'll have to do." She tapped her temple as if she'd had a stroke of brilliance. I heaved an exasperated sigh. That was Drew...living in the moment and getting us into situations we probably shouldn't be in. Maybe it had been a good thing she'd been ten hours away in Jacksonville the last few years.

"When are they coming?"

"Hopefully soon," Silas said flirtatiously. Drew shot him a scowl.

"This weekend. Gavin's driving and Tristan's sailing up the coast." She wiggled her eyebrows at me.

"He has a boat?" I asked.

"Oh, that could make for an interesting evening," Silas said.

"Straight, Silas."

"I know, I know. Has never stopped me in the past though." He winked at her.

Later that night we found ourselves seated on the porch sipping margaritas, catching up. It felt good to laugh and reminisce about old times. I'd missed having Drew in my everyday life. While we talked often on the phone, it was a poor substitute for being together in person. Silas was my best friend, and I loved him just like a brother, but it was so good to have girl time. I hadn't realized how much I'd missed that too. Apparently a lot of things had fallen out of my life over time and I hadn't realized it.

"Shopping tomorrow?" Drew suggested.

"Sounds great. There are some antique stores in town I'd like to hit first." Drew and I had talked about the overall design of the house and how to maintain the cottage feel with modern updates. First we needed to start with the living room since this is where we'd be all summer. A couch was at the top of my list, as well as overstuffed chairs, end tables and an entertainment center where we could tuck a TV that would still blend with the décor. I also needed to stop at the hardware store for sandpaper and paint to refinish the beautiful wicker set that was left behind.

We continued to drink while the tittering increased as the pitcher of margaritas dwindled.

"So when will we be graced with the presence of Kyle?" Drew inquired.

"I know, right?" Silas huffed.

"Hey." I shot them a glare.

"Kyle's a douche, love." Silas lifted his glass and took another drink. I whipped my head around and narrowed my eyes before a laugh escaped my throat.

"Total douche." Drew laughed. "So is he coming down this summer?" She watched me intently.

"Sure, probably. Don't call my boyfriend a douche." I stumbled over the last word.

"Is he mad that you bought this place?" Drew raised an eyebrow at me.

"Oh yeah." Silas' eyes grew wide. "He's pissed. They hardly talk."

"Silas." I whipped a throw pillow at him, causing his drink to splash in his lap.

"Is he that mad?" Drew asked softly. I chewed on my bottom lip and avoided her gaze.

"No, he's not mad, he's just not happy." I picked at my nails, avoiding the gazes of my two best friends.

"Do you think he'll come around?" Drew asked.

"I don't know." I focused on the cuticle of one nail.

"Douche," Silas muttered under his breath. All the drinks had caught up to me and my mood was suddenly crashing.

"I don't want to talk about it. I'm going to bed. Be ready bright and early, sunshine." I pointed at Drew.

I brushed my teeth before stripping off my jeans and crawled into bed in my tank top and underwear. I nestled into the pillow as my thoughts drifted over the past few years of my life. A few minutes later I heard my door creak open. Drew's silhouette was bathed in the light of the hallway. She closed the door behind her and silently curled up in the bed behind me.

"Are you okay?" Her voice was heartbreakingly sad.

"Yes," I whispered, failing to keep my voice from cracking.

"Doesn't sound like it," she said.

"I am." I hugged my pillow tightly.

"Have you been to see them lately?"

"No."

"You should. I think it helps."

"Really? Silas said–"

"I don't care what Silas says, what do *you* say?"

I twisted my fists together in a grip so tight the knuckles faded to the color of bone china. "It feels like I'm dwelling…"

"Did you talk to Kyle?"

"He thinks I should go. Or at least not be so quick to stop."

"I agree with him. For once." She pushed me playfully before nuzzling deeper into the pillow we were sharing.

"I'm sorry I haven't been around, Georgia."

I sucked in a sharp breath and closed my eyes as tears stung my eyelids. "I know." I took another deep breath and tried to fight the memories that threatened to invade the dark.

* * *

THE NEXT MORNING I dragged Drew and Silas out of bed at ten, and the three of us headed to town for shopping. We picked up coffee then wandered the streets, in and out of antique stores and boutiques. Our first purchase was a love-at-first-sight large, cream couch. We came across some eggshell blue and cream-striped chairs that complemented it. With the big items out of the way, we focused on smaller, decorative things. Silas spotted a weathered, wrought iron and glass side table, and I found a beautiful, vintage, mirrored lamp to place on top of it. My vision for perfect "modern cottage chic" was coming together.

With bright sunshine and a cool breeze, I breathed deeply and thought, at this moment, I was the happiest I'd ever been; life was simple as I strolled around a small seaside town with my two best friends. Tears pricked my eyes, thankful for both of them.

After lunch we went to the hardware store for paint samples. Silas and Drew went a little wild, bickering and stuffing dozens of colorful paint chips into my oversized purse. Kyle and I had moved into a beautiful, furnished apartment in D.C. where not a single thing needed to be done, so I was embracing starting from scratch with the beach house.

We headed home mid-afternoon to meet the furniture delivery truck. They hauled the old couch away and brought the new furniture into the living room, along with the oversized plasma TV Silas had insisted on. Once the furniture was in, Silas, Drew, and I spent time debating the placement of the smaller items. I cracked beers for the three of us and smiled as I watched them argue over everything. This summer would be an exercise in patience between the two of them to be sure.

THREE
Georgia

THE NEXT FEW days went by in fast-forward as college years were rewound and replayed. The only piece missing was Kyle. Once a permanent fixture of our group, when he'd finished his bachelor's degree and entered law school, he'd been all but absent. We'd become just a threesome.

Late Saturday morning, Drew and I were decked out in oversized shirts and paint-splattered shorts as we finished painting the first guest bedroom. We'd decided on a light shade of gray with pale yellow curtains and accents. Silas had just let the technician from the cable company out and joined us in the guest bedroom to chat as we worked.

We were starting to clean up when a heavy knock rattled the front door.

"I'll get it." Drew skipped out of the room. A few seconds later Silas and I heard her shriek, "Gavin!"

I scrunched my nose–the guys weren't

supposed to be here until tomorrow. I frowned, looking down at my paint-covered clothes. It would have been nice to be more presentable, but we were here to work this summer, so I wasn't overly concerned.

Silas and I stepped into the kitchen and found Drew passionately kissing a guy with broad shoulders and bulging biceps. Her fingers wound through his short, dark hair and legs wrapped around his waist, his hands holding her bottom firmly. It was slightly indecent for company, but Drew was never one for appropriate behavior.

Behind them a supermodel sexy guy stood with an amused grin on his face. Silas released a low whistle. I elbowed him with a grin, then looked back at our unexpected summer visitor. His golden hair was a bit too long, curling around his ears and skimming his eyebrows, and recklessly styled, as if he'd run his fingers through it all day. Bright green eyes mischievously assessed the couple standing in front of him. I made note of his wide shoulders and the slim cut of his shirt that hinted at a narrow waist. He wore dark khaki cargo shorts with a canvas belt that hung deliciously low on his hips. Bronzed skin and leather flip-flops finished off his casual vibe. I averted my eyes before he caught me ogling.

"I'm Silas." My decidedly gay best friend stepped around the indecent couple with an outstretched hand and flirtatious grin. I rolled my eyes. If Silas kept up these antics all summer, my eyes would be permanently set in the back of my head.

"Tristan." He shook Silas' hand and gave him a friendly nod.

"Bring your girlfriend?" Silas tossed him a carefree smile.

"Uh, no. Don't have one at the moment," Tristan answered, seemingly unfazed by Silas' overt attention.

"I'm Georgia." I held my hand out to Tristan. "I own the place," gesturing around the room with my free hand.

"Hi." He gave me a bright grin. "I'm Tristan, this is Gavin." He slapped his oversized friend on the shoulder. Gavin pulled away from Drew and gave her a lusty half smile before giving her one last peck on the lips.

"He's usually not so…affectionate," Tristan smirked.

"Well, Drew usually *is* that affectionate," I laughed.

A low chuckle escaped his throat as his eyes flashed in amusement. That easygoing chuckle had butterflies flitting around my stomach.

Silas was apparently affected too because his grin spread as he looped his arm around Tristan's elbow. "Let me show you your room."

I shook my head as Drew hopped out of Gavin's arms, smiling. "Gavin, this is Georgia. Georgia, Gavin. And the guy manhandling your best friend is Silas."

Adriane Leigh

A chortle escaped Gavin's throat as he extended a hand to me. "Nice to meet you." He wore cargo shorts like Tristan, sneakers, and a fitted blue shirt. The sculpted muscle of his biceps strained the tee, indicating he worked out.

"Do you want anything to drink? Beer, tea, water?" I offered.

"A beer would be fantastic. That drive was brutal, as was listening to Tristan moan about his latest love-gone-wrong after I picked him up at the marina."

I handed him a beer as Tristan returned to the room.

"I had to listen to you talk about Drew, so don't play like I was the only one doing the moaning. 'This summer's going to be great, man. I can't wait to see Drew in a bikini. I'm going to fu—'" Tristan was mocking Gavin in a goofy voice before I cut him off.

"Okay…beer, Tristan?" I asked.

"Sure." He crooked a grin at me and my heart thudded a few extra beats in my chest as I popped the cap and handed it to him.

"Thanks, Georgia." My name slid past his lips like warm honey. He smiled before sliding the pad of his thumb across my temple. My eyes widened, my feet rooted on the spot.

"Paint." He pulled his hand away and showed me the gray paint on his thumb. With that one gesture I knew he was trouble wrapped up in a sexy, charming package.

"Oh." The air escaped my lungs in a whoosh.

"Thanks," I whispered, turning away from him for the sake of thinking straight. "I'm going to clean up. Nice to meet you." I hightailed it out of the kitchen with Silas and Drew in a fit of laughter behind me.

"I could use a shower too," I heard Gavin say to Drew suggestively. A silly giggle escaped her throat as she and Gavin disappeared into her room behind me.

FOUR

Tristan

Gavin maneuvered the truck down the narrow drive and we turned a corner before the landscape opened up and a sprawling beach house came into view.

I whistled low under my breath.

"Yeah." He paused as we took in the house. "Drew said it was something."

"The quintessential beach house," I mumbled before jumping out of the cab of the truck and stretching my arms above my head. The cool breeze ruffled my hair and tossed it into my eyes. Fucking hair. I needed a haircut. Another thing that should have been done before I made a snap decision to take off on my boat and sail up the coast, destination this little inlet of North Carolina.

Unfortunately, time hadn't been on my side when I'd left. Sophie had morphed into a raging stalker and was knocking on my door all hours of the night, drunk and wanting to fuck, or cuddle, or anything I was willing to throw at her, which after a few nights together, I decided would be nothing because that girl was a clinger. I couldn't take it another day. Apparently she didn't take well to a friends with benefits kind of arrangement.

Gavin tossed my heavy duffel bag and I caught it just before it slammed into my chest.

"Shithead," I grumbled as he led the way up the stairs. He hustled, taking the steps two at a time. I knew he was anxious to see Drew. A few days was the longest they'd been apart in their short relationship and from the way he talked you'd think his dick was about to fall off from lack of use. I only hoped their room was out of earshot of mine.

Gavin knocked on the door and then stepped in. I heard footsteps pounding on wooden floors and then was blindsided when the petite form of Drew launched into Gavin. An *oomph* escaped his lungs before their lips connected and I heard wet tongues and small moans.

"Seriously?" I said with a roll of my eyes. Gavin's hands were already firmly gripping her ass and Drew's were tugging and twisting in his hair.

Please, dear God let their room be across the house from mine. If I had to listen to them all summer I would be spending a lot of time on my boat.

I watched them all but hump each other in

front of me before I sensed someone else enter the room. My eyes dragged across the open kitchen to land on a pair of deep brown ones watching the couple in front of me. My mind registered someone standing next to her but I couldn't be bothered to look. All I saw was long, brown hair thrown back in a messy ponytail, stray tendrils dusting her cheekbones and curling around her neck. Her full lips were curved in a frown as she watched the couple making out in the middle of the room.

I grinned because I knew already this summer was going to be interesting to say the least.

Not only would I have to contend with the Gavin/Drew fuck fest that was sure to commence as of today, but I'd be living under the same roof as this beautiful creature all summer. Somehow it had escaped me that the girl who owned the beach house was a knockout. No wonder Gavin had given me the rundown on steering clear of her before we arrived. No man in his fucking mind could stay away from this girl.

Fuck him.

Fuck me.

Why had he said she was hands off this summer? I'd only half been listening to his lecture...

I could see right now this girl was anything but average. I knew with one glance she wasn't the type that wore her dresses a few inches too short and fuck-me heels that begged to be wrapped around my neck.

There was something about her. Something that said she was...more. More everything. She had more depth. More sensuality. An unassuming beauty. She was stunning and she didn't even know it.

I couldn't tear my eyes away, but I knew I'd look like a tool if I didn't.

The guy next to her stepped up to me and thrust a hand out. He introduced himself as Silas before he asked, "Bring your girlfriend?"

I lifted an amused eyebrow before informing him that I was unattached. I liked him. I liked his forward demeanor and friendly smile. What I didn't like was that he seemed close with the gorgeous girl at his side who still remained nameless. They exchanged a glance and her lips tugged up in a small grin.

Fuck me if she wasn't even more breathtaking when she smiled.

I needed to find a way to get her to smile at me that way. I wanted to be the reason that smile tipped her lips, not this idiot. And then I instantly felt bad. This guy didn't look like an idiot at all. Although there was something between them, some connection I didn't understand. They had a way of communicating wordlessly, and I was dying to know what they were saying.

"I'm Georgia," she introduced herself with a hand shake.

The grin grew wide on my face. I offered her my name and then addressed the couple dry humping beside me. We exchanged a few words and then she laughed, the tone low, an amused smile lifting her lips. The beautiful lips that I wanted to run the pad of my thumb along right before I pressed mine to hers. Fuck she was beautiful and I was getting hard just thinking of all the things we could do together without our clothes on.

My eyes flicked down her lean form. She wore an oversized t-shirt splattered with paint and a pair of shorts that ended high on her thighs. I took in the bronze skin and shapely curve of her legs. She wasn't tall, but not short either, the perfect height to dip my head and take her lips with mine. My eyes landed back on hers and my smile widened as I thought of yanking the band out of her hair and watching it cascade around her shoulders. I wanted to fist the thick strands in my hands and hold her in place while she moaned my name in pleasure.

Fuck.

I couldn't keep on this train of thought or I was going to have a very obvious problem below the belt to deal with.

"Let me show you your room." Silas looped an arm in mine and led me out of the kitchen. I allowed myself to be ferried off by the guy who was putting off decidedly gay vibes. That was cool, maybe he wouldn't be competition like I'd originally thought. Or maybe he was bi and he was getting in her pants.

Why had Gavin said she was off limits

again?

Silas guided me into a guest room. I tossed my bag on the floor and addressed him. "And Gavin's room would be...?"

"Other hallway off the kitchen. Across the house," he answered with a smile.

"Perfect." I murmured before I heard my name mentioned in the kitchen. No way was I going to let the over-muscled fuck that was my best friend get a word in without me around to defend myself.

I walked into the kitchen with Gavin talking about all the issues I'd been having with Sophie. Jesus, five minutes in and he was already giving Georgia a bad impression of me.

"I had to listen to you talk about Drew so don't play like I was the only one doing the moaning. 'This summer's going to be great man. I can't wait to see Drew in a bikini—I'm going to fu—'" I mocked Gavin before Georgia's cheeks grew pink and she cut me off to ask if I wanted a beer. Okay, so she embarrassed easily. I loved that. I made a note to do whatever it took to have that beautiful glow highlight her cheeks again.

She passed me a beer and I flashed her a flirty, crooked smile that I reserved for women only. I knew the power my smile had and I'd used it often on the opposite sex. It had served me well, and just as I'd hoped, it worked on her too. Her pupils dilated and she pressed her lips together.

"Thanks, Georgia." Christ, that was a great

name. It was perfect for her—all wild, unassuming beauty. Before I could even think my arm rose and I slid the pad of my thumb across the skin at her hairline. I did it just as much to lift the small drop of gray paint from her skin as I did to feel her soft flesh against mine. Her eyes widened as she took a deep breath.

Fuck.

She was just as affected as I was.

I could see it in her eyes.

In every move her body made.

Even if she didn't know it yet, she was responding to me in some primal way.

"Paint," I whispered as I finally pulled my hand away.

"Oh," she said all throaty and breathlessly. Her voice caused the blood to hum in my veins. The desire to hear that sound again while I was inside her had my dick hardening.

She turned and mumbled something about cleaning up and then darted out of the kitchen. Now all I could think about was her wet body all lush and soaped up in the shower. God damn Gavin for telling me this girl was off limits.

"I could use a shower too," Gavin said suggestively before Drew giggled.

And so the fuck fest was about to begin. First stop: the shower.

Thank fuck their room was across the house from mine.

FIVE

Georgia

I scrubbed my skin raw in the shower trying to remove the paint, then slid a brush through my long, chestnut hair, dusted my cheeks with some blush, and accented my oversized, brown eyes with a hint of mascara. I threw on cut-offs and a tank top and made my way to the kitchen to find Silas and Tristan watching ESPN over beers. A moan came from the room down the hallway and I surmised that Gavin and Drew were still enjoying their reunion. I shuddered and grabbed a bottle of wine as I realized the soundtrack of my summer would include moans emanating from Drew's bedroom.

"I thought I would make dinner tonight. Manicotti okay with you guys?" I tossed out to the living room as I dug for a corkscrew.

"Sounds great," Tristan said next to my shoulder. "Let me get that for you." He took the corkscrew from my hand and worked the cork.

"Thanks," I said, pulling ricotta, eggs, and

milk out of the refrigerator and oversized shells from the cupboard.

"Do you need help?" Tristan rested a hip against the counter. His casual stance and half smile sent tingles running across my skin.

"There's a jar of homemade marinara in the pantry if you want to get it."

"Sure. I've never had homemade manicotti. Are you Italian?" he asked while digging through the pantry for the sauce.

"Uh, no. I just like to cook." I dumped the ingredients for the cheesy filling into a bowl. "The marinara is my mom's recipe."

He nodded as he twisted the cap off the jar.

I stirred quietly and shot a look over my shoulder, praying that Silas would join us in the kitchen and break up the silence. He was engrossed in his phone though, so he probably wasn't even aware.

"You live in D.C., right?" Tristan set the tomato and thyme scented sauce next to me.

"Yep." *Keep your answers short. Don't encourage him.*

"What do you do there?" He opened the box of manicotti shells and set them on the counter.

"I managed a boutique hotel."

"Managed? You're not going back after the summer's over?"

"No, I have some money saved to get me through until I can rent this out next year." I dug through a cupboard for a pan. "You live in Jacksonville?" I poured some of the marinara sauce into the baking dish.

"Born and raised." A small smile played across his lips as he watched me.

"What do you do there?" I scooped the cheesy mixture into the shells and aligned them in the dish.

"Gavin and I own a cyber security company. I work from home, my boat, or a beach on the North Carolina coast." A lazy smile spread across his face.

"Nice."

"Yeah, allows for a lot of flexibility." A roguish glint sparked in his eyes. My breath caught for a moment before I looked back to the pasta. My mind played over the strong features of his face. The sharp angle of his jaw, the way one side of his mouth lifted in a charming grin. He had the deepest green eyes I'd ever seen and sandy brown hair layered with golden streaks, probably from all that time spent on the boat. My mind soaked up the memory of his handsome face like it was starved for his beauty.

Kyle. Remember Kyle. Tristan is a flirt. Don't forget that, Georgia.

"Georgia is a beautiful name. Any meaning behind it?" My name sounded lyrical and sexy rolling off his lips. I had to stifle a groan.

"Use that on all the girls?" The words tumbled from my lips before I could sensor them.

"What?" He tilted his head in the most endearing fashion.

"Sorry, never mind. No meaning, my parents just liked it I guess." I poured the rest of the marinara on top of the filled pasta shells.

"What about Tristan? It's different..." I murmured as thoughts rattled around in my head.

"Tristan, yeah. My mom studied literature in college. 'Tristan and Isolde' was her favorite story, star-crossed lovers traveling the world to find each other." A sheepish grin lifted his lips.

"That's beautiful." My eyes were lost in his mossy green depths for a few beats longer than acceptable for a girl with a boyfriend back home. "So the wine's had time to breathe. Do you want a glass?" I stretched on my tiptoes to reach the wine glasses.

"That would be great," his voice lowered an octave from behind me. I grabbed two glasses and Tristan poured the velvety red liquid into them.

"There's a vineyard up the coast from here. We should go this summer," Tristan said.

I coughed on the bittersweet sip sliding down my throat as my eyebrows shot up in surprise. Was he asking me out?

"Yeah, maybe I can buy a few cases to keep here for guests. I'm sure Silas would be down, too."

"Silas is down for anything," my best friend said as he sauntered into the kitchen and slipped an arm around my waist. I rolled my eyes at the sexual innuendo.

"Need help with anything, love?" Silas slipped my wine glass out of my hand and took a sip. I glanced at Tristan who was watching us with intent.

"No, just putting the pasta in the oven. Forty minutes 'til we eat."

"Sounds great." Silas passed my glass back to me empty.

I scowled at him. "Wine, Silas?"

"Would love some." He grinned at me happily. I grabbed another glass and poured more wine for him and myself.

"Tristan mentioned there's a vineyard up the coast and we should go."

"Sounds great." Silas plopped down on a barstool with his wine in hand before another low moan filtered down the hallway.

"So who's going to tell them dinner's nearly ready?" I scrunched my nose, not at all eager to volunteer. Just then a whimper floated into the kitchen along with a few *yes…yes…yeses.*

A sexy chuckle escaped Tristan's throat. "Sounds like they're about done," he said, taking another sip of his wine. Heat flashed to my cheeks at Drew and Gavin's love fest down the hall.

A few minutes later Drew sashayed out of her room, Gavin's hand in hers and a dopey look on her face. Gavin wore a happy grin and raised his eyebrows when he caught Tristan's gaze. I rolled my eyes at the unspoken macho gloating that passed between them. Damn Drew and her insistence on bringing her latest man candy to moan and groan with all summer.

"That's the best manicotti I've ever had." Gavin rested his feet on the railing of the porch. We were lounging on the deck overlooking the ocean after dinner. Beer bottles, wine glasses, laughter, and easy conversation floated between us. Dinner had been a success—Gavin ate three helpings alone.

"Glad you liked it," I said as Silas lifted the wine bottle and poured more into my glass as well as his own. Drew was perched on Gavin's lap with one arm draped around his neck, her other hand holding a wine glass. Gavin caressed her thigh with one hand while holding a beer in the other. I watched and felt a yearning in the pit of my stomach for Kyle.

Silas sat in a lounge chair and I on the floor leaning against his legs. Tristan was across from us, a relaxed grin tipping his lips. The setting sun glinted off the golden streaks in his hair. I wanted to run my fingers through his tousled locks. My eyes traveled from the high cheekbones and the stubbled jaw to the neckline of his shirt. I wondered what it would feel like to run my fingers along that delicious jawline that looked like it was cut in stone and trail my tongue from his collarbone up his neck and land at the smooth skin under his ear.

"Georgia?" Drew nudged me with her bare foot.

"Huh?" My eyes bolted to the dark green

depths that were watching me thoughtfully. Damn, he'd caught me.

"Distracted?" Drew arched an eyebrow at me.

"No." I took a sip of my wine to divert myself from the Drew inquisition.

"Gavin asked when you were hoping to start renting out the house."

"It would be great if I could get some people in before the end of the season, but if it doesn't happen until next, that's okay."

Gavin nodded in response.

"We should go out tonight. Wilmington has a few clubs," Silas spoke up from behind me.

"Yes, let's go out. I want to dance." Drew wiggled in Gavin's lap and nipped at his lips. He slid his hand further up her thigh to land at her hip.

"Looks like that's not all you want to do," I smirked.

"Shut it." Drew admonished. "What do you say, G?"

"I'm in for the night. But you guys should go," I replied.

"I'm not going without you."

"Don't be such a downer, love." Silas shook my shoulders playfully.

A giggle escaped my throat as the wine's effect fizzed around my brain. "Next time I will. Promise."

"Party pooper." Silas frowned when I turned to him.

"Did you just call me a party pooper?"

"If the shoe fits, love." he said before Rihanna's *Rude Boy* chimed from his phone. "Oh, something more interesting may have just developed." He slid from his chair and answered the phone in a flirty voice. Silas had countless guys he was talking to at any given time. I'd overheard more than a few sexy phone calls that had me blushing at the memory.

I turned back to Drew and found her making out with Gavin. He'd set down his beer and both hands were caressing her body—from her legs, up her torso, around her back, and back down.

"I'm going to take a walk," I mumbled as I stood.

"I'll join you." Tristan followed me down the steps to the beach. Thoughts blurred across the landscape of my brain as I sought an excuse to bow out. *Don't get wrapped up in this charming stranger.*

"Thanks for letting Gavin and I tag along this summer. He's not much company now, but once you get to know him, he's a pretty cool guy."

"Sure. Drew would probably have driven me insane if she'd had to be separated from him all summer." I took a sip of the fruity pinot coloring my glass.

"Well, whatever the reason you said yes, I appreciate it. It's great to get away for a while. It's also the farthest I've sailed the boat, so that was a great experience."

"How was the trip up?" I could see a small

smile playing on his lips as he watched me.

"Pretty good. I'm glad Gavin decided to drive—he's a pain in the ass on a boat." He brought the glass of wine to his lips and I watched his throat move as he swallowed, thinking again of running my tongue up the line of his neck. Everything about him was unbelievably sensual.

He brought the glass down and held it lightly in his right hand, his thumb caressing the rim slowly. The thought of his fingers tracing across my sensitive skin...God, every movement he made seemed carnal. Each glance oozed with sex, like lava seeping into my bones and turning them to molten jelly.

Oh please, Georgia. He's a ladies' man. Every single move is calculated, like an African cat moving in for the kill.

"Gavin's not experienced?" I shook the erotic thoughts from my brain and continued the conversation.

"Oh, he's experienced," he crooked a grin my way with amusement dancing in his eyes, "but with sailing, no."

I laughed. "Are you experienced? With sailing, I mean?" Oh my God, was I flirting with him? I needed to clear my thoughts of this ridiculously sexy man. My cheeks flushed, a little from the wine and mostly from the delectable guy walking beside me.

"Master sailor." One corner of his mouth lifted salaciously. My stomach did a traitorous flip-flop. I turned to watch the silver rays of moonlight reflecting off the water. We walked down the beach in silence. The wet sand beneath my feet was cool and soft, the waves occasionally lapping my toes with the still-too-cool May water. Tristan laughed and shook his head every time I ran from them.

"Trade places then." I maneuvered and gave him a playful shove into the cold water. As soon as my hand connected with his bicep, fire flared through my fingertips. My hand tightened for a breathless moment before I let go. The giggle died in my throat when I thought of the ramifications of this connection I'd had with him since we'd met—dangerous things could happen this summer.

"God, that is cold." His eyes washed over me with a laugh. I tried to relax and tell myself to stay away from him to avoid the flips in my stomach whenever he was close.

"Everything okay?" he asked.

"Yeah, just thinking about things."

He nodded before taking another sip of wine. "Are you and Silas...a thing?" he asked without looking at me. I coughed on the liquid going down my throat.

"Uh, no. Not ever. Never," I laughed.

"It seems...complicated."

"It's not. He's like my brother...my family, for all intents and purposes. His family kicked him out at sixteen when he told them he was gay and he hasn't spoken to them since. He's just always been there." I shrugged thoughtfully.

"You've known him for that long?"

"No. We met in college. He's from Utah. His parents are pretty religious; they didn't take well to a gay son. His grandma in Raleigh took him in. He finished high school there and we met at Duke."

"That's good that he has some family."

"Had. She passed away our last year of college. She left him everything—she'd written his parents out of the will for what they did to him. He was sole inheritor to everything she had, which was a lot, and the reason Silas can afford to…float through life, I guess you could say."

"He doesn't work?"

"Sometimes. He's tried his hand at a few things, but it's never long before he moves on to the next. He's in between things at the moment, so he was eager to spend the summer on the beach with me."

"I'm glad he has you then. You seem inseparable."

"Where I go, Silas goes. He moved in with us for a while; Kyle didn't love that, but he knew better than to question it." *He didn't question it because he was hardly around when I'd sunken into another depression and had known if Silas hadn't been with me, I would have fallen headlong over the cliff.*

"Kyle?"

"My boyfriend. He's back in D.C., trying for a promotion at his law firm, so he couldn't come for the summer."

"Ah. You've been together a long time?" Tristan's eyes turned to meet mine. Butterflies raged in my stomach. Why was I hesitant to answer this question? *Yes, we've been together a long time. I love him. I'm going to marry him. We're going to have kids. We've planned it since we were fifteen.*

I didn't say any of those things though. "Yeah, since high school."

He only nodded in response. We walked quietly. The sun had set hours ago and only the bright light of the moon guided us along the shore.

"Drew mentioned you were escaping some lady problems in Jacksonville."

"She told you that, huh?" He ran a hand through his hair.

"She did." A wry smile curved my lips.

"I was seeing someone…sort of…briefly. She wanted more and I didn't. It didn't go over well," he finished.

My mind conjured a blonde bimbo, all long legs and platinum hair, keying his car. Whatever he'd done, I'm sure he'd deserved it. Commitment-phobes irked me.

We walked a while silently before we drifted closer and our shoulders grazed. Nerves tingled and goosebumps formed. My breathing hitched, my mind hazy with the energy that bounced between us. I slowed down and put my palm to my forehead.

"Are you okay?" Tristan placed a warm hand on my forearm.

"Yeah, the wine." The wine plus Tristan's nearness had my brain bubbling with arousal.

"Do you need to sit?" Tristan placed his hand on my shoulder, prepared to catch me if I stumbled. Didn't he know he was making it worse? His touch was the reason my head was spinning like a tilt-a-whirl.

"No, we're almost there. I'm fine." I forced a small grin.

"Okay, but if you need to stop, tell me, okay?" He ducked his head and his eyes blazed into mine. My breathing was short and erratic, but I still couldn't break his gaze. I slammed my eyes shut for a moment to shake the cobwebs from my brain.

"Yeah, I'm fine." We walked the remainder of the way back to the house with our shoulders lightly brushing. It was the most innocent and erotic touch of my life.

SIX
Georgia

THE NEXT MORNING I woke early, still foggy from the wine and the walk Tristan and I had taken. We'd returned to a quiet house and I feigned exhaustion, sending us our separate ways. I'd heard Silas murmuring on the phone to one of his boy toys back home, and soon after, intimate moans and grunts echoing down the hall from Drew and Gavin's room. Those two were going to kill me. Popping in my ear buds, I fell asleep to the acoustic vocals of my favorite band.

I stretched, facing the morning light filtering in through the window. The house was silent, but I could hear the rolling waves pounding the shore through open windows. The soothing sound of water meeting sand was becoming the soundtrack to my life. It would be sad when summer ended and I'd have to head back to the horns and sirens of the city.

I padded to the kitchen barefoot in the oversized Duke t-shirt I'd slept in. It was old and worn, but soft against my skin—a favorite to wear to bed. I bee-lined for the coffee pot and found fresh hot coffee waiting for me.

Who on earth would be up at this hour? I knew it wasn't Silas—it was a miracle if he was up before eleven. Drew wasn't an early morning person either. I glanced at the clock and saw that it was just after eight. Pouring a mug of coffee, I made my way to the French doors and found them already opened, the breeze causing the lightweight curtains to dance and twist seductively.

Tristan relaxed in a chair, his ankle resting on the opposite knee. He looked out at the water, a cup of coffee in his hand. Gorgeous, an early riser, and a coffee drinker—could he be more irritatingly perfect?

He faced me and a grin spread across his face.

"Hey." His eyes glinted in the sunlight. Oh yeah, that grin. And that delicious bed-head hair. He could be more irritatingly perfect.

"Hey." I cursed myself for taking my coffee out here. His hair was still shower damp with a few stray locks across his forehead. He was barefoot in a pair of worn jeans and a white t-shirt. He looked utterly edible.

I heaved a sigh and prayed for strength to get me through the summer in the same house with this guy.

"Morning person?" I sat and took a sip of the hot liquid.

Adriane Leigh

"Yeah, I run most mornings: run, shower, coffee, work. It's my routine. Sleep well?" he asked.

"Very well. Did you? Was the room okay?"

"The room was great. The soundtrack courtesy of Gavin and Drew, not so much."

I chuckled. "God, I know, they're awful. Are they like this all the time?"

"So far, yes."

"Great." I griped and he laughed back at me.

"But waking up to waves is amazing. I love living on the water," he said thoughtfully, returning his gaze to the horizon.

"Me too. Have you always lived on the water?" I took a sip of coffee; the warmth caused a shiver to run down my body.

"Yeah, I've had the boat a few years now and spend many nights on it during the summer."

"That sounds amazing."

"It is. Have you ever?"

"Slept on a boat, no. But I can imagine the gentle rocking lulling you to sleep." I closed my eyes and soaked up the morning sun.

"The rocking is good for many things," he crooked a sideways grin, "including sleep."

I shook my head with a wry grin. "Funny man, huh?"

He only shrugged. "You should let me take you sometime. On the boat, I mean." He bit his bottom lip mischievously. I balked at all the sexual innuendo rolling off him.

"Sounds like a good time." My voice had an

uncharacteristic lilt. Lightning jolted through my bones as my heart thundered erratically.

"I promise you it will be."

A tremor pulsed across my skin. God, this man was going to be the death of me. I cleared my throat and took another sip of coffee.

Focus, Georgia. Kyle. Remember Kyle.

"Are you docked in Wrightsville?" I queried, trying to steer the conversation back on a safer course.

"Just outside of town. Down the road, actually. We could go today if you'd like," he said.

"You're not sick of being on the boat?"

"Doesn't really happen. It's my home, more than any house on dry ground could ever be." He took a sip from his cup.

"Hmm." I sucked my bottom lip between my teeth. Was he asking me out? Or was he just being friendly? Probably friendly. I'd told him last night I was with someone. "Maybe we can ask the others."

"Well, I guarantee you're not going to get Gavin on a boat. The one time I took him out he bitched and moaned the whole trip. Thought about throwing him overboard more than a few times."

"And we'll never separate Drew from Gavin," I frowned.

"I think she mentioned something about rolling around in bed with Gavin all day today, anyway." He flinched. "But ask Silas. It's a great day for sailing." He lifted his head as puffy white clouds passed over.

"He won't be up for a while yet. Did you want to go soon?" I watched his profile. I'd never used the word "beautiful" to describe a guy before, but there was no other word to describe him. He obviously hadn't shaved since yesterday as stubble whispered along his jawline. A small moan escaped my throat before I could stop it. I closed my eyes as heat crept up my cheeks.

"Okay? Coffee too hot?" He was gazing at me with a knowing smile. I swear he knew more than he let on. A mischievous glint flickered in his deep green eyes that had my heart galloping in my chest.

"I'm going to get in the shower. Thanks for the coffee." I tipped my cup to him as I stood.

His eyes widened for a moment before an easy grin tugged at his lips. More than a little flustered, I left him alone on the porch.

There was a text message on my phone when I returned to my room.

Miss you. From Kyle. I decided to call him instead of replying to the text.

"Hey." I sensed a grin on his face when he answered the phone.

"I miss you, too," I sighed and settled cross-legged on the bed with my coffee.

"Were you up?" he asked.

"Yeah, I just got coffee. What are you up to?"

"I'm just taking a break. Going into the office later."

"You're working already?" I frowned. I could visualize him at the dining room table with his laptop and legal textbooks spread out. Those textbooks had become another design element in our small apartment. Stacks littered just about every room in our home.

"Always more to be done," he replied absentmindedly. "So how's the beach?"

"Great. I love it. I can't wait for you to see it." A smile brightened my face at the thought of Kyle here. Waking up with him Sunday mornings. Coffee on the deck watching the sunrise.

"I can't wait either. I have to get back to work. I just wanted you to know I was thinking about you. I'm glad you're having a good time."

I frowned. The way he said it made it sound like I was on spring break. "Yeah, we're getting a lot of work done."

"Great. I'll talk to you later, babe. Love you."

"Love you, too," I said before hanging up. That was Kyle, always brief and concise, a trait he'd picked up in law school. An asset as a lawyer but not so much with your significant other.

I finished my coffee, made my way to the bathroom, and stripped before stepping into the shower. I stood beneath the spray, letting the water relax my muscles and my mind. No nightmares last night—the first time since I'd been here. From the time we were teenagers Kyle had been soothing away the heartache left in the wake of my nightmares, but this time I was alone.

Shower finished, I wrapped the towel around my head, threw on my oversized tee, and stepped into my room.

"Silas," I shrieked and pulled the shirt further down my thighs. Except for my worn college tee, I was naked.

A deep chuckle echoed from the doorway and I spun to find Tristan resting against the doorjamb with a sexy grin on his face. I lost my breath for a minute as I stared at him and something down low in my belly clenched.

"Out—both of you." The haze cleared from my brain and I shot a glare at Silas who was perched on my bed.

"Don't play modest, Georgia," Silas admonished. I stared daggers back at him before pulling out a pair of panties.

"Turn around." I whirled my finger to mimic the motion of turning as I cast a stern glare at Silas.

"Nothing I haven't seen before, love."

"Well, you—you need to turn." I glared at Tristan and repeated the motion. He arched a mischievous eyebrow before his full lips turned down in a pout. God, that pout. It caused my nerves to crackle and spark.

"Turn," I repeated. He smiled briefly then turned around dutifully. Jesus, maybe this was worse. My eyes zeroed in on his ass covered in the light blue denim. They hung off his hips in a way that hinted at the delicious body underneath. I bit my lip and stared before Silas, clearing his throat, interrupted my inner monologue.

I turned back to Silas and widened my eyes. His eyebrows rose to heights I wouldn't have thought possible. I stuck my tongue out at him before pulling panties and then shorts up my legs. "Okay."

Tristan turned back around and his eyes flicked down my denim-covered thighs to bare legs. I rolled my eyes at him before another chuckle escaped his throat.

"I asked Silas if he wanted to go sailing with us—"

"And I said no way in hell are you getting me on a boat."

"Silas," I pouted.

"Seasick, love. I'll be ruined the rest of the day." He shrugged and started typing on his phone. I huffed an exasperated sigh and willed him to look up at me so I could shoot silent daggers at him. He couldn't leave me alone with Tristan. I couldn't be trusted with the Greek god standing casually in my doorway.

Wait, did I just say that?

I meant *he* can't be trusted. Obviously he was a flirt. I hated the way he had my stomach doing cartwheels with one glance.

"Sorry, love." Silas mumbled without looking up. "Have fun, though." He continued to text.

"Are you still up for it or are you chickening

out?" Tristan arched a playful eyebrow from the doorway.

"Chickening out? Never." I narrowed my eyes. I had a problem with turning down a challenge—I didn't. Ever.

"Great, I'll be waiting." And with that he sauntered out of sight. My eyes hovered on the spot he'd just occupied. Did that really just happen? Did I really just sign up to go sailing *alone* with Tristan?

"Thanks a lot, ass." I kicked Silas' leg to get his attention.

"What?" He looked up at me, confused.

"I didn't want to go alone with him," I whispered so Tristan wouldn't overhear us.

"Why not? He's delicious." He grinned at me.

"Exactly," I mumbled.

"Oh, Georgia's got a crush," he taunted.

"Do not." I unwrapped the towel from my head and threw it at him.

Oh. My. God.

I'd had a towel on my head while Tristan was in here. So embarrassing.

Wait, why do I care?

I needed to not care.

"So you just want to get in his pants then? Even better. I would hit that too." He sighed and his eyes flitted to the door where Tristan had been.

"You're a whore." A snort escaped my throat before I turned and shuffled through the closet for a shirt to wear.

Apparently I was going sailing with Tristan.

* * *

TRISTAN HAD SAILED to Wilmington from Jacksonville and was without a car so we took mine to the marina. He introduced me to his boat, *Sweet Alibi*.

"What's with the name?" I asked.

"Umm…" He crinkled his nose in the most adorable way before raising his head to look up at the sails, as if searching for the right words. "I guess you could say the boat's been my alibi on more than a few occasions." He lowered his gaze to me and a small smile appeared on his lips.

"Oh." My eyes widened in shock. Apparently Tristan was more than just a ladies' man, he'd been in some trouble with the law too.

"No, nothing like that," he laughed. "Just… I've had a few… overzealous *friends*, I guess you could call them. The boat's a good place to lay low if I don't want to be found," he finished with a flirtatious tilt of his lips

"*Oh.*" Understanding settled. Women. The boat was his alibi when he was trying to steer clear of a woman. Or women. Many women, as I'm sure he broke a lot of hearts with that hair, those eyes, that grin.

"Is this weird now?" He took a step closer to me.

"No, of course not," I answered.

A wide grin broke out across his face. "Good." He reached a hand out to me and I slid my own in his. Fire burned across my skin at his touch. He pulled me onboard and readied the boat to leave. With sunglasses on, I watched him skitter around, hoisting sails and tightening lines. His faded blue jeans and white t-shirt clung to his torso deliciously, hinting at the toned chest underneath. He wore a pair of Wayfarer sunglasses that gave him a sexy retro vibe, and coupled with the tousled, sandy blond hair, I had to force my eyes away from him.

Eyes closed, I tilted my head toward the sun and arched my neck. The breeze swirled around my still-damp hair. I inhaled the salty ocean air as Tristan started the engine and backed us away from the dock. Guilt dampened my mood for a moment when I thought of all the work that needed to be done at the house, but I forced myself to consider all the things Drew, Silas, and I had already accomplished.

Thoughts of rooms and paint colors were interrupted when a whistle snapped me out of my daydream. I righted my head and glanced at Tristan behind the wheel of the boat. He gave me a sexy lopsided grin and tilted his head, wanting me to move closer to him. I was beginning to think I could survive on a boat with Tristan if we kept some distance between us.

I heaved a sigh and made my way to him. The easy grin stayed on his face the entire time I strode over.

"Hey," he said when I got close enough to hear.

"Hey." I granted him a small smile. I kicked my sandals off and curled up on a padded bench next to the wheel of the boat.

"Great view from the water, huh?" He nodded back toward shore. We were a few hundred yards from the marina; it looked beautiful and bustling from this perspective. Seagulls dove through the bright blue sky as Tristan angled the boat north.

"It's beautiful." I looked back to shore, lost in thought.

"Are you feeling okay?"

"Great," I said.

"Good. I could probably dig up some seasickness pills, but I don't think they do much good."

I only nodded in response and snuggled my lightweight cardigan around my arms.

"You wanna drive?" He cocked an eyebrow at me.

"No, I'm good." I was happy to sit here and soak up the sea air. "What's your last name?" I asked without thought.

"That's what you're thinking about?" He laughed.

"It just occurred to me that I don't know it." I shrugged.

"I don't know yours either." His lips turned up in a smile. God, when he grinned like that it did things to my body.

"Montgomery."

"Nice to meet you, Georgia Montgomery."

"And you are?" I arched an eyebrow.

"Tristan Thomas Howell. I suddenly feel like we're on the playground for the first time." His eyes sparkled with amusement.

I laughed. It did seem exactly like that. "Georgia Hope Montgomery." My heart felt a little lighter—it felt good to live simply in the moment and laugh. That's why Silas and I worked so well—I needed someone to pull me outside myself or I would sink. And Silas liked to make people laugh. We had a perfectly symbiotic relationship.

"So were your parents hippies?"

"What?"

"Your name—Georgia, it's unique. Beautiful, but different. I was thinking only hippies would give their daughter a name like that."

"No. Not hippies. They just liked the name." I watched gulls float on unseen currents of air behind the boat.

"Where did you grow up?" he asked as he nodded at a passing boat.

"Suburb of D.C." I watched the other boats in the distance. Tristan did have a beautiful boat—rich navy with honey wood accents.

"Are your parents in politics?"

"What's with the inquisition?"

He gave a small shrug. "Just making conversation." He seemed to let my attitude roll off his back, making him even more endearing.

I frowned and then felt bad for being a bitch. "Yeah, Dad's in politics. My mom's a teacher. What about you?"

"Dad owned a construction company, Mom stayed at home with me. Can you watch the wheel a minute while I trim the sails?"

My eyebrows shot up. "I'm qualified?"

"Just keep her on course." He waited for me to take the helm. He walked toward the front of the boat and tightened some lines. As he adjusted the mainsail, I felt the boat shift. I tightened my grip to keep us on course. He continued to adjust the sails until I felt the boat pull less and we cut through the sparkling blue Atlantic gracefully.

He stretched his arms, causing his shirt to ride up and expose sharp hipbones and a sculpted V muscle that had my stomach twisting nearly painfully. I slammed my eyes closed, held onto the wheel tightly, and prayed for strength.

Kyle.

Think of sweet, loving Kyle. Always understanding. Always loving. Always there. Except now, when we were a few states apart and I was sailing on the Atlantic with a beautiful man I'd just met yesterday. Anger flared instantly but died when I remembered that Kyle was working his ass off for us. If he got the promotion, we could move outside of the city, buy a house in the suburbs, get married and have kids. That's why I loved Kyle.

"You're a natural." He returned and sat on the bench. "You seemed pretty far away." He watched me pensively.

"Just thinking." I continued to hold the wheel and focus ahead.

"Sailing has a tendency to do that to a person. I love it out here; it's the only time I get peace. The definition of unplugged. Not far off shore and cell service gets spotty—no Wi-Fi, just you and the open air."

"It's lovely." I sighed. He was exactly right. The sound of the wind in the sails and the waves slapping the side of the boat, the sea birds squawking here and there, it was simple and beautiful and allowed my mind to slow down and enjoy everything existing around me.

"I think so." He was still watching me from the bench.

"You want the helm back, captain?"

"I like the view from here." A lopsided grin lifted his cheeks. My insides coiled at the flirty inflection of his words. "I never get the chance to sit back and enjoy. I always play captain. You look good at it," he said before turning back to the water. "There's your house." He nodded as it came into view.

The beach houses packed tight along the shoreline were now behind us and my beautiful house stood nearly alone on a secluded stretch of beach. It looked large and looming but fit perfectly into the surroundings with its weathered shingles and creamy white trim.

"I love it even more from this perspective," I murmured.

"It's a great house," he agreed. "Why did you choose Wilmington?"

I caressed a thumb along the worn wood of the boat wheel. "I woke up one morning and wanted something different." My eyes trained on the distant horizon. "I went to school at Duke, and I've always loved the beach, so North Carolina seemed like an obvious choice."

"It's a nice area. And your place is big and rambling, one of those great shore houses that you don't see much of anymore. Now they're all perfect white porches and Easter egg colors."

"That house was the first that came up in results. I looked at more, but I just couldn't get it out of my head. Silas and I drove down the following Saturday. I fell in love, offered asking price and by the time we were back in the city it'd been approved." We left the house behind and an old dock jutting out of the water came into focus.

"I didn't realize I had a neighbor so close." I squinted my eyes to make out the small cottage tucked into the trees less than a hundred yards from my house. A long boardwalk stretched out over the dune grass before the sandy beach opened up.

"Looks vacant," Tristan mused. There was a white shutter hanging off a window and dune grass had overgrown the boardwalk.

"I can take over now if you want. You looked

so peaceful curled up over there," he said as he took the wheel from me. I stood beside him for a moment and our shoulders touched. I was happy, and I wasn't sure how much of it had to do with the sailing and how much had to do with the guy next to me. I had the urge to lean into his arm and rest my head on his shoulder.

"Do you want anything? There's soda and bottled water in the fridge down below." As he talked, the boat pitched to the side from a rolling wave and I knocked into him. He shot an arm out around my waist to hold me upright.

"Okay?" His hand tightened around my waist.

"Yeah. Took me by surprise."

"Takes a while to get your sea legs."

I nodded until I realized his hand was still firmly wrapped around my waist. His palm felt so warm and comforting. Fire shot through my veins, nerves prickled across my skin, and my brain fired off possibilities from that simple touch. I was just the right height to curl up under his arm. I closed my eyes, wanting so much to lean into him.

I should step away, but he felt so good, and he had just saved me from face planting on the floor of the boat. I didn't want to seem rude. A shiver rolled through my body as my shirt rode up where his palm rested and the pad of his thumb made contact with my flesh. My heart thudded in my chest and desire hit me in the pit of my stomach. His touch had electricity shooting through my body.

"Cold?" he asked before moving his palm up my arm and rubbing quickly to generate heat. I nodded and bit my lip as my brain fought to make sense of the energy bouncing between us.

"I should have told you to bring something warmer." He pulled me into him as he kept one hand on the wheel and the other wrapped around my shoulders. My head tucked into his chest felt heavenly. If I was honest with myself, it was exactly where I'd wanted to be from the moment I'd stepped onto this boat with him. He rubbed his palm up and down my back. I inhaled deeply and smelled his fresh, clean scent. He smelled like the sun and the ocean and a clean, fresh shower. It was a heady combination.

Kyle.

The man you're going to marry.

The man you're going to have kids with.

Kids that will have warm, chocolate eyes, just like Kyle's.

"I'm going to get a water; can I get you anything?" I yanked away from him and made my way toward the stairs to the galley.

"Water is good, thanks," I heard him say. I grabbed two bottles and steadied myself against the small counter. I took some calming breaths as my brain burned with excitement.

Fire shot through my body at his touch. The scent of his skin caused my brain to short circuit. I knew I was only feeling that way because I'd been missing Kyle. This was the longest we'd been apart.

Kyle was my comfort, my home. The world felt strange and awkward without him; I felt strange and awkward without him.

It'd been nearly a week and we'd been so busy we hadn't had a chance to really talk. That's what this was—I missed Kyle. I needed to remind myself not to mistake the pull I felt toward Tristan as anything other than my yearning for the sweet, dark-haired boy that'd been the first to place his lips against mine in a gentle kiss. Who'd taken me to prom and snuck into my room at night when terror tore through my subconscious and left me a crying shell of a person.

I thought of Kyle's sweet, brown eyes and the dark stubble that undoubtedly covered his jawline. I took a deep breath. Maybe I could convince Kyle to come down next weekend; he would love sailing.

I made my way up the short steps, glad that I'd managed to get control of the emotions that had momentarily been spiraling.

SEVEN

Georgia

I WOKE THE next morning bone tired. I'd tossed and turned all night plagued by dreams—some memories, some a mash-up of my worst nightmares.

Flashes of blood glistening in the moonlight haunted me. My entire body trembled with fear. Heart racing, rapid breaths, soul-stirring fear. Nightmares have a terrible way of seeping into your bones and taking root long after morning has dawned.

I clenched and unclenched my fists in an attempt to maintain control and not fall into a full-blown anxiety attack. After years of therapy I'd finally put them behind me, or so I thought, but this...this felt as near to one as I'd had in a long while. I sucked in slow breaths and curled deeper into the cool sheets trying to recover from the emotional upheaval of the night.

A smile crept across my face when I exited my room a while later and found the coffee pot full, my favorite mug sitting next to it.

My muscles relaxed as I poured myself a cup and walked to the porch, curling up in the chair next to Tristan.

"Hey," he murmured.

"Hey," I said and inhaled the warm steam, letting it wash over my face and chase the fatigue away.

"Sleep well?" He took a sip of his coffee.

"Not really." I frowned before taking my first sip of the hot liquid.

"Everything okay?" He turned to me with a concerned look on his face.

"I have nightmares that come and go. It's nothing, really, just some lost sleep." I chewed on my bottom lip, downplaying the severity. "Being away from Kyle makes it worse," I said absentmindedly. He nodded and continued to stare at the rolling waves. Long moments passed in peace as I nursed my coffee and thought about the summer stretched out before us.

"Is he going to come down soon?" Tristan asked quietly.

"Kyle?" His question shook me from my thoughts. "He's busy, but I hope so. We've never been apart for so long."

"Must be hard to be separated from someone you love."

"Yeah, it is," I murmured. "What about you? I know you're not seeing anyone, but what about family?"

"Not really much to report there. My dad still

lives in Jacksonville, but things with him are... strained," he trailed off before continuing. "My mom left when I was a kid. Just disappeared one day. She left a note, called once or twice a year after that, sent a birthday card now and again, but I haven't seen her since."

Tears pooled in my eyes at his admission. "I'm sorry." He'd talked about his mom before—that she was a literature major and had named him after the story of Tristan and Isolde, but it hadn't seemed like a sensitive subject at the time.

"Nothing I'm not used to." He shrugged. "Dad went off the rails after that. Drank too much, trouble keeping a job. He always said true love is fragile and fleeting. He is wise, but broken."

"He never found anyone else?" I watched the thoughtful, beautiful man next to me. My heart ached for the small, golden-haired boy who grew up without his mother's love.

"No, it's been hard for him. He loved her, more than himself, I think. He says it was love at first sight. She tore his heart out when she left and he's had trust issues ever since."

"Is that why you...?" I couldn't finish my sentence and locked my lips closed.

"What?"

"Don't make me say it." A smile lit my lips.

"What are you talking about, Georgia?" His grin grew wider.

"You know," my voice softened as I held his

gaze.

"Drew filled you in, then?"

"Umm," I averted my gaze.

"Have I avoided finding the right girl and settling down because of my dad?" A flirtatious glint lit his eyes, sending tingles to my lower body. "I s'pose so." He took a long draw of his coffee.

"Do you think you'll find her someday?" I asked.

I watched his fingertip trace the rim of the mug as he thought. "Maybe…" A frown twitched across his lips then disappeared.

"Have you ever been in love?" I watched him thoughtfully, trying to figure out the charming, easy-going, alluring man that sat beside me.

"I don't think so," he answered after a few beats. "Are you in love with Kyle?"

"Yeah," I said.

"Was he your first?" A teasing grin lifted the corner of his mouth.

"That's personal, Mr. Howell," I teased back.

His eyes shot up in surprise before his grin grew, revealing his perfect white teeth. "That's a yes, then?" His eyes twinkled mischievously, sending my body head first into a slow sizzle.

"Yes." I scrunched my nose up at him before shoving him playfully.

"Is he your only?"

"Are you always so probing?" I winced as the word left my lips.

His eyebrows shot up as a mischievous

sparkle lit his eyes. "No comment."

I sighed. "No, he's not my only. We've broken up a few times, dated other people, but we always came back. I guess that's how I know it's true love."

"Just because you keep coming back to the same person doesn't make it true love, it might mean you haven't found the right one yet," he murmured, his eyes trained on mine.

"Well, thanks for imparting your wisdom." I retorted. "I love Kyle. I've always loved Kyle. We're two pieces of the same puzzle."

"It's good you feel that way." He turned to look back out at the water.

"What does that mean?"

"It seems you've got it all figured out." He finished his coffee and stood. "I've got to call a client. Later, Georgia." He twisted a lock of my hair that had fallen across my cheek before tucking it behind my ear and leaving. Frowning, I considered his mysterious words. I knew Tristan was a hopeless flirt and a ladies' man, but he was also sensual, thoughtful, and emotional.

I trained my eyes on the horizon and inhaled the thick ocean air. I closed my eyes as the sweet sea breeze picked up a few stray tendrils and curled them around my neck. I was sure of two things in my life—that I'd found true love with Kyle, and buying this house on the beach had been the best decision I'd ever made.

EIGHT

Tristan

I crawled out of bed just as dawn started to peak though the curtains and stumbled to the bathroom. I splashed water on my face and scrubbed with my palms, trying to erase the memory of the beautiful brown eyes that had been haunting me since I'd stepped into this house a week ago.

I took a deep breath and pushed myself away from the bathroom counter and back into the bedroom. Tugging on a pair of jogging shorts, I headed out the door, feet pounding the sand as my thoughts ran wild about the girl I was supposed to spend a completely platonic summer with.

This girl was affected. I could feel it. I could see it in her eyes. I knew I shouldn't get involved with her. I knew it would only lead to trouble—not something I always avoided—but this girl had been hurt. She'd been broken. She thought she hid it well, but the pain behind her smile, the sadness in her eyes was always there.

I ran down the shoreline and pushed myself harder than I normally did. I ran for miles before I turned and headed back to the house, slowing my pace only marginally, both dreading reaching the sprawling beach house and wanting to get back to see her face as soon as possible. I padded up the stairs to the house just as the sun was cresting over the horizon. I passed the chairs on the deck and thought of Georgia curled up in her cute little sleep shorts and thin tank, thick waves of brown hair cascading around her shoulders, her full pink lips curved in a smile.

I loved how I couldn't bullshit her. She threw it back at me just as easily as I dealt it instead of getting flustered like most girls. Just thinking of her rolling her eyes; that indulgent smile crossing her lips, had my balls tingling.

Fuck I needed to do something about that. I headed for the shower and let the thoughts of her smooth, tanned skin overtake my mind as I took my dick in my hand and jerked myself off to thoughts of her sweet, pink lips around my cock. I finished in a few short minutes and then soaped up quickly, washing my hair and then jumping out and toweling off. I pulled on a pair of faded jeans and a t-shirt and then headed to the porch. The overcast skies had opened up and a light mist dampened the air. It was completely appropriate for the mood I was in.

I felt like a fucking teenager beating off in the shower. I couldn't even remember the last time

I'd had to do that just to relieve some pressure—but then again if this were any other girl I would have fucked her and moved on already.

But she wasn't any other girl. I couldn't just fuck her and move on. God knows I wanted to—soon and often. As often as she'd let me. Multiple times a night.

But I also liked talking to her too.

I chewed on my bottom lip thinking all of this when I heard soft footsteps on the deck. "Hey." I turned and smiled up at her. Damn if she wasn't more gorgeous every time I saw her.

"Hey. I made coffee."

"Thanks. I'm slacking this morning." I threw her that grin. You know, that one that had every girl I'd ever met dropping their panties for me.

Except this girl. This girl wasn't interested. At least she pretended she wasn't. And despite the fact that it'd felt fantastic to hold her in my arms when she'd stumbled on the boat—and I was pretty confident that she'd felt the same—she'd still jumped away awkwardly after a few moments.

"I was getting spoiled."

I could spoil you Georgia, in so many ways.

I declined when she offered to get me a cup and I placed my hand on hers to stop her from leaving. Her skin was so fucking soft beneath my fingertips I couldn't help but want to run my hands up and down her body. An image flashed in my mind of her writhing underneath me. Sliding my hands up and underneath that flimsy little tank top, my thumbs brushing her nipples, her thighs pressing together as I sucked the flesh under her ear.

Fuck me I was hard again. Thirteen. I was a horny, fucking thirteen-year-old again.

I pulled my hand away and muffled a groan in the back of my throat.

"Any reason you're sitting out here in the rain?" She said softly. The low timbre of her voice went straight to my balls.

"I like the summer rain—the smell of it—the feel of the damp breeze against your face. It's soothing, cleansing." Except right now. Right now all I could focus on was touching her again.

She murmured that she liked it too and then we fell silent. The wind whipped between us, the waves rolled up the shore and my mind was consumed with finding a way to get this girl in my bed.

My lips on her skin.

My fingers twisted in her hair.

I shrugged when she asked me if I liked the water. I ran my fingers absentmindedly along the old, weathered wood of the deck chair. I needed to do something to let out this pent up energy that was coursing through my veins. I couldn't think straight. Every spare minute was torture when I had to live in the same house with this girl.

I heard her shuffle in her seat and I turned, my eyes searching her face. Her brown irises held my own and I couldn't look away. Her soft lips opened as she inhaled and my eyes zeroed in on the tiny movement. I grinned, enjoying the moment as the energy coursed between us.

Finally she moved, pulling her thick, damp hair off her neck and twisting it to land over her shoulder, exposing the creamy skin to my hungry eyes.

"You're getting wet," I murmured before tucking a damp strand behind her ear. The barest of touches had my dick pressing painfully against the zipper of my jeans. She tugged her bottom lip between her teeth and fuck me if it didn't send my thoughts into a spiral. I needed those lips. Needed her hands on me. Needed to feel her skin against mine.

I needed her.

All of her.

Now.

"Georgia," I whispered just before I leaned into her, pressing my lips to hers in a feather-light kiss. She squirmed and I pulled only a breath away to give her an out. I didn't want to force her. I knew how she felt—or what she thought she felt anyway—and I knew a girl like her couldn't be pushed. My name escaped her lips on a soft breath and my heart pounded in my chest. It was confirmation that she wanted this. She wanted us. I could feel it. I brought my hand up to her cheek, my thumb caressing the soft skin, damp from the rain.

"I don't know what this is between us, Georgia, but I want to find out," I said as my eyes searched her face before landing on her eyes, begging her to let me kiss her again.

"Me too," she breathed before pressing her lips to mine, firmer this time. Hunger and passion ignited as our mouths opened and our tongues danced together. The blood pumped through my body at full force as I tasted her for the first time. Her soft coconut scent surrounded me, her lips like sweet sugar, the taste of vanilla on her mouth from her coffee creamer.

I wrapped my hands around the back of her neck and threaded my fingers in her hair, my thumbs landing on her cheekbones as I held her face while I explored her mouth.

Both of her hands slid up and tugged at the hair at the back of my neck. A small groan escaped my throat. She was so much better than I'd imagined. Her lips pressed to mine was fucking perfect. A perfect fucking symphony of sensation that hummed throughout my entire body.

Until in one instant her lips were pressed to mine, our bodies pulled together by some unforeseen force, and the next they weren't. She murmured something as she pulled away.

Fuck.

I watched her, my breaths coming out in shallow pants, my dick throbbing painfully in my jeans.

She mumbled an apology, saying that it couldn't happen again, before she darted back into the house.

Fuck.

Fuck.

Fuck.

It had to happen again.

Now that I'd had her body pressed to mine, her hands threaded in my hair, the taste of her on my lips, I couldn't let it go. I was even more fucked than I'd been five minutes ago. I ran a hand through my hair and clenched my jaw as I turned back to the waves rolling up the coast. The sky grew darker and the rain came down harder but I didn't notice any of it because all I could think of was getting close to Georgia again.

NINE

Georgia

SILAS AND I had spent the week organizing the storage area beneath the house and sifting through the junk left in the detached garage. We'd found outdoor furniture to refinish, and supplies from the last remodel to keep. We had donated things still in good shape, and used Gavin's truck to take discarded items to the dump.

A melodic pattering of rain woke me Thursday morning, muffling the rolling waves. I could smell the dampness in the air. It was overcast and dreary but still just as beautiful as any bright and sunny day. Every morning, I'd woken up and Tristan was already awake and sipping coffee on the porch. This morning I was surprised to find the coffee pot empty. Maybe that was only his ritual on sunny mornings, or perhaps he'd had a late night. He'd been in a corner of the deck talking on his phone when I'd gone to bed.

I made coffee, picked up the empty bottles from last night, and wiped the counters. I poured myself a cup before heading to the far end of the living room. Pulling the curtain aside, I took in the gray landscape, looking down the beach and seeing a shock of tousled, sandy blond hair out of the corner of my eye. Tristan was awake and sitting on the deck like every other morning, the second story porch sheltering him from the rain.

He was looking off into the distance. I hesitated to bother him, but had grown used to our mornings over coffee, so I opened the door and stepped out. The wood was cool on my bare feet as I made my way to him.

"Hey." His head turned and a soft smile tugged at his lips. The green of his eyes seemed exceedingly deeper in the overcast light and I couldn't help but smile at the ever-present twinkle.

"Hey. I made coffee." I tipped my mug to him as I sat down.

"Thanks. I'm slacking this morning." He smiled sheepishly.

"I was getting spoiled," I said. "Want me to get you a cup?"

"No. It's okay." He placed a hand on mine to stop me. "I'll get some."

"Okay." I settled back into the chair. "Any reason you're sitting out here in the rain?"

"I like summer rain—the smell of it—the feel of the damp breeze against your face. It's soothing, cleansing."

"Yeah, I like it too," I agreed, watching him watch the water. His strong jawline and full lips were the first things that caught my eye. High cheekbones and a softly sloped nose defined the contours of his face and gave him a boyish charm.

"You love the water, huh?" I asked thoughtfully. He only shrugged and ran his fingers along the weathered wood of the deck chair, snapping my mind to when I'd tumbled on the boat and his fingers had ghosted across my skin like the gentle caress of a lover. My breathing grew shallow imagining Tristan's hands running down my body—down the dip of my lower back, the hollow of my neck, across my hipbones.

He turned and searing eyes appraised me. I stared back, captivated by his gaze, lost in those startling eyes. I waited for him to say something to break the spell, anything to shake me out of this trance. But he didn't. The gentle thudding of rain hitting the sand and rolling waves hitting the shore were the only sounds that infiltrated our bubble.

I pulled my damp hair off my neck and settled it across my right shoulder.

"You're getting wet." Tristan lifted a finger and tucked a stray strand of hair behind my ear. I licked my lips nervously, my eyes locked with his. His touch set my skin on fire. I held my bottom lip between my teeth painfully, willing myself to feel anything other than my stomach rolling and the arousal throbbing between my thighs. His eyes darted down to watch my mouth as his lips parted lightly with his breath.

"Georgia," he whispered as he leaned into me. His lips grazed mine and my eyelids fluttered closed.

Why wasn't I pulling away?

God, I needed to be pulling away, like two minutes ago.

I should have moved my chair away from his when I sat down. Being in Tristan's space did things to me, delicious things like the hair rising on the back of my neck and goosebumps dancing across my skin. My stomach flipped, my breathing hitched, and a slow ache settled between my legs.

"Tristan," I breathed as he brought his hand to my jaw in a light caress, just like he'd been doing a minute ago to the weathered wood of the deck chair. I parted my lips and the air escaped my lungs in a rush.

"I don't know what this is between us, Georgia, but I want to find out," he said on a breathy exhale.

"Me too," I whispered and pressed my lips to his. His soft, slightly salty lips tasted heavenly as I ran my tongue along them. He opened his mouth and our tongues brushed together as his hand cupped the back of my neck, fingers threaded in my hair, thumbs brushing my cheeks. He pulled me closer to him and before I knew it I was adrift in the heady sensation of

Tristan.

I lost myself for those few blissful moments attached to his lips. I knew there was a reason I shouldn't be doing this, but for the life of me, I couldn't remember what it was. I ran my palm up his arm and over his shoulder to tangle in his hair.

But the hair was too long. It didn't feel right. It was foreign, and yet the pull I felt to continue to kiss and caress was undeniable.

"Kyle." I pulled away quickly, mumbling the name. I licked my lips where Tristan's salty-sweet taste lingered. The feelings that were swirling inside my body and filtering through my head were terrifying and new and right all in the same breath. Tristan watched as my thoughts aligned.

"I'm sorry. I don't know what just happened or why I said what I did, but it can't happen again." I stood and walked back through the French doors and into the house, more confused than I'd ever been.

TEN

Georgia

"HEY." TRISTAN STEPPED up behind me.

"Hey." I was standing on the shore the following afternoon, my sweater-covered arms wrapped around my body and toes buried in the sand while the frayed cotton of my cutoffs tickled my thighs in the brisk breeze.

"Okay?" Tristan stood next to me, eyes on the eastern horizon as the wind howled around us.

"Yeah."

"Georgia," he breathed and placed a hand on my shoulder. "Is this about—"

"No," I interrupted before he could continue. The memory of the kiss we'd shared yesterday morning had consumed my thoughts these past twenty-four hours. Shame clouded my mind, along with the overwhelming desire to feel his lips connected to mine again.

"You look so sad out here with the wind whipping around you, like you want to blow away," he said sadly. I forced a small smile before tears welled in my eyes.

"How do you have the ability to be inside my head?" I whispered as my eyes bore into his.

"I just…thought…" he hesitated, his eyes searching mine. I turned back to the horizon as my head swam with past memories—the hurt, the pain, the healing. Always the quest for healing. While Kyle had been physically present, he hadn't always been emotionally. In recent years, Silas had been a far better companion. That realization crushed my heart. I had thought Kyle was the only person I would ever need—the only person that was ever good for me, but a few mornings over coffee, a kiss, and a truckload of physical chemistry had me rethinking everything I thought I knew.

"What's this?" Tristan slid his hand down my arm and took the book I was clutching to my chest.

"I came down here to read," I answered, thankful for the distraction. He turned the book over and read the cover.

His lips parted before his eyes met mine. "Tristan and Isolde?"

"It's been a long time since I've read it. I found it in town yesterday. I'm thinking it must be a pretty special story if your mom…" I paused, hoping I wasn't drudging up a painful memory.

I watched his throat contract as he swallowed. "Do you want to read it together?"

he asked tentatively.

"You want to read it together?" My eyebrows shot up.

"Sure. It's been a long time since I've read it. My mom used to read it to me when I was a kid, like a bedtime story," he said, his finger sliding across the loving couple on the cover. I watched him, lost in his own memories.

"Sure." I took the book back and sat in the cool sand, my toes just out of reach of the waves.

I began to read.

"*Triste* means sad in French. Your name means sadness." I looked over at him after reading just the first few lines.

"Yeah." Emotion swam in his eyes and a frown crossed his beautiful features. Whatever he was thinking, I wanted to take it away, to hold him as long as needed until the pain melted from his body. Suddenly I wondered if he had the ability to take my pain away too. My heart skipped a few beats in my chest before I continued to read.

As I read, the fictional Tristan's childhood was revealed. He'd lost his parents at a young age, and was fiercely loyal to the uncle who had raised him, his sense of duty and honor unparalleled. He had first met Isolde after a battle—she'd come upon him in a ditch and nursed him back to health. He was to bring her back to marry his uncle, but on the journey they'd mistakenly drunk a love potion together—sealing their fates to each other forever.

"Do you think the potion was really a potion or just an excuse?" I asked aloud.

"An excuse?" he laughed.

"Because they fell in love even though he's supposed to be taking her to marry his uncle."

"Right." He pursed his lips in thought.

"Think about it—if a love potion caused them to fall in love, it's not their fault. It leaves them without guilt; they can't be held responsible for their actions."

"Rather pessimistic of you." Tristan bumped my shoulder with his.

"It's just convenient that they can love free of guilt. They can be selfish, betray his uncle, and tear apart a kingdom."

"But shouldn't you always follow your heart?" Tristan raised an eyebrow.

"At the detriment of others? I don't know." I frowned.

"So you're of the opinion that one should sacrifice true love for the sake of others? How selfless of you." Tristan rolled his eyes.

"You advocate lovin' all over town without care for who gets hurt?" I shot him a disbelieving look.

"Hey, we're not talkin' about lovin' all over town." He laughed. "We're talking about true love," he said with a shrug. "I don't know the answer. Just something to think about."

My heart slammed against my rib cage when he said the words *true love*. Tristan was a romantic.

"We should go in." I closed the book and stood quickly. "I've got dinner planned and I imagine Gavin gets growly without food."

"Does he ever." Tristan grinned and butterflies danced in my stomach as we headed to the house.

Forgotten was the sadness that had consumed me as I stood on the beach earlier.

ELEVEN

Georgia

"WHO'S UP FOR a night out?" Drew threw out as she bounced into the kitchen the next afternoon. I'd been cleaning the house from top to bottom. I'd scrubbed the bathrooms to gleaming before telling Drew that she and Gavin were on their own from here on out because I was not interested in coming into contact with any of their…fluids this summer.

"I'm so tired." I slid down the wall to sit on the floor. My head tilted back and my eyes closed; I was ready to sleep for a decade. I wasn't exhausted just from cleaning; my mind was still reeling from the kiss two days ago—Tristan's lips on mine, his taste, his clean ocean scent, his sexy rumpled hair. I couldn't keep my mind off him and I hated it. I tried avoiding him, or at least kept busy when he was around so I didn't dwell on every move he made.

"You promised you'd go next time, and it's

next time. We're going. Everyone in this house is going!" Drew yelled the last part to make sure she was heard.

"Going where?" Tristan stepped through the front door.

"Out—a bar, a club, I don't care where as long as there is alcohol and dancing. Where have you been?" She arched an eyebrow at him.

"I was cleaning the boat." He gestured to the bucket of cleaning supplies he held.

"Oh. So are you in?" she asked.

"Always up for a good time," he said before his eyes flashed to mine.

"Great! I'll go wrangle Silas." She bounced out of the room.

"Hey." He set the bucket by the front door and stepped toward me.

"Hey."

"Look, about the other morning—"

"It's okay." I avoided his gaze as I stood up from the floor.

"Georgia—" He placed a warm hand on my arm.

"Really, Tristan. It's okay. It just can't happen again. I'm with someone." I pulled my arm away. He stood silently before his lips parted then closed again. His eyes shifted to the bright blue sky out the window and I wondered what he'd been about to say.

His eyes clouded over for a moment before he turned back to me. "You don't have to worry about a thing, Georgia. Turns out I'm bad news no matter how you frame it—bad for you, bad at this thing between us, straight up bad for love. Message re-*fucking*-cieved."

He turned and strolled out of the room. I kicked myself for ruining something that had been so easy and simple between us. We could have been friends this summer if I hadn't been so hopelessly drawn to those perfectly full lips and deep green eyes.

* * *

THE TAXI PULLED up outside the club and we piled out. We were all dressed for a night on the town. It was unacceptable to Drew to go for a night out without getting dolled up; heels and short dresses were a requirement. Thankfully, I knew this and brought some Drew-approved clothing. I wore a tight black dress and deep red heels. My hair was pulled halfway back in chocolate waves with a few wispy tendrils.

Gavin and Drew looked adorable together as they walked hand in hand into the club with Tristan trailing behind them. Tristan wore a black, button-down shirt that clung to his lean build, with the sleeves rolled to the elbows in a way that had my stomach listing. His jeans hugged his ass perfectly, so perfectly even Silas let out a low whistle behind me. Tristan was wreaking havoc on both of us before we'd even stepped into the bar.

We made our way to a table with a view of

the dance floor where bodies were already grinding to the thumping music.

"We'll get drinks." Tristan clapped Gavin on the shoulder as they headed to the bar. I, along with every girl he passed, watched his retreating figure.

"Let's dance," Silas insisted as he grabbed me by the elbow. Drew followed us as we wiggled our way to the center and started dancing in our little threesome. It was packed and we were constantly jostled together but it only added to the atmosphere.

After a few songs, Gavin angled up behind Drew and held her close to his body. She smiled and arched her neck to kiss his lips. His hands trailed up her torso as they moved together seductively. I turned to dance with Silas before I witnessed some form of indecent exposure on the crowded dance floor. After the song, the four of us headed to the table. I took a long sip from the drink the guys had gotten me—a cherry vodka and coke. I made a mental note to keep track of how many I had before I got too drunk.

"Tristan abandon us already?" Drew looked around the bar.

"A blonde at the bar caught his attention." Gavin nodded toward a crowded corner. Behind a shock of long platinum hair I saw Tristan's honey-blond locks, a dashing smile on his face. He had an arm wrapped around the girl's waist, his fingers caressing the fabric intimately.

"Doesn't take him long, does it?" I mumbled.

"He's a whore." Drew muttered.

"With no shortage of whores throwing themselves at him," I said.

"Not with a face like that." Drew cast a glance at Gavin. He grinned and gave her a peck on the lips.

"Or that smile." I watched Tristan's hand rest on her lower back, just above the curve of her ass.

"That hair," Silas groaned and rolled his eyes in the back of his head suggestively. We all laughed again but I couldn't manage to tear my eyes from Tristan and that girl.

"Let's dance more," I said to Silas. Drew and Gavin joined us and I lost myself in the music as we howled and danced together. Gavin had his hands wrapped firmly around Drew whether she was dancing with us or grinding with him. She looked happy, and I was happy for her. They had undeniable chemistry, I just hoped she'd finally found someone she could have something more with.

I mouthed to Gavin and Drew that I would get the second round of drinks as Silas followed me to the bar. The intimate corner where Tristan and his blonde had been tucked away was now occupied by another couple that were all hands, arms, and lips. I placed an order for drinks then scanned the bar, taking in the crowd.

My eyes landed on Tristan sandwiched between two girls on the dance floor. His arms were on the hips of the blonde with his knee nestled in between her legs from behind. A brunette with long, shiny hair and a tiny, red dress was cuddled up behind him with an arm wrapped around his waist and under his shirt, her lips skimming along his ear. He wore a cocky half grin on his face, enjoying the attention from both of them. For the first time, I was seeing Tristan in all his glory. He was certainly living up to his manwhore reputation. I sucked in a breath of air as I watched him nestle into the blonde's hair.

"Something got your attention, love?" Silas asked from beside me.

I ripped my eyes from Tristan's would-be threesome and forced a smile for my best friend. "Not a thing." I grabbed my drink and downed it in one guzzle, tipping my head to the bartender for another. His eyebrows shot up in surprise before he winked and made me another. He handed it to me and we made our way back to the table.

"Letting your hair down tonight, huh?" Silas winked.

"Absolutely. Let's dance." I set my drink down and tugged him back on the floor, the opposite end from where Tristan was grinding with his new friends. As we danced, the alcohol saturated my system and left my brain bursting with happy endorphins. Silas and I twisted, turned, and erupted in a fit of giggles, laughing at other people around us. I tried to scope out hot boys for him and would lean my head and quirk an eyebrow before he shook his head in mock horror.

A handsome, dark-haired guy invaded our space and tossed Silas a forward grin. A wide smile spread across my face and I mouthed to Silas that I was going to the bathroom. His eyes were so focused on tall, dark, and handsome, he hardly acknowledged my departure.

I threaded my way through the bodies and wound around tables to get to the ladies' room. Turning down a dim hallway, I bumped headfirst into a couple making out against the wall. Hands traveling up torsos, fabric inching up to reveal damp flesh. The girl chuckled and I jerked my drunken eyes to their faces and saw Tristan's long, blond hair as he sucked on her ear. They hadn't even noticed me.

I swallowed a softball-sized lump in my throat and stood for a second too long. Before I moved around them, Tristan's eyes met mine and flickered in recognition.

"Sorry." I averted my gaze as I walked around them to the bathroom. I opened the door and landed against the wall. There was a long line and I prayed that Tristan and his blonde would be gone by the time I was done. Instantly I missed Kyle.

Thoughts rattled through my head as the line shortened and I finally stepped into a stall. I had the urge to call Kyle and let him know I was thinking about him. I missed him desperately and wanted to curl up in bed with him tonight and feel his comforting arms around me. I closed my eyes and thought of the scent of his cologne and the smooth skin along his jaw. I fished my cell phone out of my clutch, noticing it was after one in the morning, definitely too late to call.

I decided I needed another drink to stave off my depressed mood, before remembering Tristan and the leggy blonde I'd bumped into earlier. I lifted my eyes and found the hallway absent. They were gone. I mouthed a silent thank you that I wouldn't have to see them again.

Heading to the table, new drink in hand, I discovered where Tristan and his blonde had moved. She sat in my chair with her legs crossed, her dress creeping high up her thigh, and Tristan's palm placed firmly on it. I took a sip of my drink and angled my chair toward the dance floor.

"Having fun?" Tristan asked me.

"Yeah." My eyes flicked to Tristan's before landing back on Silas and his dark-haired dance companion. It seemed he'd found a new friend to keep his bed warm tonight, as had Tristan. Drew and Gavin were always a sure bet, so apparently I would be the only one crawling into a cold bed alone.

"Tristan told me you're all staying at a beach house," the blonde said above the music.

"Yep," I responded with a tight smile before dragging my eyes back to the dance floor, not missing Tristan's eyes trained on me. What was he thinking? That I was upset that he was with someone? Because I wasn't. I had Kyle, and I was missing him, the ache in my chest deep and profound. I had the ridiculous urge to inform Tristan of just that.

"Everything okay, Georgia?" Tristan asked as a small smile teased his lips.

"Yep, I'm good," I said as the music and my own heartbeat pounded in my ears.

His eyebrow lifted in doubt as if he didn't believe me. I saw his hand was still resting on her leg, his thumb caressing her inner thigh, just like it had caressed the wood that morning before we'd kissed. I shut my eyes and willed the image from my brain.

I chugged the rest of my drink. "I'm going to dance." I stood on swaying feet and made my way to Drew and Gavin. With the alcohol in my veins, I was suddenly overheating and pulling my hair off my neck. My hips swayed when a new song started and I felt hands slip around my waist. I settled into the embrace for a minute before I realized what I was doing. Turning my head to the side, I caught tousled golden hair nuzzling beneath my ear. My heart thudded as Tristan ran his nose up my neck, sending tingles exploding through my body. His breath tickled the shell of my ear and I sucked in a quick breath. Thoughts swirled in my brain as the throbbing music pumped through my veins.

I felt out of control and I loved it. I surrendered to the freedom and settled back into his chest. His hands locked around my hips, pulling me tighter into his body before I turned and threw my arms around his neck.

Inhaling his clean scent, I closed my eyes, pressing into him. His knee positioned between my thighs caused my dress to ride up. We danced through multiple songs as the world fell away. I inhaled the delicious scent that was all Tristan while my brain buzzed from my proximity to the gorgeous Greek god wrapped around me. Thumping beats of Rihanna pounded through my body, nerves tingling and my breathing shallow. My brain focused solely on the rhythm of my form against Tristan's. I shouldn't have been dancing so close, but the vodka that pulsed through me was doing the thinking for me and for once, I let go of inhibition.

Tristan pressed my body up against a wall at the edge of the dance floor and moved his hips against mine. My hands smoothed across his wide shoulders and tangled in his soft hair. He ran his teeth up my neck and scraped my earlobe as his palms roamed my body—down my back, up my ribcage, over the underside of my arms. He dipped his head and trailed his tongue along my collarbone, sending a shiver of pleasure rocketing through me.

My fingers tightened in his hair as a small whine escaped my throat.

"Do you like that?" his words escaped in a throaty whisper.

"Yes," I hissed, my eyes closed as my hips

moved against his. Thoughts dashed in and out of my head. I felt like I was supposed to grasp their meaning, but too much vodka in too little time had left me with the inability to think straight.

"I want my tongue all over your body."

My breath caught as he continued to lick and scrape with his teeth.

"I want that, too." Arousal flooded my system and landed between my thighs.

"You shudder when I touch you." He ghosted one fingertip up the underside of my arm. My head swam in a cocktail of alcohol and lust. I exposed my neck as Tristan's tongue laved up my throat.

"Oh, God."

"I've been called that once or twice." He slid a hand down my leg and gripped my thigh possessively.

"Oh, God," I said again as the fog slowly dissipated from my brain. Tristan kneaded the flesh of my thigh as his other hand held my neck. "Tristan."

"I love when you say my name." The words escaped his lips on a husky exhale.

"Tristan, stop," I breathed, my eyes still closed. His hands stilled on me instantly and he rested his forehead on mine. "I'm with someone," I whispered halfheartedly.

"He's not here tonight." His palm tightened on my thigh.

"Tristan, stop." My chest was heaving with

each labored breath. His hands slid up my arms and caught both of my wrists, locking them above my head. My eyes finally flickered open and Tristan's heavy-lidded gaze bore into mine. All trace of a smile left his face as his jaw tightened.

"You say stop, but your body says go," he whispered in my ear. "I can tell that you want this, Georgia." My name falling off his lips made my heart skip. His thigh was still wedged in between mine as his body angled over me possessively—a predator unwilling to relinquish his prey.

"No. I want Kyle."

"Maybe, but you want me too." He ran his nose up my neck as he pinned me against the wall. My hands locked above my head, my body bowed into his—trapped between him and a wall—I'd never felt more vulnerable. Or more turned on.

"What about you?" I murmured.

"What about me?"

"Where's your friend? You seemed into her five minutes ago."

"I'm not into her. Not like I'm into you," he breathed. His words sent delicious chills running down my body.

"So you won't be bringing her home tonight?" I glared at him.

"Not if you ask me not to." He pressed his hips into me more firmly, causing a new wave of delicious arousal to course through my body.

I gritted my teeth and maintained my glare. "I don't care. I'm with someone, so I don't care what you do," I spat, tugging my arms from his grasp. His gaze shot up to meet mine, a look of hurt flashing across his beautiful, green eyes. I stared at him for a few breathless moments. Guilt pressed upon me for all the mixed signals I was sending him. I had the urge to apologize, explain how twisted and jumbled my mind was when it came to him.

Instead I turned, shame bowing my head, and walked back to our small table. My head swam as I sat down. I'd chugged each of those drinks much too fast for my own good. And I'd lost count. I put my head in my hands and took deep breaths.

"You okay?" Silas slid an arm around my trembling shoulders.

"Yeah, I just overdid it," I said.

"You want to leave?"

"Are you okay to leave?"

"Absolutely." He gave me a reassuring grin. That was my Silas, always there for me, always concerned, always willing to be my person.

"Where's hottie boy?" I asked.

"Justin left. Got his number though." Silas wiggled his eyebrows.

"Justin, nice." I swatted him on the shoulder.

"I'll go tell Drew and Gavin we're leaving and meet you at the door."

He headed for the dance floor and I wound my way to the corner by the door, when I spotted Tristan with his long-legged blonde. He was sitting on a bar stool and she had her arm draped around him, her fingers tangled in his hair.

The hair my fingers had just been tangled in.

My stomach flipped painfully before I turned away. I'd come too close to making a mistake with him. Shame bubbled in my chest when I thought of Kyle at home pouring over law books. I needed to go home and sleep this night off. I needed to forget it ever happened.

TWELVE

Georgia

I WOKE THE next morning with a faint headache. I'd called Kyle last night and we'd talked for a long time about everything and nothing. It was the longest we'd talked since I'd gotten here and it felt good to reconnect. I'd realized in the bright light of morning that that had been my problem these last few days; I'd started to feel the emptiness between Kyle and I, and I'd missed him terribly. I craved his arms around my body at night and his warm smile in the morning.

I'd asked him to come for a visit the following weekend, and he promised he would do everything he could to make it work. I think he'd been feeling the ache created in my absence too.

I entered the kitchen to the smell of bacon. Gavin stood in pajama pants with an apron tied around his waist and nothing else. He held a fork in his hand as Silas and Drew sat on bar stools

Adriane Leigh

laughing. A smile spread across my lips as I reveled in the warm atmosphere of my closest friends. This is what I'd hoped for when I'd invited them here for the summer. We were a dysfunctional, makeshift family, and I loved it.

"Didn't anyone ever tell you not to fry bacon naked?" I laughed.

"I'm man enough." Gavin gave a small shrug.

"No coffee? Tristan's off his game this morning." I scooped grounds into the pot.

"Tristan didn't come home last night," Drew said.

"Really?" My head whipped around to meet her eyes.

"Probably went home with that blonde he was wrapped around…or the brunette." Drew shook her head.

"Maybe both." Gavin added and turned back to the bacon.

"Such a whore," I mumbled and tried to disguise the twinge of pain that radiated through my chest.

"Tried and true," Drew said as she flipped pages in a fashion magazine. "You'd think he'd have learned his lesson after the last one." She frowned.

"The last one?" Silas asked.

"Tristan slept with a client. They had a few meetings—"

"A few orgasms—" Gavin cut her off with a laugh.

"A few of those," Drew chuckled. "She

103

thought it was more until she flew down to surprise him one weekend and found him in bed with someone else."

"Two someone elses." Gavin held up two fingers. My eyes widened in surprise.

"Sounds like a soap opera." I turned back to the coffee pot as my mind raced with the new information. It certainly filled in a few gaps about his history, and solidified his standing as a whore. All the more reason to steer clear of those full lips and that irresistible grin.

"Tristan's life can be." Gavin poked at the bacon. "Ow! Fuck!" He jumped back from the stove and Drew, Silas, and I burst into a fit of giggles.

"Thought you were man enough," I grinned.

"I'm fine, no tears." He went back with fork in hand. "My girl likes it when I cook naked."

"Do I ever." Drew stepped up behind Gavin and slipped her arms around his waist, kissing his shoulder.

"Gotta say, I don't mind either," Silas winked at me. I laughed before pouring coffee in a mug and joining him at the island. "Less cuddling, more cooking," Silas commanded.

"Shut it." Drew glared at him as she ran her fingers up and down Gavin's back.

"Just in time for breakfast, I see." Tristan ambled into the kitchen wearing the clothes he'd had on last night.

"Late night?" Gavin thrust a hand out to fist bump his best friend. A small smile lit Tristan's lips before he knocked his knuckles against Gavin's and made his way to the coffee pot. I tried to avert my gaze from his easy smile and the perfectly tousled hair that looked like he'd just had sex, which he probably had. My stomach clenched at the thought.

"So which one?" Drew put a hand on her hip.

"Which one what?" Tristan asked with a gleam in his eye.

"Blonde or brunette?" Drew glared at him.

"A gentleman never tells." The corner of his sculpted lips lifted.

"Gentleman?" Gavin guffawed. A small smile lifted at the corner of my lips as I forced myself to pretend I didn't care. What I really wanted to do was bolt from the kitchen and force the image of Tristan's hands all over one of those girls from my head.

Tristan smirked before setting his coffee cup down. "I'm going to jump in the shower. Save me some food." He smacked Gavin on the shoulder.

"Such a whore." Drew shook her head with an amused grin on her face.

During breakfast, Drew suggested we have our first official beach day. The sun was high and the summer rain had helped warm the water. We gathered beach towels, magazines, and bottled water and made our way down the wooden walkway, over the low sand dunes, and onto the beach.

Drew and I laid down towels and watched as the guys played Frisbee in the water. All three guys were fine examples of the male form. Gavin had large biceps, broad shoulders, and clearly defined abs. His tanned skin was testament to the fact that he spent a lot of time in the sun.

Silas worked out multiple times at the gym each week and ran nearly every day, and his body showed it. He wasn't as big as Gavin, but each and every muscle in his body was well defined. He was the shortest of all three and his ready smile was confirmation of his friendly, flirty personality.

Tristan was the least defined of the three with a lean, toned body that could only be achieved by running diligently every day of the week, which I knew Tristan did before our morning coffee. The muscles were lightly etched across the breadth of his bronzed chest and he had a hint of a V across the expanse of his hips. He was mouthwatering in an I-don't-try-too-hard sort of way.

The guys dove into the surf to catch the Frisbee and we chuckled and snuck glances at them while we laid out the towels and positioned ourselves in the sun. Skin cancer be damned, I wasn't about to spend my summer on the beach a ghostly shade of white.

Tristan dove into a wave and came up, water dripping from his long hair, a carefree smile on his face. My eyes focused on him intently behind my sunglasses. He twisted his elegant body and flung the Frisbee just out of Gavin's reach on purpose, which sent Gavin diving into the water to catch it. I wondered what a relationship would be like with Tristan; mornings over coffee on the porch, days filled with sweet smiles and intimate touches, and that mischievous glint in his eye that turned my insides to mush.

"You really think Tristan went home with those girls last night?" I asked Drew thoughtfully.

"Maybe. Wouldn't be the first time." Drew turned over to lie on her stomach.

"Has he ever been in a serious relationship?" I turned over along with her.

"Not that I know of. But I've only been around them for a few months. Why?" Drew turned to watch me. "Did he hit on you?" Drew asked.

"I guess you could call it that," I mumbled as I soaked up the warm rays of the sun. The heat coursed through my body and caused every tense muscle to relax.

"Did you like it?"

"What do you mean did I like it?" I laughed.

"I meant what I said. Did you like it when Tristan hit on you?"

I frowned. "I got caught up for a moment. But it won't happen again." I sighed and nestled my head into the crook of my arm.

"You're being pretty casual about it."

"What's to say? We were drunk the second time, so that's the only reason I let it go for a few minutes too long," I mumbled sleepily.

"The second time?" Drew questioned.

"We had a thing one morning on the porch."

"A thing? What kind of thing?"

"A kiss. Just a small one. A brushing of the lips really. Nothing intense." My stomach clenched because I knew it had been intense, for me at least. "I told him it couldn't happen again."

"And then he tried again?"

"Don't they all?"

"You don't understand, G. Tristan always gets the girl. Always."

"Well, he's not getting this girl. I told him I'm with Kyle."

"Hasn't stopped him in the past," she mumbled.

The wind left my lungs at her revelation. That confirmed it. Tristan wasn't for me. Would *never* be for me. "Maybe not, but it's stopping me."

"For now."

"Stop." I flicked sand on her towel with a grin.

"Look, I don't care if you hook up with Tristan. The boy's hot. Like, off the charts hot. And God knows he must have some serious talent in the bedroom. You can see it when he gives a girl that smile and his eyes do that sparkling thing—"

"Sounds like you're interested in him," I said.

"Whatever. Anyway, I don't care if you hook up with him all summer. Kyle's not here, hasn't even seen the place, and whether you like it or not, that means something, Georgia." She tipped her sunglasses down her nose and locked eyes with me.

"It means he's busy," I said.

"So you keep saying. Anyway, my point is, don't get attached to Tristan. That's all. If you can do that then I say jump into bed with him. You need to let loose and have some fun, just for the summer. You've had a stick up your ass since the moment we met."

"Hey." I flicked more sand at her.

"Just sayin'." Her smile beamed back at me.

"So letting loose in Drew's world means *being* loose?" I gave her a grin.

"Sometimes." She pushed her sunglasses back up her nose.

"Hey, baby." Gavin dashed up and stretched his wet self across Drew's back. She screamed and punched him on the bicep.

"What are you two talking about up here?" He nuzzled into her neck and made wet kissing noses under her ear.

"I was telling Georgia she should screw Tristan this summer."

"Drew." I shot her a death glare.

"Hey, no corrupting my girl with your slutty tendencies." Silas roamed up and sat on the edge of my towel.

"Who has slutty tendencies?" Tristan walked up, spinning the Frisbee around his finger.

"Drew, of course," Silas said.

"Takes one to know one," Drew glared.

"I don't deny it." Silas winked back at her.

"You should come in the water, baby." Gavin slid his hands up Drew's back. "Considering you're already wet..." He winked.

"Christ," Tristan threw the Frisbee at Gavin's head as the rest of us snickered.

"Come on." Gavin hauled her up into his arms. She squealed as he walked her straight into the water to his waist before setting her down.

"You up for it, Georgia?" Tristan asked. Goosebumps broke out across my skin at the thought of Tristan throwing me over his shoulder and hauling me into the water like Gavin had Drew. I hated that part of me wanted him to do it.

"Don't even think about it." I shot him a warning glance. He laughed before plopping down on Drew's vacated towel.

"Water's cold anyway, love," Silas said, flipping the pages in a magazine.

"It's not so cold." Tristan passed me a brash smile. A smile that seriously had the ability to take my breath away.

"I'm good. Maybe in a while."

"So where'd you spend last night?" Why had those words just escaped my mouth? I'd only said them to fill the empty space between us. Tristan crooked his head to the side and looked at me.

"The boat."

"Oh." Alone? I burned to ask him that one-worded question. It hadn't occurred to me until now that he had a built-in bachelor pad right at the marina. I thought how romantic it would be to make love on a gently rocking sailboat, before I shut my eyes tightly in the hopes of banishing the thought from my brain. I needed to call Kyle when I got back in the house. If I was going to keep my head straight around Tristan all summer, I was going to be calling Kyle. A lot.

The silence stretched between us as Tristan watched Drew and Gavin splashing in the water. I sat up on my arms watching them. I'd never seen Drew laugh as much as she did when she was with Gavin. It was sweet, even though most of their interactions revolved around sex.

"They seem happy," Tristan mumbled.

"Yeah," I answered.

"Gavin's different with her," he said.

"Yeah?" I looked at him in surprise. He nodded without looking at me.

"Drew is too. They seem...perfectly matched."

"I think he loves her," Tristan said.

"Really?" My eyes sliced to him. He continued to watch the couple in the water. "Has he been in a lot of relationships before Drew?"

"A few, but I've never seen him like this."

I watched them. "I hope it works for them. I've never seen her smile and giggle so much."

"That's 'cause she's getting laid," Silas mumbled as he flipped pages.

"Is not." I poked him with my toe. "She only smiles when she's getting laid, she doesn't giggle," I grinned.

"I hope it works for them, too." Tristan commented. "Everyone deserves someone who makes them feel like that..." He looked down the beach and then ran a hand through his wet hair. "I'm going for a swim." He shot up and was jogging for the water before I could even respond.

Silas moved to the newly vacated spot next to me. "He can be intense." We watched Tristan wade to his waist and then start swimming in decisive strokes up the shore.

"Yeah. More to him than a sexy grin and perfect hair, I think." I watched Tristan's body cutting through the water.

"Something happen between you two?" Silas asked casually.

"He kissed me a few mornings ago," I confessed.

"Oh? Was it good?"

"Silas." I smacked him on the arm. "It was amazing," I sighed.

Silas laughed. "So you liked it?"

"What's not to like?" I shrugged. "He also got intense at the club last night."

"I did see a glimpse of that," Silas said. "You seemed...interested."

"I was drunk. I missed Kyle. I *miss* Kyle." I frowned. "But I called him when we got home. I feel better now. I think Tristan will be dangerous for me this summer. I have to keep it in check."

"Maybe Kyle should fight for what's his,"

Silas muttered.

"What?" I narrowed my eyes at Silas. "He doesn't have to fight for me. We've been together forever. We're good. He's busy."

"Maybe you don't think he has to fight for you, but a little healthy competition never hurt anyone. Let him know you're basking on the beach with a sex god while he is hunched over his books—might make him take notice is all I'm saying."

"He doesn't need to take notice. Kyle and I are good." I was growing irritated by this conversation.

"Is that why you looked so into the aforementioned sex god running his tongue up your neck last night?"

I opened my mouth to shoot Silas an angry retort but nothing came out. We continued to sit silently on the beach towels while I rolled Silas' words over in my head. He picked up his magazine and went back to flipping pages as I continued to watch the happy couple necking in the water and pondered the sexy enigma that was spending the summer in my beach house while my boyfriend sat three hundred miles away in a tiny office. Maybe the decision I'd made when I bought the beach house meant more than I'd realized.

THIRTEEN

Tristan

I'd never met anyone like her.

I'd met a lot of women, prided myself on my equal opportunity friendships, but none were like Georgia Hope Montgomery.

Seeing her rock her hips to the music at the club, watching her pretty eyes downcast had set a pot to boiling in my stomach. I didn't know what else to do, I knew only that I couldn't have her.

And damn if she wasn't determined. I knew we'd connected, I knew those mornings over coffee meant something, the afternoons on the beach with a book, not just to me but to her too. With this girl I wanted to open up, I wanted to share my feelings, I wanted to share everything with her. It was an odd sensation, one that was foreign and thrilling in the same shallow breath.

When I'd caught sight of the blonde at the club, she was everything that I normally went for. Long tall legs in a short skirt, flowing golden hair that wrapped around her shoulders, and curves that made my knees weak. But at the club, after having my lips on Georgia's, after having her steadfastly tell me that she was *not mine* and would never be, all I fought was the sense of revenge.

I wanted to make her jealous. I had so stupidly thought that seeing me with another girl would give that same feeling of dread in the pit of her stomach like it did me when I thought of her with her boyfriend

Kyle.

The name made my insides twist with pain. I wanted to pummel his face, and I didn't even know him.

I knew instantly he was too good for Georgia, hell I knew I was too good for Georgia, but that didn't mean I didn't want to be better for her. I liked a challenge, that was true, but Georgia was so much more than that.

I wanted to prove to her this summer that I could be better, be what she deserved, because I knew damn well if she was mine I would never let her spend the summer three hundred mils away from me. I would take care of her, shower in attention, please her until neither one of us could think straight. I wanted to be hers and hers alone.

I wanted everything with Georgia, and that made me determined.

The instant she'd bumped into me at the club I'd seen the look of pain radiating through her dark irises and I knew I'd fucked up. I hadn't even wanted my hands on that girl, I'd been thinking about dark brown waves and pouty rose lips that drove me insane and occupied every waking thought I had.

As soon as Georgia had bolted from the table later, stubborn fire burning in her eyes, I'd excused myself from the blonde that'd been trailing on my arm and found her.

Like a homing beacon I'd gone to Georgia, my hands around her waist, my lips dusting across the heated skin at her neck. She was intoxicating, and while I'd half expected her to punch me in the balls when she'd turned around, relief had flooded me like a tidal wave when she hadn't. Despite all my cocky airs and sarcastic remarks, I was desperate for her arms around me. If she only knew that she held all the control, I was a puppet. Every decision I made, even the bad ones, were in reaction to her. Her pain, her rebuttal, her refusal. *Her.*

Nothing hurt more than rejection from the very person you wanted the most.

I'd learned that lesson the hard way, which is why the instant Silas had left with my girl, I'd hit the fucking road, taking a cab straight to the marina and stopping at the store for a six-pack before camping out on my boat.

Alone.

I'd seen the unspoken question burning in her eyes earlier, the word on her lips.

But I didn't want to tell her, didn't have it in

me to tell her she'd crushed me when she'd pushed me away, said it would never happen. Said *we* would never happen.

So why the fuck was she consuming me then?

I shoved a hand through my sopping wet hair, having just powered through a few laps down the shore while the girls sat on beach towels up the beach. Watching Drew and Gavin this summer was like a wrecking ball to my heart, when the only girl I could ever imagine having that with walked around that big empty house, taken by someone else.

My arms ached and the salt breeze on my skin felt invigorating as I walked up the shoreline, headed back to Georgia. Headed back to the light in my life, the darkness I carried in my heart, the one girl I couldn't stop thinking about.

This summer would either be hell on earth, or some other beautiful side of paradise that I had yet to discover. The jury was still out on what would be the outcome of Tristan and Georgia.

FOURTEEN

Georgia

EVERY MORNING THE following week, Tristan and I had coffee together on the porch. Rain or shine, windy or warm, we were both there. It wasn't that we made a point of being there, we just were. While the rest of the house was silent, Tristan and I sat and talked. The first few mornings had been a little awkward after our intense encounter at the club, but we'd soon settled into a comfortable rhythm.

I made more of an effort to call Kyle on most nights to catch up. Sometimes he had time to talk, other times it was only a quick few words. The days I couldn't call, I texted. I felt comfortable in the place Kyle and I had found despite the fact that we were separated by three hundred miles. I told him about the work Drew and I were doing on the house and he listened as I described the different pieces I'd bought and my vision for each room. We were finding a way to stay close and bridge the gap that had stretched between us.

"Hey." I stepped out into the gray morning with two coffee mugs in hand, one for me and one for Tristan.

"Hey." He smiled, reaching for a cup. "Thanks." He brought the hot liquid to his lips while I sat and curled my legs up underneath me.

"Sleep well?"It was a question he asked most mornings.

"Yeah. I talked to Kyle before bed last night."

"Yeah?"

"He's going to try to come down this weekend."

"Hmm." He took a sip of his coffee. "He hasn't been here yet, right?"

"No. I was telling him about the work Drew and I have been doing. He's excited to see it."

"I'm sure he'll love it."

"Yeah." I sensed an uneasiness between us. The first in a while. "Everything all right?"

"Just a lot on my mind." He replied as he watched the white-capped waves.

"Work?"

"Among other things."

"You can tell me anything," I offered.

"Can I?" He turned and his deep green gaze honed in on me.

"Of course." I averted my eyes and brought my coffee mug to my lips. "We're friends."

"Are we?"

A knot formed in my stomach as I sensed his

gaze still on me. "Sure," I mumbled.

A few silent moments slipped between us before Tristan turned back to the water. "I hope Kyle likes this place. It's great here."

"He will. I love it here. He'll love anything I love."

He only nodded as silence descended again. I continued to sip my coffee and watch the waves roll up on the shore and then recede again.

"I'm going to head into town. I want to pick up groceries and grab paint chips for the master bedroom."

"Okay, Georgia." His eyes lifted to mine and a hint of a smile pulled at his lips. It stopped me in my tracks for an extra beat before I grinned back at him.

* * *

FRIDAY MORNING I was gearing up for Kyle's arrival. I hadn't seen him since I'd left D.C. in May. More than a month and I was missing him like crazy. I couldn't wait to wrap my arms around his neck and sleep curled against his body at night.

I wanted to make his favorite dinner—a classic pot roast with carrots, potatoes, and parsnips. It was his mom's recipe, and when we moved in together, she gave it to me. It was a simple dish that didn't take much time, other than putting everything in the slow cooker, but it reminded him of home so I loved making it for him. He said he'd need to work while he was here, but I was so excited to have him at the beach house with me that he could be doing anything and I'd still be happy.

"Working?" I said as Drew set her laptop up at the kitchen island.

"Yeah, going over the quarterlies. Tristan said Kyle's coming tonight?"

"Yep, should be here around six." Just a few hours and I could wrap my arms around him and inhale his spicy cologne—the scent of home and comfort.

"Excited?" Drew asked as she split her attention between our conversation and her laptop.

"Very. I also picked up paint samples for the master bedroom." I moved on to chopping carrots.

"You're going to wait 'til after the weekend to paint right?" Silas plopped on a barstool next to Drew.

"Yeah, I'm just getting ideas. Maybe Monday I'll start."

"What color are you thinking?" Drew asked.

"I picked up some grays; I thought some navy or teal accents would be pretty with it."

"Grey, again? You're so...depressing." Silas popped a pretzel into his mouth.

"Hey!" I pouted.

Silas shrugged as he chewed. "White Russians on the menu?"

"Kyle's favorite," I said just as my phone vibrated in my back pocket. "Speaking of," I said as his name flashed across the screen.

"Hi," I answered. "Pot roast and White Russians for you this weekend."

"I can't come, Georgia." Kyle's dejected voice echoed in my ears.

"What?" A frown crossed my face.

"Sorry, honey, work. My boss threw a case at me this morning. I have to be in the office all weekend."

"Kyle..." I felt tears prick my eyes.

"I'm sorry, Georgia. I tried to get out of it. I know you were excited."

"You haven't even been here yet," I muttered as I turned my back from Drew and Silas and walked across the living room.

"I know, honey. Really, I'm sorry. I've got to go. I promise I'll come soon."

"Fine." I stared out the window watching the waves roll onto the shore. Rage was starting to bubble inside my stomach.

"Next time. I promise, Georgia."

"Okay," I said through gritted teeth. I knew I wasn't being fair; he couldn't help it when his boss flung more work at him. But I was still angry and disappointed and hurt.

"I'll try and call tonight."

"Okay." I rolled my eyes because *he* never called *me*. Once in a while I got a random text from him but otherwise I was the one making all the effort. It bothered me that he couldn't call even a few minutes before he went to bed at night, but I'd vowed to do everything I could to keep us close, so I called him always. Even just to talk for a few minutes.

"Love you, Georgia."

"Love you too," I mumbled and hung up before the lump in my throat released an audible sob. I slid my phone back into my pocket and crossed my arms, watching the waves out the window.

"Everything alright, G?" Drew called from the kitchen.

"Kyle can't make it." I walked to her.

"What a dick," Silas sneered.

"He couldn't help it," I defended as I slumped onto the barstool next to Drew.

"So he says," Silas mumbled. I only frowned. I knew I should try to be the supportive girlfriend, but I'd been that for years now, and I was disappointed and hurt that, yet again, Kyle couldn't be there.

"Well, let's bust out the White Russians. Five o'clock somewhere, right?" Drew hopped off the stool and went for the bottles.

"I thought you were working."

"My girl comes first." She winked as she started making drinks.

An hour later, we were two drinks in, and I was feeling buzzed as the three of us sat on the floor in the living room with the paint chips spread out in front of us.

"I like Stonehenge gray." I held two paint

chips up in my hand, debating the merits of both.

"Too dark. Pewter is pretty," Drew contended.

"Maybe I want dark. Maybe I'm a dark girl." I wrinkled my nose at her before we busted a gut. "It's settled, Stonehenge gray, my room, now." I jumped up and grabbed the bucket of paint, a roller, and paint tray.

"G, you're not painting right now," Drew emptied her glass.

"Angry white woman." Silas laughed, mixing another drink for himself. I grinned and headed for my room.

"G, seriously?" Drew trailed behind me, half serious and all drunk.

"Help me move the bed."

We pushed the bed and nightstand to the middle of the room.

"Throw the drop cloth over it while I open the paint." I wedged the paint stick into the lip and leveraged it open and gave it a stir.

"I love it already," I said, finishing off the last of my drink.

"You are two crazy bitches." Silas sat on top of the drop cloth with a fresh drink in his hand.

"Can it."

"He's right, G, you're nuts." Drew laughed as she poured paint into the tray. "But no going back now."

"Start rolling." I passed her a roller. We both took turns sliding our rollers through the paint then swiped large swaths on the wall.

We painted until the largest wall was completely covered. Drew instructed Silas to make us each another drink and he did so obediently.

"Gavin is going to die when he sees this." Drew dragged her roller through more paint. Tristan and Gavin were running errands in town and had been gone for a few hours, missing the phone call and the ensuing drama.

Silas came back with drinks and Drew and I took long swigs. We were halfway through the second wall when we heard Tristan and Gavin barge into the house.

"Babe," Gavin called through the house.

"In Georgia's room," Drew called back.

"What the fuck are you doing?" Gavin entered with Tristan trailing behind him.

"Georgia is a woman scorned so we're taking revenge on the walls." She tossed him a wide smile before taking another drink.

Tristan's eyes shot to me, a question written on his face. "Kyle?" he asked.

"Not coming. Work, blah, blah, blah." Drew waved her hand. "But we've got White Russians to make up for it. He's boring anyway," she whispered to Gavin, but obviously not quietly, because we all heard her. I saw a smile on Silas' lips. I kicked at his foot but missed.

"How many drinks are you in?" Tristan's eyes trained on me.

"A few," I said. He shook his head still smiling.

"I'm sick of painting," Drew pouted.

"We can't stop halfway through," I pleaded with Drew but I knew I'd already lost her.

"We'll finish tomorrow, I promise," she said.

"I'm not sure painting while drinking is really recommended anyway," Tristan said, taking both rollers. I frowned at him, reaching for my drink.

"Gavin and I will help tomorrow," Tristan said.

"Promise, Georgia." Gavin curled his arms around Drew and gave me a sweet smile. My heart fractured a bit watching them. I'd been so anxious to feel Kyle's arms around me this weekend.

"Fine. I need another drink anyway." I looked sadly into my empty glass.

"Make me one and I'll clean up in here," Tristan offered as his sympathetic gaze caught mine.

"Deal." Our eyes held for a moment and my heart started to thud in my chest. Those eyes could really get a girl lost. And the way those lips curved up mischievously—they left me dreaming about the naughty things he could do with them.

Wait, no.

That's not what I was supposed to be thinking at all. I licked my lips nervously and left the room, bee-lining for the kitchen and more alcohol.

"Let's play poker!" Drew clapped her hands. After our paint operation was shut down, we'd refreshed our drinks and made our way out to the porch. The sun was setting and the breeze was cool as we listened to the sounds of the beach.

"Strip poker." Gavin goosed her as she jumped up and ran into the house. Tristan looked over at me and rolled his eyes. My head swam happily. If Kyle couldn't be here this weekend, I was at least thankful I'd bought the ingredients for White Russians to help me forget him.

"I am not playing strip poker." I warned as Drew tossed cards on the table and seated herself in Gavin's lap.

"Come on, G. Remember our conversation? You need to loosen up."

"I'm terrible at poker." I shook my head.

"All the more reason to play strip poker." Gavin winked as Drew smacked him on the chest. Tristan smirked, his eyes glinting in the moonlight heated my cheeks.

"You play strip poker, count me out." Silas pointed to us. "I may have a date anyway." He looked at his phone.

"Going out with Justin?" I asked.

"No." He winked.

"Someone else? You're a whore, Silas." I knocked his shoulder with mine. His grin widened as another text came in.

"We're not exclusive. Just keepin' my options open," he said distractedly as he read the text. "Strip away, loves. I'm out." He danced into the house.

"He is something," Drew scoffed with a roll of her eyes. I only shrugged. I knew Silas' game. We'd talked about it before, and he'd acknowledged that he was probably looking for love in all the wrong places, but he didn't seem to want to change and I didn't judge him. He'd been there for me way too much without judgment over the years. It was only right I return the favor.

"So, strip poker?" Gavin shuffled the deck with a grin.

"Definitely not," I took another drink.

"Regular poker?" Gavin answered.

"Sure, but I'm still terrible."

"I'll teach you." Tristan bumped my shoulder.

"I don't think she needs your kind of teaching," Gavin ribbed Tristan. We all laughed as Tristan grinned.

"Texas Hold 'Em." Gavin dealt the cards. "Ten dollar buy-in."

"We're playing for cash?"

"Always." Gavin answered as Drew slid off his lap to the seat next to him.

"No cash. At least give Georgia a few practice rounds. Can't rob the host blind." Tristan winked at me.

"Hey, I can hold my own."

"I thought you were no good?" A smile lit Tristan's face.

"I said that to get out of strip poker." I winked at him.

"God, the sexual tension between you two is making me horny." Drew took a sip of her drink.

"Drew!" I glared at her as my heart stopped. Was it really that obvious?

"I call it like I see it. Anyone need another drink?" She lifted her glass.

"I'm off!" Silas sang as he poked a head out the door.

"Be careful, Silas." I meant more with his heart than anything else.

"Always, love." He pressed a light kiss to my cheek. "You too," he whispered. This situation was getting worse by the minute. Drew and Silas were constantly giving me unnecessary warnings. Tristan and I were over any previous encounters we'd had. Sure, I was attracted to him, but I was attracted to attractive people. That didn't make me someone who cheated. Even if my significant other was a million miles away.

"Drinks anyone?" Drew asked again.

"Yeah, I'll come with you." I hopped out of my chair. "Way to make things awkward, Drew," I complained once we were alone.

"What?" She arched an eyebrow at me.

"Sexual tension between Tristan and me? We're just friends." I poured coffee liqueur into each of our glasses.

"Friends don't act like that," she mumbled. "How many drinks have you had anyway?"

"Not enough to forgive you for being a meddling bitch," I threw a crumpled napkin at her.

"Is there something to meddle in?" she asked.

"No," I raised my voice as I poured cream into our glasses. "Enough of your opinion. Keep it zipped," I said pointedly as we walked out.

We started the first round, and laughed, drank, and refilled our glasses through many rounds thereafter. My head began to feel foggy and I rolled with laughter at the banter between Gavin and Tristan. After the sun disappeared, I shivered and wrapped my sweater around my shoulders a little tighter. Another few rounds and Drew landed back in Gavin's lap, spending more time kissing than playing.

"Game over." Tristan tossed his cards down on the table.

"Night's over by the looks of it." I wrinkled my nose at the amorous couple.

"Or just beginning." He grinned that mischievous grin.

"Or just beginning," I agreed.

"Want to take a walk?" he asked, holding a hand out to me.

"Sure." I took his hand. The sudden change from sitting to standing had my head swimming as I looped my arm in his elbow and we made our way to the beach.

"No laying your moves on me." I gave him a stern glare before I burst into a fit of drunken giggles.

"I think you're immune to them anyway," he chuckled.

"I'm not. Believe me, which is why you need

to keep them locked up tonight."

"Noted."

"Good, 'cause I can hardly walk," I said as our shoulders brushed together. "We should go swimming." I veered toward the water.

"Definitely not," he replied, guiding me away from the shore.

"Why not? I've never been skinny dipping," I pouted.

"Georgia," he muttered, his arm tightening around mine. "No skinny dipping."

I stopped to face him. "You're no fun," I said as I pushed my bottom lip out.

"No fun, huh?" The moonlight reflected in his eyes took my breath away.

"No." I stared into his mesmerizing eyes.

"Georgia." He ran a warm palm up my arm, over my shoulder before his fingertips dusted beneath my ear.

"Yeah?" I watched him watching me. His eyes landed at my lips and my breathing hitched at the intensity that clouded his eyes.

He stared at me then closed his eyes tightly and opened them again. "We should turn back; you're drunk. If you pass out on me, I'm not carrying you back," he teased.

"I'm not that drunk." I gave him a playful shove. "I want to explore that house we saw from the boat." My eyes flicked over his shoulder to the cottage tucked in the trees.

"Private property."

"Never pegged you for a straight and narrow

kind of guy," I said.

His eyes glinted for a moment. "That a challenge?" He sucked his bottom lip between his teeth and pulled the flesh taut. My heart skipped a few beats as I watched the slow movement.

"Maybe," I whispered, my eyes never leaving his lips.

"Then let's go," he said without moving.

"Okay," I murmured. We stood still for a moment before I slammed my body against his and reached my hand to the back of his neck to tangle in his silky, golden hair. He pressed his lips to mine, and we kissed fiercely.

One hand pressed into my lower back, holding my body to his while the other smoothed up my back and wound my hair around his fist. He pulled gently, arching my neck, exposing my flesh to his lips. He nipped down my throat and placed soft kisses under my ear. His fingers brushed along the nape of my neck, holding me to him. I whimpered and pressed my hips into his, feeling his arousal.

Another groan escaped as thoughts of being with Tristan crashed through my brain. His lips on me. His tongue dancing across my skin. His fingertips caressing me, peeling off my panties, his eyes taking me in for the first time, running his tongue up the sensitive flesh around my hips. I brought his face back to mine in a fiery kiss, wanting everything he had to give.

His hands dropped to my thighs and lifted

me around his hips. Both of my hands wrapped around his neck and tangled in his hair, my ankles locked around his waist as he held me, one hand on each ass cheek.

"Georgia," he grunted as he kneaded the flesh.

"Tristan, please. Let's do this; I can't stop thinking about it." I nipped along his jaw. He sucked in a sharp breath, his hands tightened almost to the point of pain. He walked backward with me in his arms, kissing and sucking, until the back of his legs hit the wooden walkway of the abandoned cottage. Sitting, I straddled his waist, our lips still exploring languidly. He slid his hands inside my jeans and underneath my panties to palm my ass. His hands on my body kneading, his tongue tasting, lips caressing—drove me mad with lust.

"I can't stop thinking about you, Georgia. Every night I go to bed and think about you. Every morning I get out of bed and can't wait to see you," he murmured, dragging his teeth along my earlobe.

"Oh God, me too," I bowed into his hard body.

"I want to be with you. I can't get you out of my head." His hands slipped from my jeans and ran underneath my sweater. Fingertips skimmed my ribs and my body arched into him. His palms caressed the underside of my breasts, my head swam with lust. I wanted him to touch me. I wanted all of him tonight.

"Tristan." I moaned before his fingers traveled over my bra lightly, feathering across my painfully aroused nipples. I threw my head back and my body bowed as I rocked, seeking release of the ache between my legs. His fingers pulled down the cups of my bra and lifted my sweater just high enough to take one breast into his mouth. He slicked around the hardened peak before drawing it further into his mouth, sucking and twirling his tongue around the pebbled tip. He released it to the cool air, causing it to throb with need. His lips traveled to my other nipple to pay it the same attention while his fingers found the abandoned one, pinching and elongating it further.

"I want to feel you," I moaned, my fingers working to lift his shirt. He pulled the shirt over his head, leaving his delicious chest displayed in the moonlight—the body that I'd dreamed about for weeks. I thought of the water that had traveled down the ridges of his muscles, down his pecs, through his abs, and followed the cut of his pelvic muscle before disappearing under the band of his low-slung trunks.

"Lie back." I leaned over him, wanting my tongue to follow that same path that little, lucky rivulet of water had traveled days ago. My hair curtained around us as I teased my tongue from behind his ear, down his neck, and across his collarbone where I paused to swirl my tongue in the hollow. My hands made their way up his torso, feeling every inch of him as my tongue traveled the opposite direction, down between his pectorals, past the sharp lines bisecting his abdominals, and then across his sharp hips.

He moaned when my tongue reached the waistband of his cargo shorts. His fingers ran through my windblown hair and I felt his erection against the rough twill of his shorts. He jerked his hips when I placed a palm firmly on his cock, rubbing and caressing. Our eyes locked for a moment. His lips opened slightly, dragging his bottom lip through his teeth and my breathing picked up, my fingers fumbling with the button on his shorts.

"Georgia," he breathed.

"What?" The word escaped my lips as I worked down his zipper.

"Georgia, God, I want to, but we shouldn't."

"I want to, Tristan." I continued to palm him through the cotton of his boxer briefs.

"I know, I want to too, so bad... but you're—"

"I'm nothing. I want you." I gazed up at him through my eyelashes.

"Fuck," the word escaped his lips in a rush. "Lean up for a second."

I climbed off his lap and watched him lay his shirt in the sand at the foot of the dock. Then he stripped his cargo shorts off and laid them down next to it.

"Lie down," he murmured. I complied and he leaned over my body, his searing gaze holding my own for a few breathless moments. I wasn't sure what he was going to do. He seemed to be waging an inner battle. He closed his eyes tightly; I closed mine in defeat. He wasn't...this ended here. I threw an arm over my head to cover my eyes in embarrassment.

"Georgia," he coasted his fingertips against my stomach.

"What?" I mumbled.

"Look at me," he said.

"No," I moaned and squeezed my eyes tighter.

"Yes," the word emerging from his throat in a husky tone. He pulled my arm away from my eyes gently.

"I don't want you to this in the morning. I don't want to anything with you."

My eyes fluttered open at his words. I bit my bottom lip as my thoughts flicked through my brain. Would I being with Tristan? Would I his hands on my body? His lips trailing across my sensitive flesh?

"I won't. I won't anything that happens between us," I whispered. He licked his lips slowly as his eyes seared mine. His hands held my waist and his thumbs worked small circles on my hipbones. My breathing came out in ragged pants and I closed my eyes again, the lust becoming too much to bear.

"Will *you* regret it in the morning?"

"I could never regret anything with you," he answered and his lips caressed mine sweetly. I got lost in the sensation of the breath that passed between us, the fingers threaded in my hair, the small undulations our bodies made against each other. With every breath I inhaled the fresh, clean scent I had come to associate with Tristan.

His lips trailed down my throat taking me leisurely, tasting every inch. I exhaled noisily and pressed my hips into his, my legs locked around his waist. He hovered above me in his boxer briefs as I wrapped my body around him, still dressed in my jeans and sweater.

Tristan's lips kissed and suckled at the hollow of my neck. His palms traveled up my ribcage, lifting my sweater. I leaned up so he could peel it off my body. I lay back down and his eyes took in my chest. He pulled the straps of my bra down my shoulders and over my arms. He kissed the exposed skin then gently unhooked my bra. He laid me down on his shirt in the sand, revealing my aching breasts. He sucked in a sharp breath as he pulled the lingering fabric off and tossed it on the sand.

"You're so beautiful," he murmured. My nipples puckered from the cool air. I ground my hips into his as he leaned over and kneaded one breast in his hand, taking the nipple between his lips and swirling it with his tongue.

"Tristan, I need you," I moaned and arched into him. He switched to my other breast and kneaded and sucked, causing my body to hum. The cool air against my overheated flesh had goosebumps running across my body. His hands caressed me reverently. He reached the button on my jeans and released it quickly. Unzipping my jeans, he ran his hands under the waistband and rubbed firmly around my hips, teasing along my pelvis, alternating light caresses with his fingertips and firmer strokes. It drove me wild, made me dizzy with arousal.

"Lift up, baby," he whispered and I complied. He pulled off my jeans and discarded them at my feet. Sitting back on his knees, his hand slowly ran up my legs, chasing away the goosebumps left from the cool air, leaving a trail of hot need in their wake. Reaching my panties, his fingers brushed along the elastic. I moaned and writhed beneath his touch.

His mouth curved in a lopsided grin as his eyes met mine. "No regrets?" he murmured.

"Never," I said, my eyes pleading for him to take me. His nose whispered along the sensitive flesh above my panties before he hooked his fingers in the fabric and dragged them down my legs. He ran his hands up my thighs and kneaded the aching flesh between my legs. He looked up at me again, before brushing his nose along my exposed mound. My breath caught as he slid a finger between the slick folds.

"Like silk," he breathed. I moaned and he dragged his finger through my lips and rubbed around my clit causing my hips to buck into him.

"God," I whimpered. He ran a single finger back down before slowly pushing it inside me, thrusting and swirling. My breathing became rough pants and he lowered his mouth to the sensitive flesh before sucking my clit between his lips. My hips keened and my body rolled in ecstasy. I moaned his name as he added another finger and thrust in and out of me, probing and exploring as his tongue swirled and his lips sucked. I felt his teeth drag along my clit and tug while pressing inside me. My body rocked as an orgasm overtook me.

"Tristan," his name caught in my throat as my body throbbed while he continued to suck. My toes dug into the sand and my hands grabbed for anything at my sides. He continued to suck as my orgasm lit up every nerve in my body. My skin heated and prickled as he held my hips firmly with one hand. He slowed his ministrations and my mind floated back to the present.

"Oh, God," I moaned. He lifted his head and a soft grin played across his sculpted lips.

"You're beautiful," he breathed as he crawled up my body and wrapped both of his hands in my hair. I leaned up to capture his lips with mine and tasted my tart arousal as our tongues mingled together.

"So beautiful," he murmured against my lips as he pulled my hair to one side, arching my neck so he could suck at the skin beneath my ear.

"I want you," I moaned, my hands trailing down to his slim hips to tug at his boxer briefs. He caught one of my hands and held it firmly in his own.

"We can still stop, Georgia. This can end here." He pulled back to search my eyes, his muscles taut. His breathing was erratic as he physically held himself back, waiting for confirmation.

"No. No regrets. I promise, no regrets. I want you." My eyes were heavy as I peered back at him. His tongue ran along his bottom lip and I followed the action. I captured his lips with my own in a searing kiss, showing him just how much I wanted him.

"I've got a condom, but I'm clean, Georgia. I want to feel you, I want it to be just us." He lowered his head and kissed me slowly. "I just want me inside you." He ran a thumb across my cheekbone as he whispered against my lips.

"Yes... I'm clean too and I'm on birth control." I pressed my body to his. "I want you inside me."

A garbled groan escaped his throat as I tugged the underwear from his body. I palmed the tight muscles of his backside in my hands. He moaned and inadvertently thrust causing the heat between our bodies to double as we lay together for the first time. We both sighed as Tristan teased his length around me deliciously slowly. He ran the thick head of his erection to my clit and my body spasmed with pleasure.

I locked my ankles around his waist and pressed into him. Tristan ran his length through my wet folds as he cupped my face in his hands, tracing slow circles on my cheeks with his thumbs, his lips devouring mine as he slowly sunk into me. Pleasure flooded my brain as I took him in, my body adjusting to him. Tears sprang to my eyes as the overwhelming sensations of pleasure pulsed through my body. Feelings intensified as we lay there finally connected. He slowly pulled out and then pushed back in, his eyes watching me with each stroke.

"You're perfect," Tristan whispered as he steadily rocked in and out of me. "You're so perfect."

My eyes fluttered open and I watched him hold his bottom lip between his teeth as if he were concentrating. "It's never…this is…" he paused without finishing his thought. I ran my hands up his smooth back and dug my short nails into the muscle, needing to feel him harder, faster, everywhere.

"You're perfect, too. You feel so perfect." Hearing my words he rocked more quickly, picking up a steady rhythm, making our bodies move together blissfully. He straightened above me and ran his palms down the back of my thighs, causing fire to ignite my nerve endings. He held them firmly in his hands and leaned over me, holding my legs tightly. He worked in and out, taking on a punishing rhythm, errant strands of hair falling over his forehead as he panted above me. My hand slid down between us and I touched his base where our bodies connected. His eyes flickered open as he watched.

"Fuck," the word escaped his lips as I began massaging my clit. His eyes closed and he angled deeper and thrust faster, his face twisting in pleasure and his body shuddering with release. I closed my eyes and fell over the cliff as my own climax wracked my body for the second time. He continued to ease in and out of me slowly as my nerves tingled with pleasure. My chest heaved and I tried to catch my breath, finding him staring down at me, his expression thoughtful and sated.

"You look beautiful when you do that," he said as a small grin lifted his mouth. I bit my lip in embarrassment and covered my eyes with the back of my arm.

"Oh no, not a chance. You're not hiding that beautiful face from me." He smiled as he lifted my arm away and I rolled my eyes at him. His grin widened and he rested on top of me, his elbows holding his weight. I sighed as our cool, sweat-slicked skin made contact.

"Okay?" He lifted his head in concern.

"Perfect." I pressed his head back into my neck. Our breathing mingled together as we tried to catch our breath. The cool breeze swept up our skin, the dune grass dancing, the waves singing on the shore—a symphony to our connection. A large smile spread across my face as I threaded my fingers through his hair. We lay there for a long time, still connected, listening to the sounds of the Carolina night until finally

Tristan turned his head and I felt his lips kissing me beneath my ear.

"No regrets, Georgia?" he whispered.

I turned my face to his with a content smile and my lips traced the shell of his ear. "No regrets, Tristan."

FIFTEEN

Georgia

I WOKE IN a cold sweat. Hair sticking to the back of my neck and heart racing, I shot into a sitting position. Another nightmare. A nightmare so vivid, truth and fiction bled together into one.

Heavy boots and vacant screams echoing down empty hallways.

The clammy cool sensation of finished wood against my cheek.

I was terrified of going back to sleep. A shift was taking place in my life—the beach house, Kyle, Tristan; the tides were changing and my brain was trying to make sense of it. Perhaps my guilty conscience was working overtime. Kyle had tried to call and text a few times that day and I had avoided all of it. I just needed distance to figure out if the life we had planned for us was the life I still wanted.

I wrapped a blanket around my shoulders before I realized I wasn't in my own room. Guilt turned my stomach -- I was in Tristan's bed. After we'd walked home from the cottage, Tristan had insisted I stay in his room. The paint fumes were still strong in my own; I'd thrown the windows open to air it out for a few hours, but it hadn't been enough.

I looked around the room, wondering where Tristan was. He'd held me in his arms until I'd fallen asleep, but now there was no sign of him. I shuffled to the French doors off his bedroom and stepped onto the deck. Wrapping a blanket around my shoulders, I leaned against the railing. The moonlight, sparkling like diamonds, reflected off the silver water. I was startled to see Tristan rocking back and forth slowly on the padded porch swing watching me. My heart leapt in my throat and I wasn't sure if I should leave him or curl into his safe arms and let him ease the ache in my heart left by the dream.

"Hey." He smiled fondly.

"Hey. Sorry to interrupt. I'm heading back to bed, I just—"

"Stay, Georgia." He slid his hand along the soft fabric of the swing next to him.

"Okay." I sat, curling my legs underneath me, covering my body with the warmth of the quilt.

"I could hear you tossing and turning. Did you have a nightmare?" He watched me with concern. I nodded and looked down the beach. Shadows from the trees stretched across the sand and made for an eerie landscape.

"Do you have them a lot?"

My eyes landed back on his. I could see the concern radiating from them. "Yeah, more lately," I whispered.

"Is it because…?" He sucked his lip between his teeth. I ached to run my tongue along it.

"I don't know." I looked away. He was wondering if what we'd done earlier had caused the nightmare. If I was having regrets.

"I don't want what happened between us to be weird, Georgia. It doesn't have to be," he said as he slid his hand out and let one finger caress the blanket overtop my knee.

"I know. But it is."

"I know that you probably think—"

"You don't know what I'm thinking. I don't even know what I'm thinking," I said more to myself than him. What I did know was what I'd experienced with Tristan earlier that night was unlike anything I'd ever experienced before. Not with Kyle, or anyone else. The emotions that ran between us, the connection we shared, were profound and left me reeling. It felt like he'd unlocked a new and previously undiscovered piece of my heart.

He watched for a moment then turned his head back to the water. He left his hand on the swing next to my thigh, one finger caressing the fabric. My brain couldn't focus on anything except that barest of touches. I wished the blanket wasn't between us.

"Do you think we can go back to how we were?" I looked up at him, the moonlight washing across his face, highlighting the angle of his jaw, the line of his nose and his full lips. No matter how powerful our connection had been, despite the fact that I was upset with Kyle, I still loved him. I wasn't sure I could give up loving Kyle for the night of bliss I'd shared with someone who went through his fair share of women.

"I don't want to, Georgia." His eyes glinted in the light.

"What?" My mouth dropped open in surprise. I hadn't meant to lose him in the fallout of our one-night stand. I'd told him I wouldn't have regrets, and I was trying desperately not to, but with the nightmares and my guilt over Kyle, I didn't know if I could keep them at bay.

"I don't want to lose you as a friend," I murmured as painful tears pricked my eyelids. It had only been one month. Four short weeks since this sweet, thoughtful, endearing man had come into my life, and already I was attached.

"That's not what I meant." He looked at me with a set jaw and searing eyes.

"What do you mean?" I whispered. His eyes cut into me and I couldn't avert my gaze if I tried. Tristan had me. The energy that passed between us was palpable. My heart thudded in my chest and I swallowed a lump that had settled in the back of my throat.

"I want you, all of you, Georgia. And I want you to want me too. I know you're with him, but he's not here. He's not with you, not really. And

I am." His words blazed a path straight to the pit of my stomach. My heartbeat thundered in my ears and drowned out the roaring ocean waves.

"What?" The word escaped in a breathless rush.

"I want you." He couldn't pull his eyes from mine anymore than I could pull mine from his.

"I thought that we were…that it was only—"

"Sex? No, Georgia. I thought it would be too. But it wasn't and I should have known it wouldn't be. It could never be just sex between us."

"But those girls at the club, I thought—"

"That I took them home? I didn't. I slept on my boat. Alone." He said the last word softly.

"But I'm with Kyle," I said, my eyes still locked on his beautiful green depths.

"Do you want to be?" His question cut me straight to the core.

"Of course," I whispered and ripped my eyes from his.

"It doesn't seem like that," he said, trailing a fingertip below my ear.

"Tristan…" I licked my lips. My throat was suddenly parched.

"It's okay, Georgia. If you're not ready, I won't force you. But I'm going to spend the entire summer helping you come to the realization that you want me too." The corner of his mouth lifted in a grin.

My eyes flitted back to his for a split second.

"Now share the blanket, I'm cold." He

scooted closer and tugged the quilt from my shoulders. He wrapped me in his arms, throwing the blanket over both of us. My brain galloped into overdrive. I should stop him, but he was so safe and warm. I knew we were crossing into dangerous territory but I couldn't pull away. I gave in and snuggled deep into the crook of his arm and rested my head against his chest. I inhaled his fresh, ocean scent and sighed.

"You're beautiful, Georgia." He stroked my hair with a heavy hand and rested his chin on top of my head. I wrapped an arm around his waist and shut my eyes tightly. I should feel guilty snuggling with Tristan. I thought of Kyle pouring over his legal books in our tiny apartment. But the guilt didn't come. I only remembered Kyle's apathy the past few years and a tear trailed down my cheek. Tristan rocked us back and forth with one leg as he stroked my hair affectionately.

"There's a shooting star," he said wistfully. I'd seen it and had already wished my wish. It wasn't for Kyle or Tristan, it was for me. I wished I could find the path that I was meant to be on, and I'd find it sooner rather than later without hurting the people I cared for. I shut my eyes, realizing I was already hurting people—Kyle, and probably Tristan, before the summer ended.

* * *

THE NEXT MORNING I awoke more than a little somber. The day was overcast but still warm and humid. I stepped onto the porch expecting to find Tristan, cup of coffee already in hand, but his usual chair was empty. My heart swelled and a small sigh of relief escaped my throat before I could catch it. I knew I should feel guilty about the connection I had with Tristan but every day it was becoming harder to push him away.

Should I pretend we had never happened and step back into Kyle's waiting arms? I wasn't sure I could. The peace I felt in Tristan's arms made me smile. I walked down the steps and traipsed slowly to the edge of the water. Inhaling the thick salty air, I listened to the waves washing ashore and the birds squawking above.

"Hey."

I twisted at the sound of Tristan's warm voice coming up from behind me.

"Hey."

The early morning humidity had beads of sweat collecting on his bronzed skin. He took deep breaths and his chest heaved, emphasizing the low-riding jogging shorts and the sharp cut of his pelvic muscle. He was the finest example of the male form I'd ever seen and my belly clenched at the sight of him.

"See something you like?" His head cocked to the side, a sexy smile lifting his lips. I bit my bottom lip as my eyes caught his. Hair damp with sweat lay across his forehead and I itched to push the errant strands away and press my lips to his in a morning kiss.

"No," I choked out. A throaty laugh escaped his lips.

"Didn't look like that to me." Tristan stepped closer, invading my personal space with his heaving chest and breathless panting. The air felt thick and heavy as it filled my lungs. Was it from the North Carolina humidity or the gorgeous man standing inches from me?

"It isn't anything I haven't seen before," I whispered, shutting my eyes from his intense gaze. He laughed again and I looked up at him with a small grin. He stepped away and pulled his white t-shirt out of the waistband of his shorts and wiped his face. The move was intensely erotic and I felt a zing of fire travel straight between my legs. My breathing came out in quick pants and I closed my eyes tightly and took a few deep breaths.

"You're up early," Tristan said mildly behind me, coming closer. I knew if I leaned back his hard chest would be against my back. Suddenly I yearned to feel his fingertips grazing my skin. Across my shoulders, traveling the arch of my neck.

As if he could read my mind, Tristan touched my skin as he pulled the hair off my neck. "You should come with me next time," he whispered in my ear. I knew he was referring to his early morning run, but I imagined lying beneath his body as he rocked into me, hands clutching the sand and sea grass as I panted and writhed.

"Everything okay, Georgia?" he asked,

dusting his nose up the curve of my neck behind my ear. I swallowed.

"Yesss," the hiss escaped my throat.

"Is something on your mind this morning?" I could hear the smile in his voice as his warm palm cupped my neck. I swayed on my feet and landed against his firm chest. I closed my eyes tightly, my brain blitzed with incomprehensible thoughts.

Fire shot straight to the pit of my stomach and goosebumps electrified my skin. Tristan snaked one arm around my waist and held me firmly to his chest, nuzzling his head into the crook of my neck and whispering his lips along the skin.

"Tristan," I said in a barely audible whisper.

"Yes, Georgia?" he replied in a throaty whisper, his teeth ghosting along the shell of my ear. My heart thudded so loud in my chest I was sure he could hear it.

"I shouldn't..." my voice cracked before I could get the rest of my thought out.

"You shouldn't, but you want to," he purred and turned me in his arms. He threaded his fingers in my hair and pulled my lips to his. He kissed me slowly, as if he were tasting and savoring me for the first time. I knew I should pull away, but I couldn't. I surrendered and wrapped my arms around his torso, digging my nails into his back.

He pressed his body to mine and I could feel his erection at my hip. Rocking his lower half into me, arousal coursed through my body.

Tristan trailed his hands down my neck, over my shoulders, playing with the straps of my tank top teasingly, before continuing down my ribcage and stopping at my thighs. He squeezed tightly before lifting me into his arms. I wrapped my legs around his waist and pressed my lips firmly to his. My hands ran along the sweat-dampened skin of his shoulders, playing over corded muscles and smooth flesh. I pulled away, catching my breath. He attacked my neck with adoring kisses and sharp nips: a pleasure-pain desire tingling my body.

"Georgia?" he whispered in a husky voice.

"Yes?" Desire had flooded my brain and I rocked my hips seeking friction. I couldn't think straight; I wanted Tristan any way I could get him.

"I need coffee." He pulled away and gave me his cocky grin, my body pooling with lust before anger flared to life. I didn't know if I wanted to feel his lips on me again or smack him.

"You are a tease," I huffed. He stuck his lip out and pouted at me before squeezing the cheeks of my ass and giving me another lopsided grin. I glared at him before giving him a playful slap on the cheek. "You stink anyway." I wiggled out of his arms and slipped down his body. His arousal still very ready for action. "Go shower and meet me back here for coffee."

He shook his head and laughed before twisting one hand in my hair and pulling my lips to his in a quick kiss. Butterflies came to life in my stomach. The way he could be so sexy and sensual one minute and completely and utterly sweet the next left me in a tailspin. And I enjoyed every minute of it.

"Hey, G." Drew wandered into the kitchen a short while later with a stack of papers and a highlighter in her hand. I had two mugs and was pouring coffee into one. Tristan wasn't yet out of the shower. "You must have heard me coming." Drew set down her work and took one of the freshly poured mugs.

"Talked to Kyle?" Drew took a sip and winced at the temperature. I heaved an exasperated sigh. It had been a few days since Kyle had canceled on his weekend plans. Drew had no idea that things had heated up between Tristan and me.

"No," I answered blankly.

"You that mad that he couldn't make it?" She took another sip. I shrugged in response. Truth was I wasn't sure if I was mad or glad that he hadn't come down.

"Something else going on, G?" Drew set her coffee cup down. I fidgeted with frayed strings on my cut-off shorts. "Spill it, G."

"Nothing to spill, Drew." I brought the coffee cup to my lips.

"I can see you lying from a mile away. It's not like you to hold a grudge against Kyle. In fact, you forgive him way more than I ever would—"

"Mornin', Drew. Thanks for making coffee, Georgia." Tristan ran his fingers through his wet hair smiling warmly before strolling to the coffee pot to pour a mug for himself. Drew looked from him to me—her eyes widened.

"Georgia," she mouthed, her eyes darting back to Tristan. I narrowed mine at her.

"Did you…?" She made an obscene sexual gesture with her hands. My eyes widened at her but Tristan turned before I had a chance to answer. It didn't matter; I would have lied through my teeth.

"We should go to that vineyard today." Tristan leaned a hip against the counter.

"Yeah, sounds great," I mumbled and took another sip of my coffee, avoiding both of their eyes.

"Drew? You in?" Tristan asked her.

"Umm, yeah… sounds fun, but I've got work, so you guys go. Have fun." I could feel her eyes boring a hole into my skull, but I refused to meet her gaze.

"We'll hold off then—" I started to offer.

"No, no, no. Wine isn't really my thing. You guys go ahead."

"Maybe Silas—"

"Silas didn't come home last night," Drew interrupted me before picking up her papers and sliding off the barstool, bumping shoulders with me intentionally. I glanced up at her and she wiggled her eyebrows. I rolled my eyes at her.

"What do you say, Georgia?" Tristan's hand

traveled the short distance across the counter and his fingertips brushed my own. My gaze raced up to his dancing eyes and over to Drew, who had an interested look on her face as she backed out of the kitchen with a saucy grin. Damn Tristan for being so obvious and irresistible that my hormones didn't stand a chance against his undeniably sexy self.

"Sounds great," I mumbled as I took another drink from my mug.

* * *

SOFT STRAINS OF piano and guitar filtered from my stereo speakers as Tristan and I drove inland to the vineyard. *The D-Bags* and *Thirty Seconds to Mars* dominated on the trip, but this song began slower. It was beautiful and haunting even before a man and woman's voice sang together, the words echoing through my car.

"What is this?" My hands tightened on the steering wheel, the heartbreaking words consuming me.

"*Poison and Wine* by The Civil Wars," he answered.

"It's so sad," I murmured. Tristan only nodded in response as the man and woman continued to sing. The pain in their voices was so palpable it tore me to my core, the lyrics shredding my insides. I tried to loosen my hands on the wheel and watch the landscape breeze by.

"You okay with this, Georgia?"

"What?" I looked into Tristan's eyes as we crossed the vineyard parking lot a few minutes later.

"Being here, with me? Just the two of us?" A small frown played across his face.

"Of course. No big deal," I said then twisted my long hair and pulled it over my shoulder to keep it off my neck. The humidity was killing me. Maybe the Carolina coast wasn't my idea of heaven after all.

"Good." His mouth lifted in an endearing grin. He grabbed my hand and locked it firmly in his own. I looked down at our entwined fingers and a small frown washed across my face. I tried to banish it before he noticed.

I fell into step beside him and we walked with our hands linked. God, I hoped whatever I was doing I wouldn't end up hurting him. I'd come to the conclusion this was just a summer fling for him, and while I had no idea where I would end up at the end of the summer, namely back in D.C. with Kyle or not, I did know that Tristan would be heading back to Jacksonville.

The drive had been comfortable, if not quiet. I still hadn't spoken to Kyle. He'd tried to text and call a few times since Friday and undoubtedly knew I was upset. His last voicemail actually sounded angry that I hadn't returned his calls. Maybe I was wrong, but I was so over always being there. He went to school, he worked, he put 110% into his career, and I was left with everything else, which was nothing. I was also fighting the guilt that had grown since Tristan and I had been together. Did I regret it? I didn't want to. I'd told him I wouldn't. But I knew it was wrong being with him while I was still with Kyle, wrong to not leave Kyle first if I knew we were having problems. It was wrong not telling Kyle after it happened. It was just wrong. I found myself in a no-win situation and I was the only one to blame. I felt every decision I'd made had been the wrong one. And yet here I was, my hand locked with Tristan's because I was so inexplicably drawn to him I couldn't stay away. I was a moth to his flame.

I heaved a sigh as we stepped into the cool warehouse.

Tristan led us to a desk and paid for a tour, grabbing a map that would direct us through the vineyard. We headed out the other end of the building and walked the grass path that led to the rows of vines. At the end of every row there was a small stand set up to provide samples of the wine created with each grape.

We walked and chatted, our hands twisted together, navigating the rows. We read signs that described the types of grapes, the types of wine produced, and the flavor profile of each. We sipped samples provided by the winery and talked about ones we liked and ones we didn't. I wrote down a few that stood out with the intention of ordering a few bottles to keep at the beach house.

We laughed the more wine we sipped, the heat and humidity making the effects of the wine more potent. Weaving through rows, I laughed as Tristan plucked a purple grape off a vine and popped it in his mouth. His laid-back attitude was refreshing. I smiled more. I laughed more. I felt lighter—like the ache that had permanently settled in my chest eased when we were together. We stopped to read a sign, and Tristan's arms wound around my waist from behind and his lips tickled the skin of my shoulder. I leaned into him and he draped one forearm across my neck, pulling me tight to his lean body and nuzzling the crook of my neck. Our night together hadn't been a one-night stand, Tristan had made that clear, and now he was acting like we were more. Showing me he wanted more, but what did I want?

"I think the wine is going to my head." I leaned against a whitewashed wooden fence.

"We can take a break." He pressed his body flush with mine, wrapping his arms around my waist and locking his hands at my lower back. I laid my head on his chest and breathed deeply, closing my eyes.

"I don't think wine and heat go well together," I mumbled. A small moan escaped my throat as he rubbed his hands up and down my back. "Feels good." Tristan rested his chin on my head. We stood like that for a few minutes. The sun was starting to set and a spray of orange and pink streaked the sky. Tristan's hands settled again on my lower back and his fingertips edged under the hem of my shirt and stroked softly against my skin. His touch shot fire through my veins and sent shivers running through my body.

"This is nice."

"Mmm," I hummed in agreement.

"I like having you in my arms."

"I like being there," I whispered as I nuzzled further into his chest, inhaling his clean scent. Tristan's fingers continued to drift just under the hem of my shirt, rocking us back and forth slowly. I yawned happily and tightened my arms around his waist.

"Are you okay to walk back to the car or am I going to have to carry your drunk ass?" Tristan crooked a grin and I looked up into his eyes with a lazy smile.

"I'm good." My eyes focused on his full lips. I licked mine as my eyes flicked back to his, tentatively pressing my lips to his. He kissed me back lightly, his hands moving up to hold my face, his thumbs caressing my cheekbones as he kissed me decadently. Finally we pulled apart and I grinned at him. He shook his head before the corners of his mouth lifted in a heart-stopping smile.

"Come on, wino." He caught my hand in his own and dragged me behind him, making our way back to the parking lot. My eyes trained on his cargo-clad bottom and I heaved a happy sigh. The guy was hot, but more than that he was sweet and funny and easy to be with. He had the ability to make me feel beautiful, wanted, and special. He held me like I'd never been held, like he was holding me tightly for his own sake as for mine. I felt a connection to him that I'd never felt with anyone else, not even in the early days with Kyle.

I frowned for an instant at the realization. This day at the vineyard hadn't just been a fun day sampling wine and holding hands; we had crossed a line and there was no going back. Even if I never saw Tristan after this summer, I knew I would never be the same girl that stepped into that beach house just a few weeks ago. From this day forward I would think of my life as pre-Tristan and post-Tristan. It only remained to be seen whether post-Tristan would be happy or heartbreaking.

SIXTEEN

Georgia

"UP FOR SOME reading?" Tristan sidled up next to me as I was doing dishes the next day.

I arched an eyebrow at him. "You want to continue 'Tristan and Isolde'?"

"Sure, unless you went on without me." He bumped shoulders with me playfully.

"I haven't."

"Go grab the book." He swatted me lightly on the bottom as I hustled out of the kitchen. I swiped the book off my nightstand as I heard a text message come through my phone. Another from Kyle. He'd called and texted all day yesterday before I'd finally silenced my phone. I needed time to process my feelings, and Kyle pleading for me not to be upset with him wasn't going to get me closer to figuring things out.

I returned to the kitchen with the book in my arms, Tristan watching me with his arms crossed and a sexy smirk on his face. I rolled my eyes. How could one person exude so much sex in a single glance? He shook his head with a laugh before we stepped onto the porch. I looked up to the bright sun as the sweet ocean breeze washed over my face, inhaled deeply, and closed my eyes, soaking up the warm rays.

"You're at home here."

I turned and looked at Tristan gazing back at me with a fond smile.

"I think I am." Realization washed over me. It felt good to feel at home somewhere. Kyle had always been my home, wherever he was I felt at home, but at some point over the last few months that had shifted. Maybe even over the last few years. It had been so subtle it'd taken me a while to realize it.

We settled a few yards from the shore, perched on a small dune, the tall grass swaying in the breeze around us. I opened the book to the last page we'd read.

"My turn." Tristan took the paperback from my hands. My eyes widened before I grinned at him indulgently.

"What? Don't think I can read?" He flashed me a panty-melting grin.

"Read on, Hemingway."

He rolled his eyes in response before he began to read.

He read about Tristan and Isolde being together for the first time after she married King Mark. He read about Tristan's guilt over betraying the king, but how their love was so strong it refused to be denied.

I watched Tristan's sensual lips mouth the lines. The melodic timbre of his voice whispering the cadence of the words lulled me into relaxation and I closed my eyes, losing myself in the story.

"Do you think Tristan did the right thing?" I murmured some time later

"Leaving her? I don't know. He sacrificed himself, his love."

"Duty and honor are important," I said. "If you sacrifice those, don't you tarnish love?"

"It destroys them to be apart—'life and death together,'" he quoted.

"It's beautiful, isn't it?" I said forlornly.

"Their inseparable love?" Tristan watched me.

"The idea they can neither live nor die without each other. Their hearts are melded as one. It hurts so much to love each other and not be together she wishes she would have let him die in that ditch, and yet, she wouldn't have then known what all consuming love felt like if she had."

"Between a rock and a hard place."

"It's tragic and beautiful at the same time—'I'd never know what now I know… the love of you'… It breaks my heart." I looked at the rolling waves. "Do you think love like that exists? A love so strong that you'd rather die than be apart?"

"I don't know. It ruined my dad after my mom left…" he trailed off. "What about you?"

I sat and watched the waves lap the shore and the grass whisper around my legs. I knew what I was supposed to say. I was supposed to feel that way for Kyle. I thought I'd felt that for him at one time, but I think he had been my lifeline. His support had saved me, but had his love? Could I live without Kyle? I'd slowly become aware that maybe I wasn't as wrapped in him as I'd thought. Our lives had been intertwined for years, but maybe they weren't intertwined with love so much as a shared history.

"I don't know," I said cautiously. "Tristan left Isolde for years though, so how inseparable could they have been?" I shrugged.

"Just because they're apart doesn't mean they don't love each other. It broke them to be apart." Tristan murmured. "Do you think he was with anyone else?" Tristan's fingertip traced circles in the sand between us.

"Why?"

"'He fled his sorrow through many shores and many lands.' Sounds like a metaphor for many women." He flashed a lopsided grin.

"Is that what you do?" I held his gaze. The grin slowly fell from his mouth as we watched each other. He ran his tongue along his bottom lip.

"Maybe," he answered, never breaking eye contact with me. I inhaled a quick breath. That one word held so much more meaning than even I knew.

* * *

"GEORGIA!" DREW'S CHIRPY voice called out Monday afternoon. I was crouched down painting the porch a creamy white. The guys had sanded the railings the past week and I had finally been able to convince Silas and Drew to help me. Drew had just ducked into the house for a few minutes.

"What?" I called back as I swiped a damp tendril off my forehead.

"Delivery."

"'Kay." I set my brush down and headed up the stairs and into the house. Silas was hot on my heels as I stepped through the French doors and found a large yellow rose bouquet sitting on the dining table.

"For you." Drew nodded to the flowers with an interested look on her face.

"Did you already read the card?" I cast her a stern glance. She only shrugged in response, an affirmative in Drew's book.

I touched my nose to one of the petals and inhaled. I was sure there was a law somewhere that said you had to sniff any flower, whether they had a scent or not. I plucked the card nestled amongst the petals.

I love you. Forgive me? - Kyle

I frowned for a moment before putting the card on the table next to the crystal vase. Guilt burned a hole in my stomach like acid. If Kyle only knew I'd betrayed him after everything we'd been through, he wouldn't be begging me for forgiveness. I was instantly ashamed for ignoring his calls the last few days. And I was even more ashamed that it hadn't been difficult for me. Besides, he'd been so busy so far this summer we'd only exchanged a few quick texts and phone calls a few times a week. There was little difference between then and now.

Plus there had been Tristan.

"You going to forgive him?" Drew wrapped an arm around my waist and laid her head on my shoulder.

"I don't know," I frowned.

"Do you want to?" she asked.

"I don't know that either," I said quietly.

"I think the fact that you don't know is telling, love." Silas fingered a petal absently.

"Who are they from?" Tristan stepped into the room wearing a threadbare T-shirt and paint-splattered sweats, cut off at the knee and hanging deliciously low on his hips. He and Gavin were finishing the interrupted paint job on my bedroom. Silas had been gone all weekend—he refused to tell me who with—so I'd slept in his room the last two nights until mine was finished.

My eyes found Tristan's and held his gaze. Tristan's eyes flashed to Drew's and then back to mine.

"They from Kyle?" he asked.

I nodded in response.

"They're nice," he murmured, his gazed focused intently on me.

"Georgia hates roses," Silas grumbled from beside me.

"I don't." I jabbed him with my elbow.

"You do, and if he wasn't so wrapped up in himself he would know that." Silas glared back at me.

"I don't hate roses." My eyes found Tristan's again. His swirled with emotion before they broke our gaze and he continued to the sink, washing out a paint-covered brush. He left the kitchen a few moments later without another word.

"That's it, I'm calling it. Girls' night tonight." Drew rubbed my back with an open palm.

"Agreed," Silas chimed in and wrapped an arm around my shoulder.

"I'm fine," I said.

"You are far from fine, but if being stuck between two ridiculously hot men means fine, then I so wish I had your problem," Silas grinned.

"I'm not stuck between two men." I rolled my eyes.

"So you've chosen one then?" Silas turned a stern gaze on me.

"No, I mean—"

"That's what I thought. Girls' night!" Silas

skipped off to the kitchen and pulled the tumbler and a bottle of Kahlua out of the cupboard.

"Silas, it's not even five," I moaned.

"Rule numero uno this summer: it's five o'clock somewhere."

"You two are alcoholics." I pointed at both of them with a grin. "And I don't think White Russians are a good idea," I finished, remembering that the last time we'd drunk them Tristan and I had slept together.

"I told you, girls' night. No boys allowed, so if the drinks get you all horned up, it's just me and Drew," Silas tossed over his shoulder.

"Silas." I threw a nearby pen at him.

"I know how you get with a little alcohol, love." He shrugged before he and Drew burst into laughter.

"What's so funny?" Gavin rambled in with a grin. "White Russians? Count me in." He wrapped his arms around Drew's middle.

"No can do, big boy. Girls only," Silas said.

"But what about—"

"Silas is more girl than Georgia and I put together. He's in," Drew laughed.

"I'll take that as a compliment." Silas poured the first drink into a glass. "For the guest of honor," handing it to me.

"Why is Georgia the guest of honor?" Gavin frowned. Drew shot him a glance and shook her head. "So what are Tristan and I supposed to do tonight?"

"You'll manage," Drew said and smacked

him on the ass.

"We're being kicked out," Gavin glanced at Tristan as he walked into the kitchen. Tristan's eyebrows rose in surprise then his eyes caught mine.

"Everything okay?" He directed the question to me.

"Everything's perfect. Get out," Drew said sweetly as Silas handed her a glass.

A frown settled on Tristan's face. "Georgia, can I talk to you for a minute?" He made his way toward me.

"Nope, Georgia's off limits tonight," Drew intercepted and turned him toward the hallway. "You'll survive, lover boy." She patted Tristan's bottom for good measure. He looked over his shoulder at me with wide eyes and a sweet, boyish smile.

"You need to fill us in," Drew said. The three of us sat on the porch an hour and another round later.

"I don't want to." I scrunched my nose up at the concerned faces of my two best friends.

"Well, don't bother telling us there isn't anything going on between you and Tristan. That ship has so sailed, literally and metaphorically speaking." Silas winked at me.

"You are so corny." Drew rolled her eyes.

"But I make a helluva White Russian." Silas took another drink.

"I'll drink to that." We all lifted our glasses and clinked them together.

"Now as you were." Silas nodded to me.

"I still don't want to."

"Blah blah blah, get past the part where you play coy and onto the good stuff," Silas chastised.

I glared at him. "So we hang out. We click. But I click with Kyle too."

"Not like you've been clickin' with Tristan." Silas winked.

"Shut up." I threw a balled up napkin at him. "We click. A lot. But we click with a lot of people, right? It doesn't mean you leave the one person you've always loved over a summer... *click*." I emphasized the last word.

"I see you *clickin'*," Silas put air quotes around the word, "a whole lot more with Tristan than I've ever seen you click with Kyle."

"Me too," Drew chimed in as she took another drink. I rolled my eyes at both of them.

"What about you? You seem to be doin' a lot of clickin' with a lot of somebodies." I shot him a glare.

"You have to choose one," Silas said, completely ignoring my attempt at redirection.

I only stared at him then averted my eyes a moment later as I took another drink. I knew I had to choose one; I had a decision to make, but so far I wasn't convinced that Mr. Promiscuous was worth walking away from the only person I'd ever loved.

"You said yourself he's a manwhore. All this clickin' is all it is," I said to Drew, but I wasn't sure I believed my own words.

"Okay, enough with the clickin' already," Silas said.

"Fine, he flirts… we flirt. He's a slut. Aren't you the one that told me I should hook up with him this summer?"

"Yeah, but I told you not to get attached, and you are so attached, Georgia."

"No, I'm not."

"Oh, please." She rolled her eyes. She didn't know the half of it. She had no idea Tristan and I had slept together. I dreaded what they would say if they knew the full story. The truth was, I wasn't convinced Tristan and I hadn't been a one-night stand, despite what he said. It still meant I'd cheated on Kyle, but I didn't want to throw everything I had with Kyle away, tear his heart out, rip mine to pieces, over a drunken indiscretion.

"I hate this," I whispered.

"I know, love." Silas scooted his chair closer to mine and wrapped me in a tight embrace.

"I wish I'd never met Tristan." A tear leaked down my cheek as the guilt tightened my heart. "I wish Kyle and I could just be like we were."

"But then you wouldn't have known," Drew said softly.

"Known what? That I'm an inconsiderate bitch who leads two men on?" More tears escaped from my eyes.

"That you and Kyle weren't working. We've been trying to tell you that, but it took Tristan to make you see it." Drew reached across the table and held my hand tightly.

"But I want Kyle and I to work. We've always worked."

"But what if you work better with someone else?" Silas asked.

"Like who? Tristan? The guy who sleeps with half the county—your words exactly." I glanced at Drew.

"Maybe, maybe not. But someone." Drew's eyes swam with concern.

"I can't talk about it anymore. More alcohol." I tipped my glass toward Silas.

"You got it, love." He grinned before taking my glass for a refill.

After we'd drunk our way through a few more rounds, Silas disappeared to his room phone in hand, avidly texting with a grin. Gavin and Tristan had returned from wherever Drew had hustled them off to and joined us in a last round of drinks. I was curled up under an afghan and nearly passed out on the couch. Gavin and Drew had left for a beach walk, and Tristan sat in the chair opposite, sipping the last of his drink and watching me. I could feel his eyes but I refused to meet them. I couldn't talk to him right now, not about anything serious. My talk with Silas and Drew was still rolling around in my brain. I knew I had to choose, but at this point I couldn't choose anyone but Kyle. He was my everything and had been for most of my life. What Tristan and I had was fun and sweet, but nothing more.

The waves on the beach echoed through the stillness as the breeze blew in the windows, twisting the curtains and accentuating the silence that stretched between us.

Tristan finally stood and I chanced a glance at his shadowed form walking into the kitchen. He set his glass in the sink then turned back to me. Our eyes locked for a moment before he spoke.

"I'm going to head to bed," he murmured.

"Okay," I answered and curled up tighter in the blanket.

"You're not sleeping there are you?" He nodded to the couch.

"I can't sleep in my room. The paint fumes." Silas was staying home tonight, so I'd moved to the couch.

"Sleep in my room, Georgia. I know after the flowers and whatever…we don't have to…I can sleep here," he rambled before motioning again to the couch.

"I'm not running you out of your room." I tucked my head further into the pillow. The high from the drinks had worn off, and Silas and Drew's lecture hadn't much helped. I just wanted to curl up and fall asleep and hopefully forget about the painful decision that lay ahead of me.

"You can't sleep on the couch, Georgia." He stepped toward me. "I insist. Come on. Don't make this weirder than it has to be." He held a hand out to me. My eyes shot up to meet his and I could see the determined set of his jaw. I rolled my eyes and took his hand, standing up and curling the blanket around me as we walked down the hall to his bedroom.

"I'll just change and be out of your hair." He grabbed a pair of sleep shorts and walked into the en suite bathroom. Returning a few minutes later, he found me curled up on the bed before he sighed and walked toward the door.

"Tristan?" I called timidly.

"Yeah?" He stopped at the door and turned to me.

"You don't have to go." I scooted over on the bed.

"It's okay. You've got a lot going on, Georgia. I'm not here to complicate it."

"It won't. I just feel bad for you sleeping on the couch."

"Wouldn't be the first time." He shrugged.

"Come on, I won't bite." A smirk tipped my lips as I lifted the blanket up.

"I don't want… things are so—"

"Just sleeping, Tristan," I interjected.

"Okay," he walked back to the bed and slipped under the comforter. I tucked my head into the pillow as Tristan lay stiffly beside me.

"Didn't know you were so square." I turned toward him. He lifted an eyebrow at me before he stretched his arm out and I tucked into it.

He laid his palm on the back of my head and stroked my hair before tucking his nose in and inhaling. The notion of him taking in my scent, seeking comfort from it, left a warm feeling in my stomach.

"I don't want to make things harder for you, Georgia." His lips moved against my hair.

"You're not. I like us," I said before stretching an arm over his stomach and holding him tightly.

"What is us?" he murmured.

"Friends," I answered instantly.

"Who kiss?" he said faintly. I frowned without responding. "And sleep together?" he murmured.

"We're just sleeping," I said quietly.

"If that's what you want to think."

I heard him but I was too drowsy to respond. Tristan's fingers continued to stroke through the strands of my hair as I drifted off to sleep surrounded by his ocean-fresh scent that was fast becoming comforting.

"Georgia," a deep voice whispered. My neck was damp with sweat and I kicked off the twisted covers. My hand ran across a hard shape next to me and I inhaled a familiar, clean scent.

"It's okay," Tristan reassured as he stroked my back.

My heart was pounding in my chest. "Did I… did I say anything?" I managed through quick pants.

"I couldn't tell what you were saying. You sounded terrified. You're crying, Georgia." He swiped tears away with the pad of his thumb then pulled the hair off my neck and swiped the damp locks off my forehead. "Is it the same dream you always have?" he asked. The bright moonlight reflected off his searing green eyes as he watched me closely.

"Yes." I shut my eyes tightly and took a deep, cleansing breath.

"I'll get you some water." He hopped out of bed, ran to the bathroom, and returned a minute later with a cup in his hands. I took long swallows as the cool liquid washed away the ache in my chest and calmed my nerves. He set the cup on the nightstand and lay down in the bed beside me, wrapping an arm around my shoulders, pulling me tightly to him. I pressed my face into his chest and tried to take deep breaths.

"Do you want to talk about it?"

"No," I answered quickly.

"I'm here if you want to."

"I know."

"Have you ever talked to anyone about it?" he asked hesitantly.

"About a dream? No," I said in a clipped tone. He continued to run his hand down my hair; the motion was comforting and I was thankful I had woken up next to someone after that dream.

"This seems worse than before," he said, referring to the last time I'd woken from a bad dream and found him on the porch swing. This had been worse, so much worse.

"It wasn't," I lied. "Can we go back to sleep?"

"Okay," rubbing circles on my back.

The sun peeked through the curtains what felt like hours later, but could have been minutes. We both stretched and yawned and pretended we were just waking up from sleep, but the dark circles under our eyes confirmed that neither of us had slept well after my nightmare.

SEVENTEEN

Georgia

AFTER TRISTAN AND I had silently gotten out of bed, he made coffee, I took a shower, then we met on the deck as usual. Except this morning coffee was quieter than normal. The dream was on my mind. Tristan had been right, it was more intense than they've been and I had a feeling it was because I was so chewed up about making a decision. But after lying next to Tristan all night, I'd made up my mind. Still reeling from the nightmare, lying in Tristan's arms while he comforted me, my decision had been made.

Gavin and Tristan had locked themselves in the spare bedroom where they'd set up their office for the summer. They were both on the phone off and on, and I heard keyboards clicking away. Silas and Drew crawled out of bed later and I sent them into town to pick up more paint to finish the deck. Once they cleared out and I was sure the guys were immersed in work, I scrolled to that familiar name in my contact list.

Seeing Kyle's face come up had my tummy twisting uncomfortably.

By the time I'd hung up with him more than an hour later, my stomach had settled. I knew I'd made the right decision. The nightmare last night had been the catalyst. It'd told me all I needed to know; who I should be with and who I shouldn't.

There wasn't really another decision that I could make. I had to follow my heart, and my heart was fully and completely devoted to Kyle and our future together. The nightmares had been getting worse, so much worse—two in the short time since Tristan and I had slept together. Two vivid, terrifying dreams that left my heart pounding, fear and adrenaline rushing through my system. I knew my subconscious was trying to tell me something—it was telling me that the path I was on was the wrong one. My nights were peaceful when I was with Kyle, but the nights when I'd been wrapped in Tristan's arms the nightmares had been nearly unbearable.

I knew Tristan would be upset, but thankfully things hadn't gone too far before they'd ended. We'd had one night, but it was just that—one night. We'd been drunk, I'd missed Kyle, and I'd made a bad decision. I didn't look forward to telling Tristan, but he would move on. There was no doubt in my mind that it wouldn't be long before he had someone else warming his bed.

I smiled contentedly at the memory of Kyle's words in my ear. The reassurances that once we got through this summer, once we were back in the same city, things would be better. The soothing timbre of Kyle's voice sent warm tingles coursing through my body, reminding me of summer nights lying in the grass looking at the stars and talking about our future.

"Hey, G." Drew wandered out on the deck with a glass of sweet tea.

"Hey," I said brightly. My shoulders felt so much lighter for the decision I'd just made. Kyle was my home. He knew me—my history. He'd been my everything for as long as I could remember. He'd pulled me through in hard times and never turned his back. Just because he was working a lot of hours didn't mean I could turn my back on him—on us. He was working hard to build our future. I knew that. I couldn't let my loneliness get the best of me. No more drinking around Tristan, I vowed to myself. He was hot every day, but when I was drunk, he became irresistible.

"Who was on the phone?" She threw herself into the chair next to me.

"Kyle." I sighed happily.

"Really?" She arched an eyebrow.

"Really."

"You seem pretty happy to have just gotten off the phone with that douche—I mean Kyle." She smiled with fake sweetness.

"Kyle's my boyfriend, so play nice."

"So you chose?" Drew asked with concern.

"You don't approve?" I glared at her.

"I didn't say that. I just hope you're making

the right decision," she said before taking a sip of her tea.

"I am. Kyle is it for me. I know that now more than ever," I said with a tender smile.

"You and Kyle are back together?"

I winced when I heard his voice. "We were never really apart…," I muttered. Tristan stood with two glasses of sweet tea in his hands. I could see his jaw tighten as a range of emotion flashed across his eyes.

"I'm sorry, Tristan. I didn't want you to find out like this, but after last night—"

"Did you tell him?"

"What?" My eyes bore into his, pleading with him to not do this here, in front of Drew.

"About us? What happened on the beach—"

"No," I cut him off. "But I will."

"You think he'll be forgiving then?" His green eyes blazed into me. They cut straight into my stomach like a blade.

"I…I don't know. I just couldn't tell him over the phone," I whispered, the look on his face stealing the air from my lungs. Tristan was hurt because I chose Kyle.

"I hope you'll be happy, Georgia. Here," he shoved the sweet tea at me then turned and stalked into the house. I watched him leaving and my heart clenched at the pain that I'd seen etched across his face.

"What happened last night?" Drew asked.

"We slept together," I said, still watching the door he'd disappeared into.

"You what?" Drew's voice rose.

"Not like that." At least not last night I thought to myself. "Because the paint fumes in my room, I just slept in his bed," I trailed off and then shut my eyes. I had so royally fucked this summer up. I'd hurt two men that cared for me, trampled over their feelings because I couldn't let either go. "I didn't think he would be so upset," I mumbled.

"I knew he would. He wanted you to choose him."

"I didn't think—we were just hanging out. Friends. I thought that was it." I turned to her.

"Not to him. You didn't see the way he looked at you? His eyes light up when he's with you. He watches you when you're not paying attention. It's adorable. Or sickening. I'm not sure which really. I feel bad for him." Drew took another drink.

"What? He's a manwhore, Drew. I'm sorry if I hurt him, but I'm sure I was nothing more than a fling, it's a long summer, he'll get over me just fine. Trust me."

"Are you sure you trust yourself?" Drew asked.

"Of course," I scoffed before standing and marching back into the house and into my bedroom.

Kyle said he would be down for the Fourth of July weekend, only a few weeks away. It felt like a lifetime, I was so anxious to see him. I knew I'd have to tell him then what had happened between Tristan and me. Kyle and I had always been honest with each other and I knew I at least owed him the truth.

I set my tea on the nightstand and my eyes settled on *The Legend of Tristan and Isolde*. The memories of reading on the beach flooded my brain. I closed my eyes and heaved a sigh. I'd hoped our friendship could remain intact after the brief fling we'd had, but now I knew that was too much to hope for.

I glanced back at the paperback with the lovelorn couple on the cover. A couple tortured and broken by their love. I frowned and dropped the book into my duffel bag and then shoved it under my bed.

* * *

"HEY, GEORGIA. BEEN a few days." Tristan's lopsided grin greeted me as I stepped into the balmy morning.

"Hey." I forced a smile. "I was just checking the temp, I'll leave you—"

"No, join me," he said as he patted the chair next to him. I clenched my teeth together as I made my way closer. He'd been avoiding me since the awkward confrontation on the porch.

"I'm sorry, Tristan. I really didn't want you to find out like that. Kyle's just always been my person, and what we had was nice, but I can't just leave him. I love him and I just want you to know, you can move on. I mean, I won't be upset. I don't expect you to not date anyone the rest of the summer just because you're staying here." I knew I was rambling but the situation had been so awkward between us, all of my thoughts had escaped in a rush.

"Not a problem, Georgia. We were just a fling. It's cool. Happens all the time." He grinned that heart-stopping, lopsided grin before taking another sip of his coffee. My heart clenched at his words. I'd suspected that we'd just been a fling, even said it out loud to Drew, but hearing the words from his mouth hurt. It was confirmation that I'd been one in a long line of one-night stands for him.

"Okay," I murmured.

"Any plans for Fourth of July?" he asked.

"Um, Kyle's coming down, but otherwise, no," I said before turning my gaze to the grey-blue water lapping the shoreline.

"Mind if I invite a few people over? We've got prime viewing location for the fireworks."

"Uh, sure." I wasn't expecting that. "People from Jacksonville...or...?"

"From around here. Kelsey and Briana, maybe." He shrugged.

"Kelsey and Briana?"

"The girls from the club," he responded before grinning that charming, lopsided grin again that stole my breath every fucking time.

I frowned for a moment before catching myself. "Right, Kelsey and Briana. I'll tell Silas and Drew."

"Sounds great. Thanks, Georgia."

I frowned as I watched him saunter back into the house. His demeanor was so off. This wasn't the Tristan I'd become close with over the summer. Was this the real him? He'd never been like this toward me before, but what was he being? Friendly? Open? Honest? What was missing? Was this the Tristan that wasn't trying to get in my pants—treating me just like one of the guys? The thought sat uneasy with me.

I sighed and took a sip of coffee. If this was how it was going to be between us I'd have to get used to it. I wasn't sure if I preferred this or the awkward tension that had permeated the house the last few days. I would miss the sweet, thoughtful, friendly Tristan from earlier this summer.

* * *

I WAS IN the kitchen chugging a glass of water when Tristan wandered in a few nights later. His hair was perfectly tousled with a few stray wisps falling over his forehead. All the time we'd been spending in the sun had streaked his hair golden and brought out the bright green of his eyes. He looked devastating.

I had finished painting the porch in unbearably humid temperatures and was still in a grungy, paint-splattered tank top and a pair of ratty shorts, my hair in a floppy ponytail with loose chunks falling out. I looked a hot mess, minus the hot. Or if the hot referred to the temperature of my skin, in that case, then yes, I was a hot mess.

"What's up?" I gave him my best bright grin.

"Headed out." He flipped through his wallet before sliding it in his back pocket.

"Date?" The word escaped my mouth before I could stop it.

He quirked one eyebrow at me before responding. "Something like that," he answered.

"No time for dinner?" Here I was, making awkward conversation with Tristan.

"Sorry. Leftovers maybe?"

"Okay. Have fun." And now I sounded like his parent.

"Always."

I looked up after a few moments when he hadn't moved or said anything else.

"You okay, Georgia?" He came a few steps closer. I backed away immediately, afraid to get into his personal space. My brain had a history of going fuzzy when I did.

"Great," I forced a smile.

"You're not lying?" His gaze traveled up my body, heating my skin, before landing on my eyes.

"Why would I lie? I'm with Kyle and you're with...whomever." I finished awkwardly. His eyes seared into me. The emotion swirling in them was mesmerizing. I wanted desperately to know what he was thinking but I couldn't bring myself to say the words. It didn't even matter. I had chosen Kyle. And he was with anyone he wanted to be with.

A horn honked outside. We both looked to the door then back to each other.

His lips parted as if he was going to say something and then closed again. I gave him a small smile to ease the tension between us.

"Sounds like you're wanted," I whispered, still unable to turn away from his gaze.

"Seems so. Later, Georgia." His eyes held mine for another breathless moment before he turned and strolled out the front door.

I leaned over the sink to look down to the driveway. A shiny, red Mustang sat idling with a long-legged blonde in a short mini-skirt waiting at the door. She wrapped her arms around Tristan and pressed her lips to his. When she pulled away, a sexy grin lit his face as he ran a hand up her thigh and over her ass. I swallowed back the painful ache in my throat and backed away from the window. I headed for the hottest shower I could possibly take, trying to focus on anything other than the image of that girl's long legs wrapped around Tristan's waist tonight.

* * *

"RISE AND SHINE, cupcake!" Drew and I knocked on Tristan's door early the next morning with paint cans in tow.

"Maybe he didn't come home last night?" Drew said as she knocked on the door again. Still no answer.

"I told him we were painting his room today, so maybe he stayed on the boat last night," I said.

"He had a date, didn't he? I didn't hear him come in—" Drew opened the door and we walked in.

"Oh my God." I stared at Tristan's naked body, a white sheet draped below his hips, barely covering his lower half. One tanned forearm crossed over his eyes to block the light in his sleep and another stretched out on the pillow next to him. His bare torso was deliciously tan and chiseled with the lightest dusting of hair that disappeared below the white sheet at his waist. My body would be in full-blown lust mode if it wasn't for the pale arm draped across his abdomen. Long, blonde hair fanned across the pillow and one perfectly curvy leg was thrown over his legs.

My heart leapt into my throat at the sight before me. It felt like I'd walked onto the set of a porn movie. Some terrible morning-after scene that would be burned into my memory forever. Whenever I closed my eyes I would see them lying like this. I would picture them fucking all night, in all different positions; moans and grunts and the smell of sex filling the room. Was he sweet to her like he was to me? Did he use a condom with her? Or did he beg her to go without like he had me? Tears stung my eyes at the thought.

Just then Tristan heaved a sigh and rubbed his eyes before they flickered open and caught sight of Drew and I standing in the doorway. I suddenly felt like I needed to throw up.

"Way to bring your skank home, Tristan." Drew shot him a glare. I stood motionless beside her, my eyes boring into his, imploring him to say something, or nothing, I wasn't sure.

"Sorry," I finally choked out as I grabbed Drew and backed out of the doorway. Tristan's eyes held mine the entire time. Was he mad that we'd barged in? Maybe he was still drunk from the night before. Or had a hangover. I was going to kill myself all day with the thoughts running through my head.

"We're painting." Drew lifted the can in her hand. "You've got fifteen minutes to get her out," she spat. Tristan's eyes shot up in surprise before Drew slammed the door on his beautiful face.

"Another cup of coffee?" I set the paint can in the kitchen and made my way to the coffee pot. I needed something to occupy my mind and my hands.

"Sure," Drew answered as I filled our cups and we made our way out to the porch.

"So that was awkward." Drew cast a sideways glance at me.

"Not really," I lied, something I was doing often lately.

"Definitely, really. You don't have to pretend, Georgia. It was awkward for me; I can't imagine what it must have been like for you."

"It wasn't like anything for me. We're nothing, friends at best and some days I'm not even sure we're that."

"Hmm." Drew took another sip.

"Later, babe." We heard Tristan's voice in the kitchen. Drew and I both peeked through the open windows. The breeze blew the curtains so we caught only glimpses of their morning-after goodbye. The unnamed girl laid a passionate kiss on his lips and he slapped her on the bottom playfully. She still wore the mini-skirt from the night before.

"He is such a slut. I hate him," Drew said as Tristan's date left. A giggle burst out of my throat at Drew's declaration. Tristan must have heard us because he turned and arched an eyebrow. He looked seven shades of sexy first thing in the morning. It didn't help that he was dressed only in his jeans from last night—no shirt. Perfect just-had-sex hair. I rolled my eyes at his ever-present flawlessness. I kind of hated him too.

"Something funny?" Tristan grabbed a cup of coffee then joined us on the deck. He stood at the railing and took a sip, looking at the water.

"Can't you put on a shirt?" The words slid out of my mouth before I could stop them. He turned to me before a smile lifted the corner of his perfect, sculpted lips.

"How drunk were you last night to bring that

home?" Drew sneered.

"Not drunk at all, actually," he responded. It was like a punch to my gut. He'd been completely sober and brought someone home, had a long night of crazy sexy sex in my house with no remorse, and allowed us to walk in on him. I thought I might throw up. A drunken hookup would have been so much easier to handle. The realization dawned: that's what he and I had—a drunken hookup. We'd both been wasted the night we'd been together. Tears burned behind my eyelids and I jumped up, sloshing the coffee from my cup.

"Fuck," I swore as the hot coffee burned my hand.

"Are you okay?" Tristan cupped my burned hand in his.

"I'm fine. We have lots of painting to do. Sorry we woke you, Tristan." I launched back into the house, dropped my cup in the sink and grabbed the paint cans, making my way to Tristan's room.

My plan of escape was, however, not well thought out; his window was wide open and I could hear every bitchy remark Drew was throwing at him.

"Are you fucking kidding me, Tristan?"

"What?" he replied.

"You're hurting her."

"Hurting her? She's with Kyle. She chose Kyle."

"So why do you have to slut all over town?"

Drew seethed.

"I'm doing what I've always done, Drew. Lay off. Not your business or hers. I'm sorry you had to walk in and see it, but maybe next time you'll think twice before opening my door."

"You can bet on that. I'm going to have to scrub the image of your skank-fest from my brain."

There was no response from Tristan.

"We didn't think you were in there," she said quietly. "And we especially didn't think you would have someone in there with you," Drew finished.

"Sorry you had to see it," he said frankly. He had no remorse whatsoever and why should he? This was his room for the summer and he'd said himself, this is what he did. And he was right, I had chosen Kyle. I had no right to be upset over Tristan being Tristan. But I was.

Drew walked into Tristan's room a minute later. "Sorry, G." She rubbed my shoulders.

"For what? We shouldn't have barged in. He's entitled to bring whoever he wants home. Can you help me push the bed to the center?" I started pushing the bed Tristan and his blonde beauty had fucked in all night long. I winced when I saw an empty condom wrapper on the floor.

"Here," Tristan's eyes flickered down to the ripped foil on the floor before he swiped it up and shoved it in his pocket. His eyes lifted to mine and a look of shame crossed his face. "Let me help," he whispered before stepping next to me to push the bed across the room. I held my breath—if I smelled his delicious, ocean scent I would lose it. Tears sat on the edge of my eyelids and a painful lump the size of a softball was lodged in my throat. His scent had started to feel like home to me and I couldn't smell it now, not when it was mingled with the scent of some expensive perfume his bed companion had worn last night.

"Thanks." My eyes met his. They held a look of sadness and remorse. My heart tightened in my chest. "We've got it from here," I whispered before opening the paint can.

"Gavin and I will be in the office. Call if you need anything," he said mildly. I glanced up as he pulled a faded shirt over his shoulders then left the room barefoot with his laptop under his arm. I heaved another sigh before passing the roller through the paint and attacking the walls with a vengeance.

EIGHTEEN

Georgia

"HEY," TRISTAN SAID to me on the deck later that week.

"Hey," I whispered as I curled up on the chair next to him. I knew he'd be out here, coffee was made and the French doors thrown wide open— a sure sign that he was on the deck. I'd been avoiding him the last few days but I knew I couldn't keep it up for the rest of the summer, and despite the awkwardness of the other morning, I couldn't hold it against him. I had no reason to.

"Look, Georgia, I'm really sorry you had to see that the other morning—"

"It's all right. No harm done."

"Well, I wish it wouldn't have happened. I was going back to my boat because I knew you were painting in the morning but I forgot my keys. I feel like a dick."

"You have every right to expect privacy. We

shouldn't have barged in."

"I don't mean that, Georgia." He laid his warm hand on mine. It caused shivers to jolt through my body and I pulled my hand away immediately.

"Well, whatever you mean, it's not a big deal. No need for things to be weird between us."

"Okay," Tristan said.

"What are your plans for today?" I diverted the conversation.

"I have to make a few calls this morning, test security on a few websites then I was going to do some things on the boat."

"Nice day for it." I indicated the bright blue sky above us.

"You can come if you want," he trailed off.

"No, I have a lot to do around here. I'm behind schedule. I'll be lucky if I can even rent it out next season at this point." I sipped my coffee and looked down the shoreline. The wooden walkway for the cottage next door was barely peeking out of the dune grass. Now that I knew it was there, I could spot it if I looked closely enough, and unfortunately, I was intimately aware of its existence after the night in the sand. I watched the grass lick the weathered wood and remembered Tristan's tongue trailing the planes and hollows of my body. My nerves tingled and my tummy clenched at the memory.

I felt a featherlight touch and saw Tristan's finger drifting across the weathered wood of my chair.

"You okay?" he asked.

"Yeah." I averted my eyes but when I looked into his I knew he knew where my mind had been. Not a million miles away but a few short weeks ago when we'd been together. I sighed, knowing the remainder of this summer would be hard and I didn't think I had the strength to withstand it. I wanted to crawl back in my bed and spend the day reading, but doing that may send me headlong into a depression. And reading reminded me of reading on the beach with Tristan. Everywhere I looked I was reminded of Tristan. Everything I did, everything I thought. I was drowning in the memories we'd made this summer.

"Are you sure, Georgia?" His eyes searched mine. He'd always been so sweet and attentive with me. Always so concerned, his beautiful, green eyes searching my face to make sure I was okay.

"Yeah, I'm going to call Kyle." I heard Tristan suck in a quick breath as I stood and walked into the house. If I let my mind travel down that path I'd want to have Tristan's arms wrapped around me the remainder of the summer.

"Morning, love," Silas said as I curled myself around him in his bed.

"Morning," I whispered into the crook of his neck as a soft tear trailed down my cheek.

"Are you okay?" Silas rubbed up and down my back.

"No," I squeaked.

"Is it Kyle?"

"No."

"Tristan?"

"I wish it wasn't, but I think so," I said.

"Are you having nightmares again?"

"Some."

"Did something happen with Tristan?"

"Yeah," I answered, barely above a whisper. "I slept with him, Silas." The ache in my chest felt like it was crushing me from the inside out. It'd only been a week since we'd been together but I was craving his touch, his body hovering over mine, his lips on my skin.

"Oh my god, was he good?" he continued without waiting for my response. "Fuck, I knew he was good. I need details. I'll die a happy man if you give me details."

"Silas," I whimpered.

"Sorry." He stroked the hair spilling down my back.

"I can't leave him, Silas. I can't." I shook my head as tears fell.

"I know, love," he said. "Maybe you should tell him?"

"Kyle? No."

"Not Kyle, love."

"Tristan?" I jerked my head up to look him in the eye.

"Maybe you should tell him everything."

"No." I shook my head emphatically.

"Maybe it would help if he knew—if he

understood why you don't think you can leave Kyle."

"It doesn't matter, it's over with Tristan. It never even really got started."

"Do you really think that, Georgia?" Silas's brown eyes burned into mine.

"Yes…" I whispered, still holding his gaze. "I don't know."

"Do you want to know what I think?" he asked gently.

"No."

He chuckled. "I'm going to tell you anyway."

"You always do." I rolled my eyes.

"And it's exactly the reason you keep me around."

"I need to work on that." I frowned.

"I think the nightmares are back because you're torn. I think you're forcing yourself to stay with Kyle because of the past, not because of the future. And you need to stop living in the past, Georgia. It's poisoning you. If you stayed with Kyle you would have a nice life, boring maybe, but perfectly, normally nice. But if you let go of the past—let go of the pain—if you followed your heart, you may find something beautiful."

"I know, but Kyle—"

"I know. Kyle was always there, but it doesn't mean you owe him your future."

"I'm happy with Kyle."

"If you were happy, love, that night with Tristan wouldn't have happened."

"I can't leave him, Silas." I buried my head in

Silas' neck.

"I know. Promise me one thing?"

"Hmm?"

"Love yourself this summer. Love yourself enough to follow your heart…"

"Silas…" I whined.

"Just try," he said as he smoothed his hand down my hair. "Just try for something beautiful."

* * *

IT'D BEEN AN exhausting week between working and nightmares and Kyle and Silas and Tristan and Tristan's whores. He'd been out every night this week. I'd told him to move on and date, and he was doing just that. The only problem was that I'd told him I wouldn't be upset, and yet every night he didn't come home I got more upset.

Tristan's dating was eating me up inside.

Every night I went to bed and imagined a different, beautiful beauty with her legs wrapped around his narrow waist. I imagined dainty fingers threaded in his beautiful, tousled hair, tugging while she screamed his name. His lips on her body, his hands caressing her skin. My stomach was in a constant state of upset. I was now having nightmares every night and last night I'd made Kyle stay up and talk to me on the phone. Next weekend was Fourth of July and he was coming down, the first time he'd see the beach house. I'd babbled endlessly about the updates on the house, the surroundings, some of the local shops—anything to fill my head with thoughts other than Tristan. Finally Kyle had begged for sleep and we'd hung up. But that wasn't it for me. I'd tossed and turned, listening to the rolling waves, trying to time my breathing, willing myself to fall into a dreamless sleep when I heard a car door slam. After a few minutes I heard keys rattling and footsteps, giggles, and bodies bumping into things. My rage peaked in that instant. I threw the blanket off my body and stomped down the hallway into the kitchen. Moonlight washed across the room, making their outlines easy to see.

Tristan stood in front of a brunette propped up on the counter, his hips nestled in between her thighs, her skirt riding high up her legs. His hand trailed high up her thigh, fingertips disappearing under the tight fabric of her skirt. She moaned into his mouth as they kissed. His other hand was wrapped around another brunette at his side, her lips attached to the skin under his ear, her hands threaded in his messy hair. He pulled away from the girl on the counter and moved his lips to the other girl, twisting a hand in her long hair and bending her neck to his sensual mouth. She moaned as he dragged his teeth down her neck while she slid a hand down his back and cupped his ass tightly. Her body writhed against his as the brunette on the countertop arched her body into him and slipped a hand down the front of his pants.

Bile rose in my throat as I watched, unable to tear my eyes from the erotic display in my kitchen. The only thing that had a stronger hold on me was the anger. My rage at him bringing those girls into my house in the middle of the night, letting them writhe all over my countertop with him nestled between their legs.

"Can you take it elsewhere?" I flipped on the light and crossed my arms, my gaze boring into the back of Tristan's head. He turned slowly, his eyes coming to rest on mine, blurry and unfocused. He was clearly drunk. As drunk as I'd ever seen him.

"Georgia." The heart-stopping smirk that normally made my stomach do delicious flips spread across his face, but tonight it only caused rage to pool in my belly. "Wanna join?" His eyes flared as his gaze trailed down my body. I realized instantly I was wearing a tight tank top without a bra, the cool breeze washing across my skin had my nipples standing at attention. I crossed my arms to cover myself. Tristan's eyes traveled down my legs where my tiny sleep shorts hardly covered a thing. His thumb traced small circles on the thigh of the girl on the countertop. My stomach boiled in anger.

"No, you're a whore. Take your skanks elsewhere."

"Bitch," the girl standing next to him huffed with a hand on her hip.

"You're always welcome, Georgia. Just say

the word. All you ever had to do was say the word."

I stared at him, my eyes blazing as it registered that he referred to more than just the situation playing out before me.

"I hate you," I hissed and turned on my heel to leave.

"Georgia, wait. Can you give me a minute?" He turned to the girls. "Down the hall, second room on the left." He swatted one of them on the bottom as they hustled out in a fit of annoying tittering.

"What are you doing?" I glared as he came closer to me.

"Am I doing something wrong?" he said as he reached me, invading my personal space. I could smell the flowery perfume on him and it made me want to throw up.

"Bringing those skanks here," I sneered.

He arched a surprised eyebrow at me. "I'm doing what you told me to, Georgia."

"I don't recall telling you to whore all over town." I chewed the inside of my cheek.

"I'm moving on, Georgia," he whispered. "Sorry if you don't like the way I go about it." He cupped my face, smoothing his thumb over my cheekbone. "It didn't have to be like this, Georgia." He rested his forehead against mine. I closed my eyes and took a deep breath. Despite everything, despite the girls and the vile suggestion he'd just made about my joining them, I could forgive him. I knew that I could.

This wasn't my Tristan. This was someone who was in pain, seeking an outlet in the only way they knew how. I ran my hands up his neck, both of my thumbs brushing along his jawline.

He sucked in a quick breath and then touched his lips to mine in a featherlight kiss. "I wanted it to be you. I always wanted it to be you," he mumbled. I swallowed the lump in my throat. Tears burned my eyelids. I wanted it to be him too. I wanted to give myself to him and only him.

"I'm sorry," I murmured before pulling back from him. I wiped the tears from my cheeks and watched hurt shoot across his eyes. He shut them as if pushing the pain back from the surface. His eyes opened slowly and he made his way to his room. I watched him and my heart tightened in my chest. The pain he'd left me standing in felt so real, like I'd crumpled on the floor and melted into a pile of tears.

"I hate you," I whispered to no one but myself, flicking off the light and heading back to my room. I slammed the door and threw myself in bed. I waited for sounds of a threesome to reach me from a few rooms away but they never came.

NINETEEN

Georgia

"MORNIN' GEORGIA," TRISTAN smirked, stepping into the kitchen. He looked wildly sexy in a V-neck shirt and a pair of cargo shorts.

"Hey," I mumbled as I poured grounds into the coffee filter. I hadn't gotten much sleep last night, my thoughts consumed with my run-in with Tristan. Drew, Silas, and I were going to the garden store to buy landscaping supplies so I'd need copious amounts of the black brew to get my ass in gear.

"Thanks for making coffee this morning; I was up late last night," he said as he walked past me, caressing my lower back on his way to the fridge. His touch sent shivers coursing through my body. I gritted my teeth together and concentrated on measuring the right amount of water to pour into the reservoir.

"Vanilla or caramel creamer?" he asked, leaning into the fridge. I only scowled at him.

He waited another minute before turning to

look at me. "Grow up, Georgia. Vanilla or fucking caramel?"

"I've got it." I sneered as I reached into the fridge and pulled out the caramel.

"What's the problem, Georgia?" he whispered in my ear as his hand came to caress the exposed skin of my lower back where my shirt had ridden up.

"The problem, Tristan, is that you're a whore," I seethed, our faces so close, lips nearly touching before I ripped away from him and a cocky grin lit his lips. The more he smiled the more I hated him for it, yet it was the one thing that made hating him impossible.

"Anything I can do to change your mind about that?" He used his body to push me back into the counter. I bit down on my lip to concentrate on anything other than his hard body pressing into me. "Come on, Georgia. Tell me," he taunted as he ran his hands up my torso slowly, tantalizingly. His hands made their way up my ribcage, his thumbs brushed the sides of my breasts as my breathing hitched, and butterflies scattered in my belly.

"Stop marching the slut parade through my house," I whispered as I closed my eyes and shifted, rubbing my thighs together to ease some of the ache that had settled there.

"It's just sex, Georgia. Two people, or three as it were, looking for a good time." His thumbs danced softly on the skin next to my breasts, dangerously close, yet not nearly close enough.

He ran his nose up the line of my neck until he reached my ear. "I told you I was never good at saying no," he whispered, his nose ghosting along the shell of my ear. My heart pounded furiously in my chest. "I'm not sure you're good at it either. I can feel what I do to you: your heart pounding, your chest heaving, your nipples hardening," he breezed one thumb over a sharp, aching peak, "your legs shifting back and forth, begging me to touch you." He ran one fingertip between my breasts, down my stomach, past my waistband, grazing high up on my thigh, nearly touching my throbbing center through the fabric of my shorts.

A groan escaped my throat as I arched my neck. I couldn't think straight with this incessant pounding in my chest, the raging thud in my ears. "Aren't you worried about safety? Catching... something?" I whispered.

"I'm always safe, Georgia. With every one of them," he whispered seductively, tauntingly, causing my blood to boil every time he mentioned the other girls he'd been with. Every time I thought about their high heels locked around his waist. Him peeling the sexy underwear off their bodies.

"You weren't with me," I whispered as I rocked gently into him, my eyes closed, my brain swimming with desire and lust and the fading vestiges of anger.

"I couldn't think straight when I was with you," he hissed in my ear, his warm breath washing over my skin, sending tingles through my body. "Say yes, Georgia, and I'll do whatever you want. There's so much I want to do to you. I dream about all the ways I can take you." Two long fingers caressed the seam of my shorts, causing fire to race through my veins and lust to spike through my entire body. I thrust my hips at his touch involuntarily. "I'll take you right here on this counter if you let me." He lifted and set me on the counter, spreading my knees and resting his hips between my thighs. "You just need to say the word, Georgia, and I'll show you how good it can be. I can make you forget him. I can make you forget everything if you just let me. I would slide in slowly, your back would arch, your breathing would hitch." He thrust his hips into me so I could feel his rock hard arousal. A choked whimper escaped my throat. "I can make you scream my name, Georgia." He wrapped one hand around my neck and held tightly as he dragged his tongue across my sensitive skin and breathed hot in my ear. The action had me sitting on the edge of release. So close, I could fall over into him. It would only be a minute, if I just said yes, I could be his, he could make me lose myself, and isn't that what I wanted? To be lost? To forget? To have the pain taken away? Tristan was my drug if I'd only let him in.

"I don't want to be one of them," I moaned.

"You aren't. You never were." He husked and I arched. I ached for him. "Come on,

Georgia," he whispered. My eyes flickered open as he moved his hands to the top of my thighs and held firmly, tightly enough that it almost hurt. He continued to rock into me, his straining erection sliding against the seam of my shorts, providing almost enough friction. His eyes revealed determination and anger and lust and need, all brewing under the surface. The intensity in those green irises held me chained to him. I couldn't look away if I tried.

"God, Tristan," I hissed through clenched teeth.

"Let me help you. Just say it. Say yes and that's it." He rocked harder and my breathing came out in furious pants.

"No, Tristan." I ground my teeth together as anger and fear and shame spiked tears behind my eyelids. "No, I can't... I can't... Please." I held his upper arms tightly, pushing him away yet clutching him for dear life. "Please stop," I whimpered. He stood away from me for a moment before the tension left his body and he wrapped his arms around my trembling body in a tight hug. I locked my hands behind his back and held him to me. I knew it was unfair; I was torturing him as much as I was torturing myself, but I couldn't let go. I couldn't take the leap like he'd begged me to.

TWENTY

Tristan

I regretted every fucking minute. Why did I find myself regretting so many things with her when she was the one person I wanted the most? I craved her love, I craved her mind, I craved everything about her while she abused my emotions like a rag doll.

I'd made a rainfall of bad decisions lately, starting with taking that girl home after I'd forgotten my boat keys, but I'd been so angry I couldn't see straight, and while I hadn't planned on Georgia catching me in the act like she did, naked bodies strewn across cotton sheets, some sick part of me had wanted her to catch me just the same.

But the look on her face had said it all. I'd gone too far, I'd stepped over bounds, and for once it'd actually made me feel good. I'd gotten a reaction from her and that's all I'd ben looking for.

I had anger burrowed deep in my gut, anger

at her refusal to acknowledge my feelings. I may have a checkered history with women, damn Drew for telling her any of it, but Georgia had just met me, why was I being judged by my past sins?

I knew deep down that if things were different, if we'd had a different start, a better start, we could have been different together. I could see us falling together, both single and unattached, my heart soaring with every kiss, her body coming alive under mine with every stroke of my fingers. We would have been kinder, no season of pain between us, more in tune, we could have been great. And suddenly meeting Georgia felt like a lifetime too late.

Georgia and I deserved that life, I could see it plainly in my mind, but it was if fate had other plans. But fate had to be so mother fucking wrong, why else would it hurt so much? Not having her was like a physical pain I could hardly bear, the only thing deferring the heartache was inflicting it on her. It was messed up, so wrong, and horribly selfish, I just couldn't see it for what it really was, me barely keeping my head above water without her.

It was fucked up, it made me bad, wrong in every way, but it was the only reaction I had. It was pain and desperation and desire all rolled into a tightly wound ball. I couldn't decipher my way in or out, I just knew I had to throw with everything I had.

Maybe my emotional compass was off, but I

was fucking lost.

I needed Georgia to tell me what was right and wrong, how to help her, how to save her, how to keep her. I could feel the love between us in my bones, but she was just too stubborn and loyal to admit it.

But not so loyal that she wouldn't give her heart to someone else.

I'd fucked up with her already, maybe irreparably, but it didn't mean I wouldn't keep trying. I could be better, I would be, if I could only get control of these raging emotions. If I could only make her see that we could be right, we could be everything.

If she'd only say yes.

Just say yes.

Just give me a chance.

I just needed one chance to give her everything, and I knew then she would never walk away again.

TWENTY-ONE

Georgia

"YOU LOOK EXHAUSTED, G." Drew and I sat on the beach a few mornings later. I hadn't slept for shit in days and Tristan's most recent indiscretion with the threesome was eating away at me. Another image that'd been burned in my brain. Every time I settled into bed and closed my eyes, the images played of all of the girls and the positions he could be in in that very moment.

"I haven't slept."

"At all?" Drew sipped a spritzer through a straw.

"Pretty much. Don't you think it's too early to drink?" I nodded to her drink.

"Nope," she answered.

"I orchestrated this girls-only beach day so now it's your turn to dish."

I heaved a great big sigh in response.

"Silas will be pissed we had a beach day without him." I was trying to divert again.

"Silas is off getting laid somewhere, so he's

shit out of luck. Come on, G, this summer was supposed to be great. And it has been for everyone but you."

"Maybe we should invite Justin over. I like him; I think he and Silas could be really good together." I continued to shift the topic of conversation away from myself.

Drew wasn't having it. "Things are getting worse, Georgia," she said. "You're having nightmares every night, honey. I hear them."

"I'm sorry for waking you up." It felt like the weight of the world sat on my shoulders. I needed to relieve it with someone. Anyone. I thought I would go crazy keeping everything locked up in my own head like this.

"It's not that, G. I'm worried. Silas too. Maybe if you told Tristan…" she trailed off.

"Told him what? Everyone wants me to tell him something--what am I supposed to tell him?" I raised my voice.

"Tell him why you can't be with him. Or why you think you can't anyway." She took another sip of her drink.

"I've never told anyone, Drew. Just you, Silas, and Kyle."

"I know, but maybe that's the problem. I think that's why the nightmares are getting worse. I think a part of you wants to let Tristan in, but you're so afraid…"

I looked at the rolling waves licking the sandy beach. "I'm angry that Kyle hasn't been here," I whispered.

"I know, I am too," she said.

"I'm afraid to tell Tristan, I'm afraid he'll walk away. Things are so fucked up."

"I know you're afraid of that, but he wouldn't," she rubbed my arm gently.

"You don't know that. What happened was fucked up, Drew. It fucked me up for years. It still does."

"I know."

"It's a lot to deal with and it isn't even over. It comes up to bite me every few years."

"If he doesn't want to put up with it then at least you'll know he was never worth it. But as it is, Georgia..."

"So I'm supposed to gamble on Tristan and fuck up what I have with Kyle? Kyle can't forgive something like that. Not ever."

"Ironic, really," she murmured. "So were you never going to tell Kyle? Was that your plan? Because it's eating away at you. Whether you choose Kyle or Tristan, I know you, Georgia, and it's going to eat away at you."

"I don't know. Part of me thought if Tristan and I never happened again..." I hesitated. "I cheated on Kyle, Drew. I'm not worthy of either one."

Her eyes softened as she took in what I was saying. I'd never told her in so many words, but I knew she'd suspected that Tristan and I had slept together at some point. "You made a mistake, that doesn't mean you don't deserve love. It means you're human. And I think you'd be surprised what Tristan can handle—and what he'd be willing to handle." She cocked a brow at me. "Just talk to him. He's pretty fucked up right now. Gavin said he's never been like this…"

"Like what? A whore?" I mumbled.

"No, he's always been a whore, but not like this. Not every night. Not different ones like this. He's in rough shape." She frowned. "Just talk to him. I think he needs to know why you didn't choose him."

I frowned and worked over her words in my mind for a few moments. "I need one of those." I pointed at her drink.

"Great! Take mine." She handed me her drink. "I'll go make another." She sped up the stairs to do just that.

I reflected, waiting for her to return. I dragged my fingertip through the sand and made random shapes. A sailboat. The letter T, the letter G, the letter K… I swirled before brushing it all aside. My brain was so jumbled and confused, I wasn't sure what was up or down anymore. Kyle entered my life when I was twelve and my life had changed for the better. Months before, I'd been in such a dark place. Hopeless was the only way to describe it—dark and hopeless. I had stopped talking for nearly a year, but when I met Kyle, he didn't care. He talked to me even when he knew I wouldn't answer, but he knew I was listening. I was hanging on his every word. He was my light in the dark recesses of my mind.

Slowly I began to open up, but only to him.

We talked about nothing in particular, and certainly not what had happened to me. Everyone wanted to talk about what had happened, but he didn't. It made all the difference…Kyle made all the difference in my life.

One night he'd finally asked me why I had nightmares. He had heard me scream from his next-door bedroom window one summer night. The next morning he'd asked me and I'd told him. It'd all come flooding out. I couldn't stop it, and I didn't want to. He sat and listened to everything but his face betrayed nothing. Finally, when I'd finished, he asked me if I wanted to walk down the street for ice cream. He treated me as if nothing had happened at all, as if I hadn't just laid my entire horrific past at his feet, and it was exactly what I'd needed.

From that day on, Kyle became my protector. When the kids bullied me at school for being quiet, he stood up for me. When things at home got tough, I crawled into his bedroom window and he held me all night and kept the nightmares at bay. He was my savior in the darkest time of my life. He was my knight—always there to protect and defend. It had only been the last few years that life had taken us down different paths.

I knew Kyle must have felt it, but we didn't talk about it. And I tried to overlook it for as long as I could. I still held tightly to those memories I had from when we were kids. I couldn't let go of Kyle. He'd been the only person to pull me out of the darkness. What happened if I went there again and I didn't have him? Would I get lost in it? Would I lose myself? I was too afraid to find out.

* * *

DREW AND I had spent the day cleaning out the upstairs to ready it for remodeling. Gavin and Tristan had worked all day in their makeshift office, and Silas had done whatever it is that Silas does while he's in between jobs. Kyle was set to come down in a few days for the Fourth of July weekend and things with Tristan were strained. We'd been trying to work through it the best we could, which meant avoiding each other, but I quickly found that wasn't going to work. It made for awkward tension that permeated the entire mood of the house.

"Will you walk with me?" Tristan approached me on the deck a few evenings later. The sun was just beginning to set, bright pinks and oranges streaked across the sky.

"Sure." I forced a smile. I flinched when he placed a steadying hand on my back as we made our way down the steps and out to the beach. The day had been humid, nearly stifling, a typical southern summer day. A thin sheen of perspiration clung to my skin and had me itching to head straight into the water, but I knew we should talk if we wanted to survive the rest of the summer without driving our friends insane.

"I just wanted to say sorry, Georgia, about how it's been. I wish we could go back. I miss how easy it was between us."

"Me too." A lump of tears collected in my throat as we meandered down the shore. I walked ankle deep in the water, the waves licking my feet with each pass.

"I know you chose him, Georgia, but I just wanted to tell you that I can't go back to before. I'll never be the same. What we had, how we were, no matter how brief, was...different for me."

I stumbled at his words. My eyes trained on the gentle ripples the waves had etched in the sand. Imprinted like Tristan and I had imprinted on each other. Whether I liked it or not he'd imprinted on my heart. But did I tell him? Could I? Did I want to? Would it change anything? "It was that for me too," I whispered so softly I wasn't even sure that he heard me. The only sign that he had was his jaw working back and forth in thought. We walked in silence longer.

"You can tell me," he gently urged.

"What?"

"About whatever happened to make you this...sad..."

"I... I don't tell anyone." I was mildly surprised he was bringing this up.

"I know, but you can't keep it forever."

"Yes, I can."

"It'll poison you." He slowed and I matched

my pace to his.

"It already has," I whispered. What was it about Tristan that had me so willing to open up to him? "Besides, Silas and Drew know. They're all I need," I gritted my teeth.

"What about Kyle?"

"What about him?"

"Does he know?"

"Of course he knows, he's been there since the beginning," I snapped.

"Did he do something to you, Georgia?"

"No. It's not like that." I stopped and looked at him. His eyes bore into mine, imploring me to open up. And what surprised me more than anything else was that a part of me wanted to. "I can't."

"Can't or won't?" he asked.

"I can't. I want to, but I can't. You don't know…" I trailed off. If I opened up to him, my soul would crack wide open and shatter at my feet in a thousand pieces, never to be repaired.

"Talking may help heal the pain."

"I don't want to heal the pain. If it heals I'll forget, and I don't want to forget."

"Healing isn't a betrayal of the memory."

"Stop talking. Please, stop talking." I turned and walked away from him.

"Well, I'm here and I can wait." He caught up to me and snagged my hand in his own. Holding tightly he said, "I'll wait for you, Georgia."

Pain and anger and frustration and confusion

swirled in my mind. I wanted to open up to
Tristan. I wanted to believe him, but could I risk
it all for him? His history wasn't promising, not in
the slightest. How could I know that he wouldn't
go back to his old ways? How could I know he
wouldn't get sick of me in a week or month?
How did I know Tristan wasn't the type of guy
that lived for the chase? He'd told me we were
more to him, but I'd only known him since May.
Maybe he told all of them exactly what he'd told
me. I was growing so frustrated with living inside
my own head, mulling things over constantly.
For once I wanted to live recklessly. I'd had
twelve short years of innocence before it was
ripped away. Tears pooled in my eyes and
perspiration beaded at the back of my neck.

"I'm so fucking hot." I planted my feet and
tugged my shirt over my head, whipping it to the
ground. "Let's go swimming." I wanted to live in
the moment—needed to. All this thinking was
suffocating me.

"Georgia," Tristan said with a frown. I
smirked before hooking my thumbs in the
waistband of my shorts and pushing them down
my legs, then turned and walked straight into the
water.

I walked until the waves lapped at my waist,
then slipped under, feeling it wash over me:
refreshing me, reinvigorating me, cleansing me.
The water rippled over my lean muscles as I
swam underneath as far as my lungs would
allow. I bobbed up for air and turned and swam

back, again as far as I could go before my lungs screamed in protest. I stood, my toes digging into the soft sand beneath my feet. I slicked my hair back and opened my eyes to find Tristan still frowning from the shore.

I unhooked my bra, sliding it off my wet body and throwing it up on the shore. It landed in a wet thud at his feet. His eyebrows lifted in surprise before looking back to me with a frown.

A small grin flitted across my face and I dove under the water again, swimming as far as I could. The water caressed my body, soothed and assuaged the pain that clenched my heart. I swam back and bobbed up, my lungs aching from being pushed to their capacity, finding myself staring eye to eye with Tristan. His eyes, hooded with a mix of anger and lust, stared back at me. My chest heaved as my lungs sucked in air then released it. The hot Carolina breeze washed over my skin, causing my nipples to pebble. We stood inches apart, the energy between us humming, threads of desire stretching between us—pulling us together like a magnetic field. I clenched my fists reflexively at my sides and then pressed my body flush to his: skin to skin, chest to chest, thigh to thigh, our lips caressing and tugging at each other.

I wrapped my fingers in his hair and pulled, his hands held my waist in a firm grip, then slid down the hollow of my back, fingering the waistband of my panties before slipping in and clutching the cheeks of my ass.

Pressing my body to his, wrapping my arms around his neck, I pulled his head to mine. Embracing and kissing, we consumed each other for as long as our lungs would allow before pulling away.

My body wracked with breathless pants as I trailed my tongue across his collarbone, up the line of his neck, across the chiseled angle of his jaw, finally kissing his earlobe. I dusted along the shell of his ear before pulling his earlobe between my teeth with a tug. A rumble escaped his throat as he clutched my backside fiercely, almost painfully.

"Please help me forget."

"I can't say no to you," he mumbled against my lips.

"Don't."

"I can't have you part way anymore. It's not possible for me," he murmured.

"I know." I breathed as I clawed at his skin, begging for more of him before sliding my hand down the front of his boxers. His erection grew when I made contact with the sensitive flesh. He threw his head back and sucked his lower lip between his teeth. It was the most erotic image I'd ever seen and had my heartbeat racing double time. I kissed up the line of his neck and sucked his lip between my own.

"Georgia—"

"Stop talking." I tightened my grip around his cock and he sucked air between his teeth. I'd lied earlier—this was the most erotic image I'd ever seen. His breath came out in ragged pants as I started to work up and down his length before I backed up, smiling. I walked backward, my fist wrapped around him until the back of my knees hit my target. I leaned back on an abandoned dock that floated half-submerged in the water. I pressed his length between my thighs and worked it back and forth against the damp fabric of my panties.

"Georgia." His eyes flicked down my body laid out before him, down to his arousal pressed between my thighs.

"Please," I whispered before releasing him and hooking my fingers in my panties. He grabbed both of my hands and brought each up to his lips, kissing my wrists tenderly before placing them at my sides. He hooked his thumbs in my underwear and pushed them down my legs. I kicked them off my feet and felt them float away in the water. My fingers scrambled to release him from his boxers. I pushed the wet cotton down his thighs, leaving them there.

"Do you want me to use a condom?" He mumbled between pants.

"No, just you. I just want you."

He slid one palm up my thigh and hitched it around his hip, his other hand wrapped around my neck and tangled in my hair. He held my head firmly to his, pressing our lips together fiercely, rocking his erection back and forth, teasing my sex. I arched as he rocked, pressing harder and deeper as he reached my aching clit.

My breath caught in my throat as he continued to caress me then lowered his head to suck a nipple into his mouth. I caught my lip between my teeth, fighting for control over my raging lust.

"Are you going to come, Georgia?"

"Yes," the word hissed between my teeth.

"Let go. Let me have it... let me have you," the words rumbled out of his throat as he thrust his length between my swollen flesh. I cried as pleasure and sensation rushed through my body. I panted as my nerves tingled and fired off. He pressed his forehead to mine and held me as I felt the release calm and soothe my body. Our breaths mingled together as Tristan's cock moved against me slowly before he finally slipped inside, groaning as he filled me. We moved together, slowly and reverently, worshiping each other. Tears stung my eyes as I realized what was happening. We we're trying to keep each other in any way we could. There was no going back so we were trying to find something new. Something that would work, help fill the void of pain and anger that had settled between us. Maybe this was our goodbye. Maybe it would be best if he went back to Jacksonville. Maybe these past few weeks were all we'd ever know of each other.

Emotion rushed through my system at the possibility.

Not having Tristan in my life felt unbearable.

Tears flowed down my cheeks as we rocked together, clutching one another, holding on as if our lives depended on it.

"We're so good together, Georgia. We're perfect," he whispered against my lips, his hand still wrapped in my hair, our chests touching as we found each other on a hot summer night in the Atlantic.

"I know," I whispered and shut my eyes more tightly as my tears fought for release. Our bodies dancing together in a way I'd never felt with anyone else. It tore at my heart and shame bubbled in my chest knowing I'd never felt this with Kyle. More tears ran down my cheeks because I'd wanted desperately to, but the truth was I hadn't.

"Stay with me, don't go back to him. Stay," he murmured and I felt his entire body shudder with release. I moaned as my release rolled through me: toes curling, goosebumps rising, body panting, breaths mingling together, bodies twisted in a sensual embrace. A lump knit together in my throat, the feelings I felt for Tristan were the ones I'd wanted to feel for Kyle.

"Stay with me tonight."

"What?" Our lips touched as we spoke.

"Right here on the beach. Stay with me," he murmured before capturing my lips with his. "I'll be right back." He jogged out of the water, pulling his boxers up as he ran up the shore. No sooner had he shot up the steps to the house than he was jogging back down again with a blanket in his hands.

I smiled when he laid it out on the sand and

came back to me. He wrapped both his arms around my waist and cuddled my neck. His lips ghosted along the skin, a tremor of arousal surged through my veins. He hugged me tightly and lifted my feet, walking me onto the shore and laying me on the blanket. He lay next to me and we snuggled together. He wrapped the blanket around us: feet tangled together, bodies still wet from our evening swim. My unruly, wet hair was sticking to my neck and his face. He brushed it aside with a smile, green eyes dancing in the moonlight. His other hand was wrapped firmly around my waist, my leg hitched over one of his. I inhaled his clean, ocean scent and snuggled into his warm body as he stroked my hair.

"Thank you," I whispered against his skin.

"For what?" I felt the echo of his words against my lips pressed at his chest.

"For helping me forget," I said with a yawn.

Relief washed over me. A sense of release, a moment of healing.

The ocean hadn't been the only thing to help cleanse me. Tristan had too.

TWENTY-TWO

Georgia

THE FOLLOWING MORNING I woke wrapped in Tristan's arms, our feet tangled together, his arm still around my waist, just as we'd fallen asleep. I yawned and smiled and turned into his neck. I sucked in a deep breath and relished his natural, beachy scent. My mind replayed our frenzied lovemaking in the ocean, the overwhelming feelings I'd had for him, and the shameful realization this was now the second time I'd slept with Tristan and cheated on Kyle.

Flames ripped through my veins, my brain finally registered that Kyle was arriving tonight. I suddenly needed space, distance, time to think. I tugged my lip between my bottom teeth, wondering if I should wake Tristan. I couldn't possibly untangle myself without waking him. But I needed a moment, time to think and process. My body ached to stay wrapped in Tristan's arms with the roaring waves just beyond our feet, but my brain needed time to process the position I'd put myself in.

I liked Tristan. A lot. The happiness I felt in Tristan's arms brought tears to my eyes. Kyle—every fiber of my being needed him. I was afraid to live without him. He was my rock, my protection, my knight. True, we'd had a rough time the past few years, but I had faith it was temporary. My life with Kyle wouldn't always be like this, would it? I didn't want to believe so, but the truth was I just didn't know.

Tristan's fingertips swept along my torso tenderly. I smiled and my eyes searched his face. He was just waking, his eyelids still closed, delicate eyelashes shadowing high cheekbones. He was always beautiful, but in this moment when he was asleep and peaceful, his beauty took my breath away. I lifted a hand and traced my finger along his lower lip. Tears pricked my eyelids when I thought of walking away from him for good. I didn't know if I could do it, even for Kyle. My stomach rolled with anxiety because I knew I couldn't keep doing this, couldn't keep going back and forth. I was in far too deep with both of them. Someone would be hurt and the blame would rest solely on my shoulders.

Tristan's eyes flickered open and focused on mine.

"Mornin'," he whispered.

"Mornin'." I smiled back at him.

"I could lie here forever with you," he said as his thumb worked small circles on my waist. His touch had goosebumps running up and down my body.

"Me too," I said honestly. I wanted to break myself in two. I wanted to give my heart to both of the men in my life. I wanted to give Kyle the part of myself that needed the safety and comfort of his arms, and I wanted to give Tristan the piece that craved the sense of lightness and happiness he made me feel.

I stared into his beautiful eyes and I wanted to choose him badly, but I was terrified that I couldn't trust him with my heart. My heart already held enough pain to last a lifetime and I was sure it couldn't survive another heartbreak.

"Kyle is coming tonight," I murmured.

"Yeah?" Tristan's gaze never wavered from mine. I could sense his question. I knew he wanted to ask. He wanted to know what that meant for us.

"I don't know what to do," I trailed off and finally broke my gaze from his.

"I know what I want you to do," he trailed his fingertips up my ribcage and his thumb brushed against the underside of my breast, causing my heart to thud erratically. I looked back into his eyes and felt waves of emotion swirling between us. His eyes implored me to choose him, choose this moment. I'm sure my eyes revealed that I wanted that too, but I'm sure they also were a window into the pain and anguish I felt at telling Kyle. Leaving Kyle.

"I need to tell him, but I don't know if I can

this weekend."

"You can't put it off, Georgia. It's not fair to anyone, especially him." His jaw clenched and I could feel the air shift between us. The tension was back. I was also a little angry with the notion that Tristan cared about what was fair to Kyle, because when he'd slept with me, flirted with me, he hadn't been concerned.

"I just need time," I whispered, my eyes searing into his, silently pleading with him to understand. "I can't spring this on him when he's been working so much, we've been apart for so long…he won't expect this from me. It would ruin him. I just need time."

"He's a fool if he doesn't expect it," Tristan said through gritted teeth.

"What?" My mouth hung open in surprise.

"There's a reason you're down here without him. A reason you bought the house without even telling him. Don't kid yourself, Georgia."

"How can you say that? You don't know. You have no right to make assumptions." The truth was Tristan was right. Kyle and I hadn't been working for a long time.

Starting in college Kyle had taken too many classes, picked up internships, spent late hours at the library or in his advisor's office studying and setting the wheels in motion for his future. For nearly a decade I'd heard 'Just let me get through this semester, just 'til I graduate,' and then it'd become 'When this internship is over, after my first promotion.'

"I need you to make a choice." Tristan's strained voice tore me from my thoughts. "And if not now, when? The end of the summer? Will you string us both along for that long? Sleep with me on the beach and have him waiting back in the city?" The anger in his voice struck me to the core.

"I'm not listening to this. I'm telling you I need time." I pulled away from him and grabbed my shirt, slipping it over my head before I stood and shimmied my shorts over my legs.

"Georgia, please, I'm sorry. I didn't mean to upset you, but I need to know. I can't keep living like this. I can't see you in the house and not touch you. Not be with you. I need to know," he whispered the last sentence, his own eyes now pleading for me to understand. Tristan stood and reached for me, wrapping a hand around my cheek and threading his fingers in my hair. "Choose this, Georgia. Choose us."

I bent my head to stare at our bare feet in the sand.

"So this is it for the weekend?" He lifted my chin up to meet his eyes. Tears pooled behind my eyelids as I watched his green depths blazing into me. I felt pulled to him, some forcefield at work between us. No matter how hard I tried, no matter how hard we tried to be apart, we couldn't. It was an impossibility.

"I'll miss you," he said sadly as his thumb ran across my bottom lip. His eyes flicked across my face, into my hair, his fingers gently kneading the nape of my neck.

"Me too," I said quietly before he placed a chaste kiss on my forehead. His lips lingered, pressed to my skin for a long moment before he pulled away and dropped his hands.

"I'll get this." He nodded at the blanket twisted in the damp morning sand. Silence ballooned in the distance between us. He was waiting for me to say something.

Anything.

Everything.

But I couldn't. As strong as my pull was to him, the fear I had that he would shatter my heart was just as strong.

"Okay," I forced a smile to lift my lips while my heart ached in my chest. I turned and walked back to the house and up the stairs, heading straight for the comfort of my own bed.

* * *

"GOD, I'M SO glad you're finally here." I leapt into Kyle's arms before he had a chance to shut the car door. I wrapped my legs around his waist and he held me. I nuzzled into his neck and inhaled the familiar scent of his cologne. "I've missed you so much." Tears streaked down my cheeks. I'd been a bundle of anxiety all day, torn between Tristan and Kyle. Life was so much easier when they could be kept separate. My past and my present were colliding this weekend and I was a ball of nerves over it, guilt burning in my chest and choking my throat. But with Kyle standing right in front of me, it was so easy to jump into his arms and take comfort like I always had.

"Georgia," he whispered and ran his hand down my hair soothingly. "Don't cry, I'm here now, baby." He shushed in my ear and the tears only came faster. I held him as my body shivered. He waited patiently, rubbing my back and stroking my hair. It felt good to be in his warm and comforting embrace. It was the one thing I'd been missing more than anything all summer.

"Why did it take so long for you to come?" I whispered when the tears finally subsided.

"I know, I'm sorry, but I'm here now. I'm here." He set my feet on the ground and held me in his arms. I smiled up at him through teary eyes and then gave him a playful smack on the cheek.

"Do it again and I'm kickin' you to the curb," I said sternly before smiling. He smiled sweetly at me and pulled my face to his, taking my lips with his own. I opened and my breath caught as he slid his tongue into my mouth, our kiss lingering and easy and reassuring. Kyle was always what I needed, always what made me feel better, and right now was no different. All thoughts of Tristan fell from my mind as I embraced the sense of calm and serenity that came from being back in Kyle's arms.

"So introduce me to these roommates of yours." Kyle finally broke our kiss and swatted me on the bottom. I smiled and pecked him on the lips one final time before he followed me into the house with an overnight bag on his arm.

I introduced him to Gavin who was typing on his laptop feverishly at the dining room table. Silas and Drew were playing cards and had already started on margaritas. I wasn't at all disappointed that Tristan had been on his boat for the day. I think he was giving me the time I'd pleaded for earlier this morning. I knew I'd need to introduce him to Kyle at some point this weekend, but I hoped Tristan would make himself scarce. I felt a pang of guilt for wishing Tristan would stay away after everything we'd been through this summer—everything we'd shared. But this was Kyle. This was the boy who'd captured my heart at the age of twelve and held it in his strong and steady hands.

"Mexican and margaritas tonight." I wrapped Kyle's hand in my own.

"Sounds great, baby. I've missed your cooking."

"Hope that isn't all you've missed," Silas grumbled while Drew huffed. I shot them both a death glare but neither met my eyes. I wasn't sure if Kyle heard, but he ignored them if he did.

"Sit and play cards, I'm going to throw the enchiladas in the oven. I'll bring you a margarita." I said before kissing his lips tenderly.

"Play cards, Kyle. Let me cater to your every

whim," Silas mumbled under his breath. I was sure Kyle had heard that but like the good boyfriend he was he chose to ignore it. He wasn't one for confrontation, and even so he would never put me between him and Silas.

"You sure, baby?" Kyle slid an arm around my waist and pulled my body flush with his.

"Positive." I said before Kyle pulled away and slid into a dining chair next to Silas.

"You in, Kyle? $100 buy-in." Silas grinned.

"Silas," I hollered from the kitchen. They knew Kyle was shit at poker and could take him for all he had.

"They're not playing for cash, Kyle. Don't let Silas bullshit you." I glared at my best friend who only winked back at me.

"Don't you have another roommate?" Kyle asked before taking a bite of the steaming Mexican food a short while later.

"Did I miss dinner? I knew you were making Mexican tonight, Georgia—I wasn't about to miss it." Tristan burst through the door and then halted when he saw the new guest at our table.

"Speak of the devil," Drew murmured. I bit my lip and glanced to Silas who had a shit-eating grin on his face.

"Kyle, this is Tristan Howell. Tristan, Kyle Collins, my boyfriend." I forced a smile as my insides rolled over.

"Kyle." Tristan nodded as he took a seat.

"Tristan." Kyle held his hand out to shake. A lump rose in my throat as their hands locked together. "Dig in, Georgia's a great cook." He nodded to the platter of enchiladas on the center of the table.

"That she is," Tristan said. His eyes scanned the table and fell on mine for a lingering moment before he shoveled food onto his plate. "So how long you in town for, Kyle?"

"Just the weekend. It's hard for me to get away, I'm up for promotion at the firm and it was tough for me to get this weekend off but I know Georgia's been missing me so I made it a priority." He grinned and slid his hand up my thigh lovingly. I smiled and turned back to my food.

"Surprised she finally made the list of priorities," Drew whispered to Silas at the opposite end of the table. I wasn't sure if they'd meant for me to hear or not but I had and shot them a dirty glare. I would need to talk with them; they were only making a bad situation worse.

"Well, great timing. We're having a party tomorrow night, watching the fireworks from the beach, should be great." Tristan continued the conversation flawlessly.

"Party, huh? Georgia's not usually much of a party girl," Kyle said.

"I had to cajole her. She's a tough cookie, but with a little sweet talk, I had her." Tristan's eyes met mine, his lips curling slightly as if amused by a private joke. My cheeks heated and I took a long swallow of my margarita. Was everyone in this house pushing for Kyle and I to fail?

"Georgia's always been easily swayed," Kyle said sweetly, as if he were talking about a child. Was he always this condescending? I didn't recall it ever bothering me before.

"You think so? She seems to be pretty capable of standing her ground when she wants. And stubborn as hell some days," Tristan said. I knew this conversation carried much more innuendo than Kyle realized. If Tristan was going to be like this all weekend, we were going to have major issues. I took another swallow of my margarita and emptied it, stepping back from the table hurriedly to refill my glass. I needed to escape that conversation.

"We should take a walk," I said with a smile at Kyle.

"Sounds great." He wrapped an arm around my hips as I stood next to him at his chair. "I've got a call to make but then I'm all yours." He placed a protective hand on my bottom before standing and making his way to my bedroom. Drew and Gavin headed out to the deck while Silas meandered down the hall to his bedroom.

"I'll help you clean up," Tristan said as he pushed back from the table, his plate in hand.

"No, I got it. Thanks." I flashed him a tight grin.

"I insist. Least I can do to repay you for the delicious meal." That sexy smile of his lifted at one corner of his mouth. I stood at the sink rinsing plates and loading them into the dishwasher.

"Kyle seems nice," Tristan's breath caressed the sensitive flesh under my ear. He trailed a tentative fingertip down my neck, past my shoulder blades, dragging the hair to one side and over my shoulder. He placed a soft kiss in the middle of my neck before whispering in my other ear. "Tell me, Georgia, does he make you come so hard you forget your own name?" His fingertips slid up the back of my thigh tantalizing every nerve until they slipped under the hem of my shorts. "Does he make you feel like this, Georgia? Do you shiver when he touches you? Does your heart pound and your breathing accelerate?"

I bit my bottom lip and held my back rigid. "Don't touch me," I gritted through my teeth.

"Ah, definitely not what you were saying last night." His fingertips trailed higher under my shorts between my thighs until he'd almost reached my very center. I swallowed and meant to turn and push him off me when suddenly his fingers were gone. I shut my eyes tightly and took a deep breath before opening them to turn and tell him he couldn't do things like that but he was gone. He'd disappeared like a dream. A fantasy. A nightmare. I wasn't sure which.

"Fuck," I whispered to the empty room.

"What was that, babe?" Kyle walked in and wrapped an arm around my waist. I leaned into him and sighed, but less out of comfort over being in Kyle's arms and more out of frustration for the havoc Tristan wreaked on my body.

* * *

"MORNING." I WOKE the next morning curled around Kyle's body, his arm beneath my head, my hair spread across my pillow and his chest. I inhaled deeply and a bright smile crossed my face.

"Morning," I smiled and tucked into his shoulder further.

"Beautiful as ever in the morning." He placed a kiss on my head.

"I missed waking up with you," I whispered.

"I missed it too, baby," he said as he stroked my hair with one palm. We sat silently for a few minutes, the waves crashing outside of the open window a constant hum to the soundtrack of my new life on the beach. I loved it.

"Open your eyes." I could feel his lips moving against my hair. I inhaled a deep breath of his skin before my eyes fluttered open. I turned to look up into his face but my eyes landed on a black velvet box sitting on his chest.

"Kyle." My mouth dropped in shock.

"I missed you, Georgia. So much. I hated coming home and you not being there. I want you to always be there. This was the longest we've been apart and I never want to be apart again." He lifted the box with his free hand and snapped the lid open. "Will you marry me, Georgia Hope Montgomery?"

Tears welled in my eyes as I stared at the stunning oversized princess cut diamond shining back at me.

"Kyle." My eyes rocketed to his and I got lost in their chocolatey depths. I saw emotion pooled in them and I flung myself onto his chest and pressed my lips to his. "I missed you so much." The levees burst and tears streamed down my face, but I refused to remove my lips from his. He kissed me back, holding my head tightly, his fingers twisted in my hair.

He finally pulled away. "Is that a yes?"

"Kyle, I don't know. I want to spend my life with you, but this is all so much. This summer has been so hard—"

"I know, baby. That's why I'm here. Being apart from you made me realize how much I need you. How much I've missed you—missed us -- over the last few years. I'm not going to work as much. Once this promotion business is off the table, that's it. We get married, we move to the 'burbs, and we have babies. That's what I want, and I want it with you." His eyes held mine, pleading, searching, waiting. My emotions swirled, the thoughts spun through my head. Glimpses of my life played before my eyes. Kyle when we were young, kisses in the parking lot before school, summer nights under the stars, high school graduation, college graduation, finding him bleary-eyed at the dining room table hunched over law books, the beach house, Tristan, sailing with Tristan, reading with Tristan, the vineyard with Tristan. The laughter, the smiles, the flirting—all with Tristan. Kyle had soothed my soul, been my reason for living for many years, but I couldn't deny that in the recent past there'd been a shift. Kyle had come to represent sadness and bitterness in my life, and Tristan had been the one to shine a light. There was also my life at the beach house. A life that Kyle wasn't interested in and never would be because his job, his career, the career that he wanted—the one I could never ask him to leave for me—was in D.C.

"I want that too, but I need time, Kyle. It's been hard being apart from you this summer. I've missed you more than anything, but things have been hard for me, and they've been that way for a few years now—"

"I told you, Georgia, no more long hours—"

"It's more than that, Kyle." I leaned away from him and traced my fingers along the line of his stubbled jaw. "It's just that…" I said sadly. Do I tell him? The words were on the tip of my tongue.

It's Tristan. I don't know what I have with him, but I don't know if I can let him go. I don't know if I want to. I slept with him.

The words sat on my lips, begging for release. I opened my mouth to say something, anything. Apologize because I couldn't say yes? I wasn't sure.

"Don't answer now. You can have time. Take time, Georgia. We can have a long engagement, no pressure." I could tell he was begging. He wasn't letting me get a word in for fear that word would be a no.

I opened my mouth to say I wasn't sure before he interrupted me. "Just try it on, Georgia." He slid the ring on my finger. I looked down as the diamond caught the light, refracting it in a million directions. My hand sat in Kyle's, his thumb caressing my skin. "I can't wait to marry you, sooner or later, whatever you need. I'll wait as long as you need me to, baby." He lifted my hand and kissed the ring on my finger, never breaking eye contact. "Will you wear it?"

I swallowed the lump in my throat, glancing from the ring on my finger to the beautiful, brown eyes that I'd been lost in my entire adult life. I nodded nearly imperceptibly, the only admission I could give him, because I wasn't brave enough to say more. I couldn't give him the yes he wanted, and I couldn't crush him and say no. So I said nothing.

Kyle slid up to the headboard and hauled me on top of him, devouring my lips in a passionate kiss. "I love you so much," he murmured as he wrapped his arms around my back, rubbing his warm palms over my sensitive skin. Tingles erupted over my body as he kissed me while tears simultaneously seared behind my eyelids. Kyle was so comfortable, yet I wanted more. A sense of guilt washed over me that I wanted more—what else is there? How could I be so shallow as to throw away what Kyle and I had on a sexy guy with tousled hair and a cocky grin? But I had, and I couldn't go back, but part of me wanted to, and part of me didn't, because Tristan had made me feel alive. Kyle had given me breath to resuscitate me when I needed it all those years ago, but Tristan was the rehabilitation necessary to make my life worth living again.

The realization choked my throat. I didn't want to believe it. I couldn't. Because believing that meant I loved Tristan. And I didn't want to. I so desperately wanted to feel alive with Kyle.

He twisted a hand in my hair and nipped underneath my ear before capturing my lips with his own. The heartbeat roared in my ears and I leaned on him for a moment to strip my panties off and slide his boxers down before settling on top of him. I pressed his length between my thighs and rocked. I needed to make this right. I needed to do what I could to feel the passion with Kyle that came so easily with Tristan.

He slid the tank I'd slept in over my shoulders and attacked my nipples with his tongue. I arched my back into him and twisted my fingers in his short hair. Straight-laced Kyle, my rock, my comfort, my everything. I kissed along his neck and inhaled his cologne and had a moment of longing for a clean, ocean scent that I'd grown accustomed to all summer. Shame tightened my throat. I swallowed it down and continued to grind against Kyle.

"Georgia, wait," He murmured before fishing a foil wrapper out of the pocket of his jeans that lay in a heap on the floor. Kyle insisted on using condoms, preaching that the pill wasn't one hundred percent and he didn't want to start a family until we were ready. He rolled the latex down his length and then lifted my hips in his strong hands and slid into me.

He filled me and I rocked my body against him, arching, moaning, grinding while trying to fight the image of tousled, golden hair and sparkling, green eyes that threatened to consume me.

* * *

"GEORGIA AND I have an announcement to make." Kyle held my hand under the table. I watched in silent horror, begging him to turn and look at me, pleading with him not to reveal what I thought he was about to reveal. Everyone at the kitchen table—Drew, Silas, Gavin, and Tristan all turned as they shoveled bacon and eggs into their mouths.

"I finally got a ring on her finger." A wide grin spread across Kyle's face as he lifted my left hand to show off the glinting diamond on my finger. I plastered a small smile on my face as I avoided the eyes of everyone at the table.

"Huh." Silas sat directly across from me and when the single syllable escaped his mouth my eyes found his. My stomach rolled painfully; I knew that look on Silas's face. It was all judgment. And I couldn't blame him, even if I hadn't said yes.

I didn't do this. I didn't agree to this, not like you think.

I silently pleaded as I maintained eye contact with my best friend. I couldn't even bring myself to look at Tristan. I was terrified of the expression I would see directed at me. I imagined the hard set of his jaw, his eyes glaring, hurt and anger reflecting in them.

"Congratulations," Gavin said before passing another forkful of eggs into his mouth.

"Yeah, congratulations, Georgia," Drew spit from beside Gavin.

My eyes finally landed on Tristan's. He sat at the head of the table, kitty corner from Drew and Kyle. I sucked in a sharp breath when I saw his beautiful, green eyes burning into mine—staring unabashedly, unwilling to turn away. It was obvious he was angry and I silently pleaded for him not to make a scene, not here, not now.

His jaw was clenched tight, his face held in a controlled, expressionless mask. I'd never seen him that way and it frightened me. I felt instantly terrible that I'd made the beautiful, laidback guy so angry. He didn't deserve that. I never should have done what I did. And Kyle's announcement was only twisting the knife. Anger with Kyle boiled in my stomach, so palpable I could taste it.

"Congratulations, Kyle, Georgia—I hope you both get everything you deserve." Tristan patted him on the back, but his eyes stared at me unapologetically. The anger and hurt swirling in his green depths was clear. But I hadn't even said yes. "If you'll excuse me, I've got some work to do." He stood and turned away, dumping his plate in the sink before walking out. He hated me, and yet I hadn't even done anything. But by doing nothing I had allowed the world to fall out from under me. I had allowed Kyle to make this decision for us. I'd allowed him to put the ring on my finger. I'd given him the proof necessary for the announcement. And hadn't I acquiesced—wasn't my answer as good as a yes when I'd let him slip that ring on my finger?

My heartbeat roared in my ears, my breathing escaping in quick pants. I needed a break, I needed to get away from this table, I needed to scream, or run, and most of all I needed this ring off my finger. Kyle was rambling about wedding ideas, but I didn't hear any of it. My gaze shot to Drew's as fear clenched my stomach, a lump of pain stuck in my throat. Mist mingled in my eyes and threatened to overflow. Drew's gaze penetrated mine; she was angry, that was clear, but after a few moments her features softened, and I could feel the compassion pouring off her.

"G and I will clear the table. We'll bring coffee out on the deck."

"I wasn't done." Kyle stopped mid-sentence

and shoveled another pile of eggs into his mouth.

"Done now. Great, let's go." Drew swooped his plate from him, and I walked dutifully behind her into the kitchen.

Once the guys were on the deck, Drew dropped the plates in the sink and wrapped me in her arms. Sobs wracked my body as she held me.

"It's okay, Georgia. It's going to be okay," she said soothingly.

"No, it's not. I'm such a fucking horrible person. I've ruined them both. Tristan never deserved this. I never ever should have done what I did. And if I ever told Kyle, it would destroy him. They'll both hate me forever."

"Shh, it's going to be okay, G, I promise. Things seem fucked right now, but however they work out, they'll work out," she murmured.

"I didn't say yes, Drew. I didn't say I would marry him, I just needed time, but then he slipped the ring on my finger and guilt came crashing down on me this morning, and when we made love, all I thought about was Tristan. I never said yes." Heaves wracked my body, my shoulders hunched into her small frame, her arms rubbing circles on my back.

"Oh God, Georgia, things are fucked up." She held my cheeks in her hands and looked me in the eye. "Why did you keep the ring on, honey?"

"I love him. I've always loved him. I just couldn't bear to tell him no." I wiped the tears from my cheeks.

"And what about Tristan?"

"I don't know. I thought we were a fling, but I can't stop thinking about him. We slept together on the beach, and it was different. It was…everything," I sobbed. "This morning, I told him I needed time. I gave him hope, and then Kyle's announcement… I didn't say yes, Drew. But Tristan will never believe me. The anger in his eyes at breakfast…" I trailed off.

"He was pretty obvious. He couldn't take his eyes off you. Do you want to marry Kyle?"

"I don't know. Before this summer, without a doubt, but now…since Tristan…" New tears streamed down my cheeks.

"God, G, we've got to figure this out."

"I can't leave him, Drew. I just don't think I can. If things get bad again and he's not there…"

"I know you think that now, but maybe you should give the ring back, tell him you need some time."

"That's not an option. Kyle will take it the wrong way and you know it."

"Well, I don't know if there is a wrong way to take it. You sort of did the worst thing to him imaginable," Drew gently reminded me that I'd cheated on the man that had just announced that we were getting married.

I frowned but remained silent, working over her words in my mind. "Where do you think Tristan went?" I finally asked.

"I don't know, but you should probably talk

to him. He didn't look good when he left."

"I will. I feel terrible, Drew." A pit of despair settled over me. "I don't think I can give the ring back, not yet, not this weekend," I mumbled.

"I know, Georgia."

"I can't live without Kyle."

"I know it seems that way, but—"

"I can't, Drew. I know that. It's not possible." I looked at her with determination in my eyes.

"Honey, if you can't live without Kyle, then you have to give up Tristan."

I swallowed the painful lump in my throat and nodded. I wished desperately that I could keep them both, but I knew with every fiber of my being that there was never anyone else for me but Kyle. He'd been my everything since I could remember. I'd started living again when Kyle came into my life and I feared I'd stop if he ever left.

TWENTY-THREE

Tristan

Georgia had made her choice.

Georgia had made her fucking choice alright, and it wasn't me.

I stomped down the steps of the beach house, barely refraining from kicking at the railing as I went. I hit the driveway and aimed for the old sandy road that led in here. I'd fucking walk to the boat if I had to, I had to escape them. I'd put myself through god damn torture being in the house with them the last few days, but I'd wanted to stay, to show Georgia I wouldn't leave, to prove to her that I was in for the fight. I wouldn't give up until she told me, and last night, we'd been so close. I'd touched the heart of her, I could feel it.

I'd touched the live wire that was raw and uninhibited, buried deep inside her heart that she failed to show anyone. I'd touched it, felt it, held it in my arms all night and woken up with it this morning, but just like she always did, Georgia had turned her back and like that she was gone.

Out of sight, out of mind is apparently what we were, and I didn't think I could bare it anymore.

She'd fucking promised me she'd choose. And for a minute, just a fraction of a fucking second, I'd thought she would choose me.

My stomach rolled with pain as I treaded on the sand, suddenly feeling like I could use a run. Pound away the pain clinching my heart.

I picked up speed and rounded the twisting road until more beach houses dotted the lane as I approached town.

"Need a ride?" A voice called from an idling car before I'd even realized one was upon me.

I caught a glimpse of blonde out of the corner of my eye and inwardly groaned. "Nah, I'm good thanks."

I continued jogging as the red car coasted beside me. "Sure? We could grab something to eat? Go back to your boat?"

Fuck, I'd forgotten I'd told Briana I had a boat. It was usually one of those lines I used to pull a girl in, but just like every thing else this summer it was one more decision I regretted making.

"Pretty busy actually. Thanks for the offer though." I waved then turned a sharp left down an alleyway that I knew would come out near the marina.

Fuck that girl. Fuck all of them.

Fuck Georgia and Kyle and every dark-haired

girl with brown eyes that cracked my fucking heart in two.

I couldn't stand to look at the female form right now, the thought of the gentle lapping waves and quite solitude of my boat the only thing keeping me going. Maybe a dog. Dogs were way more loyal than women.

I finally hit the dock and slowed to a walk, fishing the keys out of my cargo shorts and picking my way through the boats until I reached mine. I climbed on board, not at all concerned with sailing, just desperate for the escape when I plopped onto the bench Georgia had perched on while I'd manned the wheel on our first excursion.

I sighed, leaning back against the pillows and tossing my forearm over my eyes, blocking out the bright rays of the sun and the dark memories.

Georgia had imprinted on me. She was everywhere, I couldn't get away from her no matter how hard I tried. And the real son of a bitch of it was, I didn't even want to. I was a god damn masochist for her.

I grunted when I remembered I had the fucking party tonight. Flipping the top off a beer, I took long draws form the bottle, relishing the bitter taste on my tongue just like the bitter bite Georgia had left on my heart.

Damn her.

Damn me for falling for the one girl I couldn't have.

Damn *him* for being three-hundred miles

away and a thousand miles out of her league.

I chugged the rest of the beer, tossing the empty bottle into the garbage can before cracking another. Resting back against the pillows I turned my face to the sky, sun kissing my skin, reminding me of the warmth that burst through my system with Georgia's touch.

I shook my head and took a few more long pulls from my beer before a flash of white caught my eye. Dark, chocolatey waves fell down her back, a narrow waist and creamy thighs I would sacrifice a limb to get lost in.

Could Georgia possibly have come after me? Left that arrogant fuckwad and come to tell me she was mine forever?

I narrowed my eyes just as the brunette turned, my paper-thin hopes dashed to find a stranger's face returning my stare. Her eyes held mine for an extra long instant, causing irritation to form in my stomach before a thought occurred to me.

I had to go to that god damn party.

What better way to show how unaffected I was by bringing a certain dark-haired date?

I chugged the rest of my beer, then gave a friendly wave before standing and making my way off the deck and down the dock, rejection forming a solid mass of anger-fueled revenge in my stomach. It was time to make the best of a bad situation. Georgia and Kyle be damned.

TWENTY-FOUR

Georgia

PEOPLE WERE ARRIVING for the party that Tristan had planned, and Tristan still wasn't here. He hadn't returned since leaving the house this morning, so I still hadn't had a chance to talk to him. Part of me was angry he hadn't returned, hadn't given me a chance to explain. But did I deserve one? Did he owe me one? Things were confusing and complicated, so much pain wrapped into history—it colored my past and my present, and I still hadn't found a way to stop it from poisoning my future.

Drew was manning the stereo off the deck as people mingled. The sand was lit with the golden glow of tiki torches, and Drew had hired a bartender who'd set up a makeshift station on the beach. The day had been humid and windy so Drew and I were dressed in lightweight summer dresses. Mine was purchased in town this week for Kyle, he always loved when I wore white. The dress was relaxed and flirty and blew around my thighs in the wind, the next best thing to wearing nothing on a humid July night.

Knowing I was stressed, Kyle and Drew were trying to wrangle me. Silas had invited a few friends, and Drew and I had been shopping with some of the girls, but other than that, I'd never met most of these people. I recognized one of the girls Tristan had been making out with that night in the kitchen and rolled my eyes. He would invite one of the slut parade. I wondered if he'd show at all. Guilt stabbed my chest that perhaps I'd hurt him so deeply that he wouldn't even show to his own party.

Drew recognized my pain and handed me a margarita. Silas stepped up and complained about the music when the golden-haired god of my dreams, or my nightmares, I hadn't yet decided, walked around the edge of the deck with a girl on his arm. A new girl. A dark-haired girl, with full curls down the middle of her back, a tight white dress, and deep, brown eyes.

Silas finally realized I wasn't paying attention when he turned and found Tristan. "Georgia," he breathed. "She looks—"

"Like me," I whispered. Except she was taller, much taller. Nearly as tall as him, whereas I barely passed his shoulders. I felt a stabbing pain in my heart when I saw his arm locked around her tiny waist.

"I need another." I passed my drink to Drew.

"Georgia, you're engaged, remember that," she said as she took my drink from me.

"I didn't say yes," I mumbled.

"You're still wearing the ring, love." Silas lifted my hand, the large diamond glinting in the yellow light. I gritted my teeth together and snatched my hand from him. Tristan passed the girl a drink from the bar and then took a Heineken for himself without making eye contact with me. His smile was easy, his eyes twinkling. He looked sexy. Heartbreakingly sexy.

The two of them walked closer and Tristan's eyes dragged across the crowd before his gaze swung around and crashed into me. His stormy green eyes seared a pathway straight to my aching heart before he dipped his head in acknowledgement and turned away. I blinked, unsure how to react, and quickly turned away, rushing through the French doors to chase down Drew and my drink.

Silas followed behind me. "You gonna be okay tonight, love?"

"Perfect, Silas. Even more after another drink." Drew passed me a fresh margarita and I took a gulp.

"Hey, Tristan." Drew glanced over my shoulder with a smile.

He stopped at my side. "Thanks for letting us have the party, Georgia." He took another swig of his beer.

"No problem." I looked to Drew and Silas, desperate to escape Tristan and his heartbreakingly easygoing demeanor. He'd been upset when he left this morning, but easygoing

Tristan was unsettling. What, or who, had he done to get him over his anger so easily? My stomach lurched at the thought. I think I had my answer in the leggy brunette, sipping a cocktail on my deck.

"Anyone seen Kyle?" I asked.

"He and Gavin went to get more ice. They're hauling it to the back now," Drew answered.

"I'm going to see if they need anything." I registered a frown splashed across Tristan's features before I turned and shot out the French doors.

Drew had set up a small dance floor on the patio that extended out to the beach. Kyle and I danced and drank more margaritas. After the fifth, I'd lost count, but I'd slowly been able to forget about Tristan and the slut parade he was bumping and grinding with on the porch and patio, in the house, really anywhere he could get his hands on them. It was mostly just the girl in the white dress—the girl I imagined he'd been with earlier. He'd probably taken her to his boat and fucked her on the deck. Wouldn't that have been romantic? He'd said the rolling waves were good for more than just sleeping. I wanted to believe the things he said to her didn't matter like they did to me—that I was different, but then I'd shake myself out of my liquor-induced haze and Kyle's happy smile would snap me back into the moment.

I smiled up at him and curled my hands around his neck, playing with the hair at his nape. He grinned as his lips met mine as our bodies danced a little too slowly for the music Drew was playing. I treasured being in Kyle's arms because I knew he had to leave tomorrow. I didn't know what I would do then, where that would leave me, but I wanted this night to be ours. I only wanted to focus on the boy who'd captured my heart when I was twelve.

I pressed my damp body into his and he smoothed his palms low on my back, clasping them at the top of my ass. I stood on tiptoes and tasted along the line of his neck with my tongue. His sweat-dampened skin was salty, his cologne invading my nostrils caused me to sigh contentedly.

"Missed you so much, Georgia," he muttered as I trailed from his neck to his ear.

"I missed you too." I ground my hips into his, feeling the erection straining his shorts. He slid his hands up my torso and over my ribcage, his thumbs resting on the outside of my breasts.

"I can't wait for you to come home," he whispered as he pressed my body into his and moved his hips seductively. My breathing hitched for a moment when he said the word home. I no longer thought of our apartment as home; I thought of the beach house as my home.

"Maybe we could spend summers here," I hummed through my margarita fog.

"I can't, baby, I'd love to, but all the hours at the firm…" he trailed off as he nibbled on my earlobe. Suddenly I found myself needing another drink.

"I'm going to get another margarita, you want anything?"

"A beer would be good, but I'll come with you." He started to escort me from the makeshift dance floor to the stairs.

"No, that's okay. Stay here. I'll just be a minute."

"Okay, don't be long, Mrs. Collins." I forced a smile before he swatted me on the ass as I turned and made my way up the stairs.

I stepped into a surprisingly empty house. Drew had smartly kept the lights dim to discourage partygoers from wandering in. I pulled the pitcher of margaritas from the freezer and poured more into my glass before opening a beer for Kyle. I pressed the beer to my forehead to relieve some of the heat dampening my skin.

I made my way through my bedroom, checking my phone, then stepping out the French doors. This part of the porch was quiet, the noise of the party was muted and the light of the tiki torches didn't reach this far. I stood at the rail and looked out down the beach toward the cottage. Memories of that night slammed into my brain as I watched the dune grass sway in the breeze while the white-capped waves rushed on shore. It really was an idyllic setting. I wondered what it would be like to spend the off-season here.

"I think about that night all the time—how you tasted, the sound you made when I sank into you, the way your back arched," Tristan's purred in my ear as his fingertips trailed along my waist. The lightweight cotton of my dress did nothing to dull the sparks from his touch.

I sucked in a sharp breath as he moved his body closer to mine, breathing in my ear, his nose skimming the line of my neck. My eyes fluttered closed, and I curved my neck to the side.

"Congratulations on your engagement by the way," he mumbled right before he tugged on my earlobe with his teeth. My heart pounded furiously in my chest and heat prickled through my system. Fire shot a path to my core and had my stomach doing flip-flops. I pressed my thighs together to relieve some of the tension.

"Are you having fun, dancing with him? Kissing him? Pressing your hot, little body against his?" His palm trailed over my ass and curled around my leg. "I bet you're wet right now, aren't you, Georgia? You get off on fucking around with both of us, don't you?" He slid a fingertip lightly up my inner thigh and under my dress. I pressed my lips together painfully. He was right, I was wet but not for the reason he thought, not because I got off on both of them—it was just him. He has me turned on, all hot and wet and needy.

"I'm engaged," I whispered. I'd come to the conclusion that while I hadn't said yes, I'd allowed Kyle to put that ring on my finger, the one that was like a weight weighing down my left hand at this very moment, and that was as good as engaged in anyone's eyes.

"Oh, I'm aware," he growled as his fingers continued teasing up my thigh. "I crave the smell fo you on me."

"I have to go," I moaned as my heart pleaded for him to take me. His breath, his touch, his scent were all so intoxicating.

"Then go," he said as his tongue trailed over my collarbone, catching a bead of sweat that was headed for my cleavage.

And then his fingertips reached my panty line. "Stop," I breathed.

"Should I fuck you while you wear his ring on your finger? I think you'd like that," he whispered, and the words bit into my gut.

"Stop. I'm not yours," I whimpered. "I'm not yours." I pulled away and glared at him, gripping the margarita and the beer in each hand tightly, trying to maintain control. His eyebrows arched and his gaze held mine.

"You're right. You never were." The spark in his eyes burned out. His gaze turned to the cottage down the beach, our cottage, and then flickered back to the beer in my hands. "Have a good night, Georgia," he said in an emotionless voice before grabbing the beer from my hand—Kyle's beer—and sauntering off around the house and back to the party. I watched the space he'd just occupied and gritted my teeth.

Why was I so goddamn powerless around him? What the fuck kind of hold did he have over me? Why did it feel like he was shooting sparks straight into my bloodstream every time he touched me?

I gnawed my inner cheek and felt the coppery taste of blood. Tears puddled in my eyes, and I wanted to burrow under my covers and block out the world. I wanted to be in that place where I'd lived when I was a girl, before I'd met Kyle, when I'd blocked the pain and felt nothing. Numbness would be preferable to the pain I was causing. I needed that place now, more than ever. For the first time in fifteen years I needed that place.

"Hey babe, what took so long? And where's my beer?" Kyle slid an arm around my waist and kissed me on the forehead.

"God, I forgot, I'm sorry, I'll go get one."

"No, it's okay." Kyle chuckled. "Had a little more to drink than you thought, huh?" he asked. I shook my head and squeezed the tears behind my eyelids. I laid my head on Kyle's shoulder and leaned into him, allowing my body to sink into him, allowing him to support me, just as he always had. An image popped into my head of a wavy, brown-haired thirteen-year-old. The gap between his teeth, the Washington Nationals baseball cap on his head, his ready smile, the easy-going banter. The memory made me smile. My life was effortless with Kyle, he turned me into the new me, the girl I'd become *after*. I couldn't go back, the pain was too deep. It'd rip my heart out if I went back, but I could go forward, and Kyle allowed me to do that. All those nights spent in the backyard counting stars and losing count and starting over again. Nights spent in the ramshackle clubhouse his dad made, the old oak tree he'd kissed me under for the first time when we were fifteen. My heart swelled as all the memories rushed back. I tightened my arm around his waist and he looked at me with a loving smile. I smiled as tears sprang into my eyes.

"I love you," I whispered.

"Love you too," he said. "You okay?" A frown crossed his face.

"Perfect." I tucked underneath his arm. A guy came up on Kyle's other side and they started talking about a case in the media. Kyle faced him with his arm still draped across my shoulders. I took another drink and scanned the crowd. Drew and Silas were on the dance floor giggling and grinding. Gavin was standing at the edge talking to a group of people, glancing back to Drew every few minutes and smiling. My heart ached thinking I was supposed to leave this all behind come September. And this could be my only summer here. Kyle was right -- it wasn't feasible for us to spend summers here unless we wanted to live apart. Even spending summers here and Kyle coming down on weekends wasn't practical, the drive would cut so much of his time that it wouldn't be worth it. I would have to give this up; there was no other option.

This would be a perfect house to bring kids

to, maybe a dog. I could envision kids running down those porch steps toward the ocean with floaties around their arms, pails and shovels in their little hands, but my breathing caught in my throat when I realized they weren't little dark-haired, brown-eyed kids. They had beautiful, sandy blond hair that glinted in the sunlight, and deep, sea green eyes. I think I stopped breathing for a moment as I watched them giggle, building sandcastles, and jumping waves, Tristan's toned arms lifting them over his head, an easy smile on his face, his skin a perfect, sun-kissed bronze.

Tears flooded my eyes. "I have to go, I'll be right back." I rushed away from Kyle before he had a chance to say anything. I angled around the house and into the sand. My pace slowed as tears blurred my vision.

Stepping up to the outdoor shower wall, I turned and ran right into Tristan, leaning against it, one leg bent at the knee, the foot resting against the wall. He was just tipping a beer bottle to his lips when he spotted me.

"Fuck," I groused. A cocky smile lifted the corner of his mouth.

"Problem, Mrs. Collins?" His beautiful, green eyes flared.

"Fuck you," I spit out.

"I'm not the one you should be mad at, Georgia." He set his beer on the ledge and turned to me.

"Who should I be mad at then?""

"Yourself."

"Me? Not a chance. You come in here and stay at my house for the summer, and… you say things, and do things, and the slut parade…" I trailed off as I ran out of steam. I knew I only had myself to blame. I wanted to lash out at him but I couldn't. I couldn't hate him for the tender touches, the gorgeous, green eyes I so easily got lost in, the sexy, turned-up grin that had my tummy flipping deliciously. I couldn't be mad that he had such a profound effect on me.

"That's ridiculous, Georgia." His green eyes flared with anger, his jaw clenched. Just then fireworks rang off in the distance and we turned toward the sound. Fireworks shot from the harbor of the next town up the coast. Bright bursts of green, blue, and red lit the sky as we heard the partygoers cheer.

"I hate that you came here this summer. I hate that you turned everything upside down." I glared back at him. His eyes flashed again before he hauled my body to him. His lips met mine and our tongues tangled in an erotic dance. He tasted of beer and Tristan, a combination that left my head swimming with lust. I melted instantly in his arms just like I always did. I tangled my hands up behind his neck and in his hair, the hair I longed to run my fingers through each and every day. I smashed my lips to his so tightly I knew they'd be swollen in the morning. I didn't care. His hands caressed my back, my ribcage, my breasts, and my ass.

"I hate that you smell like him." He growled

and nipped at my ear almost painfully before lifting me off my feet and backing us into the shower stall. We stumbled in, lips still connected, arms groping wildly at each other, moans echoing in the humid air, and fireworks shooting off in the distance.

"I only want my scent on you." He slammed me against the door and held me firmly against his lean body. I pulled his shirt off and a flood of arousal hit me between my thighs. My heart thudded in my ears as we stared at each other, lost in a momentary lust-filled gaze. "Just my taste on your lips." He claimed my lips with his. Tristan slid his hands up my thighs and lifted me against the door, a thigh in each hand. I sat suspended, his hips snugly between my legs, my arms around his neck. We kissed and I tugged his hair, whimpering into his mouth and rocking into his arousal. I panted as he held me high on my hips, his cock pressed against the thin fabric of my panties. "Just me inside you." He angled his body into me and rubbed erotically. Lust consumed me, causing my hips to move in rhythm with his of their own volition. My brain was foggy with need and lust and alcohol and Tristan. I wrapped an arm around his neck and kissed and nipped his ear before tugging with my teeth. He heaved a noisy breath when I scraped along the sensitive flesh, then he hooked a hand in my panties, tearing them from my body. I heard the zipper of his shorts come down, and he sunk into me. Finally he was there, and it was blissful. It felt like exactly what I needed it to feel like, not wrong, but the best thing on earth. The thing I needed more than anything else.

He held my thighs tightly, his fingers digging into the supple flesh as he rocked into me. His jaw clenched tight, my moans echoing off the walls of the small shower stall as the fireworks boomed down the beach.

"Fuck, Georgia." He grunted as his hips thrust against mine. He angled into me, hitting a new and delicious spot somewhere deep inside, every thrust hard and fast and erotic. Reckless, lustful abandon echoed off the four walls surrounding us.

"I feel you everywhere. When you're not around I feel you. I need you. I fucking need you so much," he whispered between pants. I moaned and bent my neck, feeling his tongue travel the line of my throat before nipping at the flesh. He sucked at the base of my throat as he powered into my body and an orgasm overtook my senses, traveling from my head to my toes. Fire burned through my system and I shuddered and moaned his name, my breath heaving in my chest. Tristan slowed his assault as I came down from my release but kept pushing into me, a slow and gentle rhythm that prolonged the delicious sensations rolling through my body.

I panted and clutched at the straining muscles of his biceps as his tongue trailed down my chest. He pulled away for an instant, angling his hips into mine to hold me against the wall, and took one hand to lift my lightweight summer dress over my head, tossing it to the floor. He unhooked my strapless bra with a flick of his fingers and it fell to the ground around his feet. I bowed as his lips attached to my nipple and sucked fiercely, elongating the pebbled peak further. He slowly built up a steadier rhythm with his thrusts as he sucked and nipped and teased with his tongue. I held his head tightly to my chest, my body begging him for more even though my nerves were so oversensitive I wasn't sure my body could withstand it before crumbling at his feet.

He pulled at my nipple with his teeth, the pain shooting through my body and landing in a new and delicious sensation of pleasure at my clit. My eyes focused on his beautiful lips as he pulled away and sucked his lower lip between his teeth, his eyes trained at the point where our bodies were connected. He had a clear view thrusting in and out of me, worshiping me, pleasuring me, and my heart leapt into my throat as I watched him watching us, an errant lock of hair falling into his eyes, the shadow of his eyelashes caressing his cheekbones. He was biting his lip so hard it was turning white as I took pleasure from the pleasure he got watching us.

"Fuck," he gritted through his teeth. He looked up at me and a smile lifted his beautiful, sculpted lips. I captured them with my own. I needed to feel them. I never wanted to stop feeling them on my skin—my body—my lips. He continued to slam into me methodically, as one of his palms slid down my leg to reach my clit. He massaged and pinched and slid his fingers through my swollen flesh and back up again. Choked groans escaped my throat as he played my body like an instrument.

My fingers clenched in his hair and I leaned my head into the crook of his neck and bit into his shoulder as another even more powerful wave of pleasure cascaded down my body, the sensations wracking every nerve I had. I cried out in pleasure as his body held me tightly and he came with a shudder. I held him in my arms as his body shook and he emptied into me.

Our breathing came back to normal, we held each other, me still wedged against the door, his head still tucked firmly into my neck. His sweat-slicked skin beneath my fingers, his damp, golden hair tickling my cheek, our bodies pressed together skin to skin. Hard and soft. Dark and light. We were a contradiction in every way.

I ran my fingertips along the skin of his back, my fingernails raking along his muscles. I kissed along the line of his neck. I fucking loved him and I hated it. I hated him for making me love him. I hated Kyle for leaving me alone so many nights for so many years. And mostly I just hated myself for doing this to all of us.

I lowered my legs from around the sharp line of his hips and fumbled in the dark for my clothes. After pulling my panties up my legs and my dress over my shoulders I smoothed my hair behind my ears, fidgeting in the small space.

I needed to go.

Needed to leave.

Needed to escape.

A jolt shook my body when Tristan skimmed his thumb along the line of my jaw. "Georgia, I–"

"Babe! You back here?"

My heart lurched and my hand pressed to my lips. "Kyle." I mouthed the word, my gaze searing Tristan. He stood still, his index finger lifting to press to his lips in the universal sign for *shhh*.

I nodded and waited. I deserved this. I deserved for Kyle to find me and Tristan, our skin damp and flushed from fucking.

We listened to shuffling in the sand in between the echoing booms of the fireworks. My heart raced and my chest heaved with erratic breaths.

Oh god.

Not now. Not an anxiety attack. I bit down on my bottom lip, trying to stifle the sensation. Trying to swallow down and hold it in.

"Georgia?" Tristan ducked his head and took my shoulders in his hands. My limbs shook with fear, anxiety pulsed through my veins, I shook from my fingertips to my toes. "Georgia." He whispered louder, his eyes searching mine. I only shook my head. I couldn't form words. Couldn't even take full breaths.

"Kyle!" Tristan bolted around me and threw

the shower stall open.

I slid to the door.

Oh God, he would tell him. He would confess everything. He was throwing me under the bus. Forcing my hand.

I couldn't. I couldn't. I couldn't.

I slid to the sandy tile floor and stuck my head between my knees trying desperately to focus on my breaths.

TWENTY-FIVE

Georgia

THE NEXT MORNING, I had a splitting headache. I threw a pillow over my head, willing the throbbing to subside before deciding that a tall glass of water and Advil were in order. I sighed, stretched, and then slowly opened my eyes to find Kyle next to me. I rolled to my side and placed my palm lightly on his chest, the diamond ring sparkling in the light that suffused the room. His deep, rhythmic breathing told me he was still sound asleep, so I snuck out of bed and padded into the bathroom. I stumbled in front of the mirror and assessed the damage from the night before.

I rubbed my hands over my face, willing the sleep away. I touched the dark circles under my eyes and frowned; getting old was a bitch and I had a feeling the alcohol wasn't helping matters. My eyes trailed further down my reflection in the mirror and landed at my hips where the hem of my T-shirt met the pale pink of my panties. I squinted at my reflection.

"What the hell?" I leaned in to get a closer look.

Bruises.

Fucking bruises on my thighs. Perfectly round bruises.

I turned to the side and found more where the top of my thighs met my hips.

Suddenly last night came crashing back to me. I remembered walking around the side of the house, Tristan leaning against the wall of the outdoor shower looking sad and broken.

Our fighting. Our kissing. Our fucking.

Kyle. Tristan. My breakdown.

"Oh God." I covered my mouth with one hand as bile rose in my esophagus.

I remembered all of it.

I closed my eyes and replayed the scene in my head. When I opened them the evidence of our wild, forbidden coupling was on my thighs. I peeked out the bathroom door and found Kyle still sleeping. What had happened? Had Tristan told him? Why was he...how could he be...here? In bed with *me?*

I shut the door and slid down to sit on the cold, tile floor. Shoving my head in my hands I tried to calm my breathing. I had to talk to Tristan. Had to find out what had happened after I'd blacked out. After we'd....and then Kyle had...

Bile lurched into the back of my throat as I realized I'd had sex with Tristan the night that Kyle had proposed to me. The day of my engagement I'd had sex with someone else.

I willed myself to breathe deeply while my mind raced. I was having a panic attack; if I didn't get ahold of myself I would be an incoherent blob on this bathroom floor, in the same state I'd found myself in just last night.What the fuck was I supposed to do? My fiancé—the man I'd loved and cheated on—slept in the bed right outside this door. And the man I'd cheated on him with was in this house somewhere. What a fucking mess. I was no more than a whore who had trampled all over the hearts of each of the men she cared for.

I had the urge to puke.

"Georgia?" Kyle tapped on the door.

"Yeah?" I croaked.

"You okay?" he asked.

"Yeah, just don't feel very well."

"Okay, can I get you anything, babe?"

Babe. He was calling me "babe." That meant he didn't know. But how could he not? How could he possibly not know what Tristan and I had done?

"Georgia?"

"No, thanks. I'm fine. I'll be out in a minute." I answered as my mind raced.

"Okay." Kyle's footsteps padded out of the room. I gritted my teeth and tried to breathe deep and slow through my nose, filling my lungs, expanding my chest cavity, closing my eyes, and thinking serene thoughts. I can fix this. I can do what's right. I can still make the right decision.

I'd made the wrong fucking decision at every turn this summer, but there was still time to make the right one.

I lifted myself off the floor and opened the door, making my way to the closet. I pulled on a pair of long shorts. Most of the shorts I had were too short and would show my bruises.

"You're up early," I mumbled to Silas sitting at the kitchen island with a cup of coffee. I poured one for myself, and a glass of water.

"Early night." Silas shrugged.

"Seriously?" I swallowed two Advil and gulped the glass of water.

"You don't remember? Justin and I had a spat, apparently dancing with someone else—even if you're not exclusive— is not okay with him," Silas grumbled.

"Didn't see that." I frowned, taking a sip of my coffee. I wondered if Tristan was already awake. I glanced at the closed French doors, an indication that he was probably still sleeping.

"Where did you disappear to? Kyle was looking for you during the fireworks." Silas took another drink from his mug.

"I wasn't feeling well, I laid down for a while." *Or got laid.* I heaved an exasperated sigh.

"Hmm, come to think of it, I didn't see Tristan either." Silas looked me squarely in the eye.

"Hey, babe, feeling better?"

Kyle drifted into the kitchen in a T-shirt and shorts.

"Yeah, I'm okay," I responded weakly.

"Too much to drink, huh?" Kyle asked and leaned in for a kiss, sliding both his hands up my thighs and under my shorts. Kyle stroked his thumbs along my flesh, in the same area Tristan's hands had held me against the wall the night before. I cringed.

"I guess so."

"You should probably lay off the hard stuff. Remember your therapist said alcohol can increase the likelihood of a panic attack?"

"What?"

"Last night. Tristan said he found you on the floor of the shower in a full blown panic attack. You looked bad, babe. I don't want to have to worry about you down here if you're going to be drinking like that." Kyle worked slow circles on my shoulders with his thumbs.

"You had a panic attack last night?" Silas' voice rose in alarm.

"Oh, yeah. It wasn't a big deal. It hasn't happened in so long, I guess I just blocked it out." I placed a hand to my forehead and feigned confusion. I was lying to my fiancé, and now my best friend.

"No more drinking?" Kyle caught my chin between his thumb and index finger.

"No more." A small smile curved my lips.

Was I really going to get away with this? Was Kyle so trusting of me that I could sleep with someone right under his nose and he wouldn't bat an eye?

I couldn't think about it anymore. "Want me to make some breakfast? Pumpkin pancakes?" I pulled away awkwardly. I couldn't stand his hands or his lips on me right now.

"You okay to cook?" Kyle poured coffee.

"You should rest, Georgia. If you're not feeling good..." Silas placed the back of his hand on my forehead.

"I'm fine." I swept his hand away. "Go bang on doors and wake everyone for breakfast." I stood and headed for the pantry.

"It's just Gavin and Drew. Tristan didn't stay here last night," Silas said.

"Really? Where did he stay?" I spun around quickly, catching myself. Silas noticed my reaction, but Kyle stood oblivious, sipping his coffee and looking out at the beach.

"No idea, he left just after the fireworks..." Silas said pointedly.

"Oh." My mind raced, a thousand thoughts bouncing around. I turned back to the pantry as anger prickled my skin, the blood scorching in my veins. He was gone. He'd gone home with someone else. Would Tristan do that? Would he be with me, then fuck someone else after? I didn't remember how we'd ended things. I was so fucking drunk I didn't even remember anything until seeing those bruises this morning. But maybe he'd been so drunk he didn't remember either. Pain sliced my heart open that he could forget our coming together last night.

I need you. His words echoed in my brain.

I fucking need you so much.
I need you.
I need you.

What did that mean? In that moment? For a while? The rest of the summer? Forever? My hands started to shake and tears pricked my eyelids as I reached for the flour on the top shelf. My breathing sped up and I found myself at the onset of another panic attack. The image of his arm wrapped around the beautiful brunette he'd brought last night flashed before my eyes. My heart ached at the possibility that he'd been in her bed last night, or he'd brought her to his boat. That he'd had both of us. Blood surged through my veins and my limbs began to shake in anger, pain, and anxiety before the sack of flour hit the floor and exploded all over my feet.

"Georgia?" Silas and Kyle hurried into the pantry after me. I'd dropped to my knees on the pantry floor, my legs covered in flour, tears flowing silently down my cheeks.

"I don't feel well." I avoided Kyle's eyes and looked only at Silas. I pleaded with him to understand, to help me, to protect me from myself. I was no good at operating my life; I needed someone to do it for me. For so long I'd relied on Kyle, but I'd fucked that up this summer. The only person I had left was Silas, my best friend who never judged me, only loved me. "Can you help me to bed?" I murmured.

"Come, love," Silas whispered as he lifted me into his arms. Kyle watched us leave with a confused look on his face. Silas carried me down the hallway and set me in bed. I curled up and nuzzled into the pillows that still smelled of Kyle, falling asleep with this desperate notion that everything I'd thought about my life was now turned upside down and on a collision course—an impending explosion the only foreseeable outcome.

* * *

I SAT SIPPING coffee on the deck, staring off into space. Kyle had left yesterday afternoon after I'd insisted I was fine. I'd told him it was probably just dehydration from the drinking the night before and the ever-present humidity. He'd finally left, giving Silas strict orders to call him if anything else happened and to make sure I drank plenty of water.

I lifted the coffee cup to my lips, my thoughts moving to Tristan. Our night in the shower, the passion, rage, and anger swirling around us as we connected like we never had before. He was rough, but I understood why. He wanted to stake his claim. Our emotions had been out of control all summer, and finally when I'd given him that little piece of me on the beach—the night we slept wrapped in each others' arms, the morning that I'd given him hope that we could be together—it'd crushed him when Kyle had announced our engagement. We were so frustrated that we'd taken each other in the shower stall with abandon. Claiming each other with everything we had in us, all of the pent-up frustration that had simmered all summer had come out in those long breathless moments when we'd connected. And I still had the evidence on my thighs, a reminder of how Tristan had made me feel. The pool of love and lust he'd thrown me head first to drown in.

I sensed him sitting on the chair beside me. I didn't turn, I didn't need to. It was him, there was no question. We sat silently. I didn't want to know where he'd been. I didn't want to talk about what had happened between us. I didn't even know if I wanted him next to me. I'd tried to blame him for causing my heart to crack wide open this summer, but it had been my own fault, and in all honesty it had probably been a long time coming.

"I'm sorry, Georgia," he murmured after long minutes of silence stretched between us. He reached one hand out and caressed my skin with a tender fingertip. "I can't be here anymore," he said in a broken voice. My heart fragmented in my chest, cracks breaking open and causing fissures to splinter and bleed.

"No," I whispered.

"I have to go, Georgia. This is destroying both of us," he murmured.

"You can't. I'll... I can't..." I was sure my heart was physically shattering into a thousand tiny shards. They were falling and shredding the organs inside me. My body was crumbling, and I was losing the man that had made me feel so much more than anyone else. He'd offered me the chance to forget. He'd pleaded with me to choose him, and still I hadn't. I'd led him on and still chosen who was safe. I hadn't been willing to gamble, even for Tristan.

"You chose him, Georgia." Each word passed his lips on a painful breath. His eyelids at half-mast, he looked completely defeated. I had broken him. "I tried to get over you. I wanted so fucking bad to forget you. But every time I was with someone, it was you. Your hair, your eyes, your touch. You're all I fucking saw. You have a choice, Georgia, but I don't. I don't have a fucking choice, I never did. It's always been you. You're it for me, but you still chose him. I'm fucking lost without you. You destroyed me. I'm not the person I was before I met you and I can't go back. Nothing works anymore without you." His words seared a pathway to my heart. Like fire raging inside me, burning me from the inside out. The pain I'd put him through I felt acutely in my chest.

"Tristan," I whimpered.

"Don't ask me to stay, Georgia. I can't stay. I want to stay for you, but I can't. I can't stay for me. This is crushing me. You're not mine to want."

"I'm sorry," I whispered as hot tears fell down my cheeks.

"I'm sorry too." He stood and was gone. His words replayed in my head as I gazed out at the ocean, seeing nothing but him, his words, his pain. He was leaving, and my heart had stopped beating for the first time since I was twelve.

* * *

TRISTAN HAD BEEN gone for days, and as each ticked by I stayed in bed. I hardly ate, hardly spoke. Kyle called me every day, usually when he was crawling into bed at night. He knew nights were the hardest for me, but even hearing his soothing voice before I turned the lights out didn't help. Silas and Drew checked on me, played cards in my room while I watched them silently from underneath my bed sheets. But nothing made a difference; I'd turned numb.

I'd also succumbed to nightmares every night. The most horrific I'd ever had. I'd lay in the partial state between sleep and wakefulness. I knew I was dreaming, but I was powerless to stop the inevitable. I waited as terror caused my heart to race, my breath to heave painfully, my skin to prickle with fear and sweat. The nightmares were ravaging my heart like a tornado hellbent on destroying everything in its path—they took it all.

I grew terrified to sleep. Dark circles had taken up permanent residence under my eyes.

My brown irises dull, my skin pale. I was exhausted, but each time I burrowed into my pillow and closed my eyes, the nightmares returned, converging with memories. I became a shell that my pain echoed through.

Silas lay in bed beside me, stroking my hair, pleading with me to call Kyle. Pleading with me to go home to D.C. I couldn't bear the thought. Drew grew desperate and sent Gavin to speak to me. He begged me to let him call Tristan, said he was sure Tristan would come if I needed him, but I refused. I couldn't take any more from any of them. I'd broken them all. I'd done things to both Tristan and Kyle that were unforgivable, and their lives would be better without me.

I padded to the kitchen in the early dawn hours a few days later. Diffused rays streamed through the curtains. I opened the French doors and shuffled to the deck. I inhaled the humid ocean air, sucking it into my lungs and begging for it to heal me—to do anything to erase the pain that was suffocating me. I moved down the porch steps and made my way to the beach. I walked and walked, trailing my feet through the gentle waves that lapped at my toes.

I passed our cottage. Sparing it a single glance, I felt the pain of that night stab me in the heart. We'd shared a few beautiful, stolen moments, and then he'd moved on, just like everyone had warned me he would. The very last thing I could handle and he'd done it. The lightning bolt that had seared a path to my heart at the memory of our time together eased into a dull ache until it evaporated into numbness. A hollow, black hole of blessed nothingness.

I turned to keep walking. I walked until the beach house was nearly out of sight before I stopped and looked out at the horizon. I was sick of the nightmares, I was sick of hurting the people I loved, I was sick of being unable to make up my mind. I took a few tentative steps out into the gently lapping waves. Small strings of seaweed curled at my ankles. I kept walking. I walked until I was up to my thighs, the cotton, summer dress I wore dampened at the hem and sticking to my legs. I brushed my fingertips in the water and stood quietly. I watched a gull land and the ripple that trailed behind him as he drifted.

I took a few more tentative steps and then sunk down in the cool ocean, my white dress plastered to my wet body, the loose fabric drifting in the water around me. Floating on my back with arms outstretched, I looked up at the stark, white clouds passing above my head. I inhaled the ocean scent and closed my eyes, a constant burn behind the eyelids from the tears I'd shed over the last several days. I didn't know what I wanted anymore, didn't know who I needed, before realization hit me. I needed myself, whoever she was, I needed to find her and nurture her. I needed to make her worth loving before I could love anyone else. An invisible weight seemed to lift as I floated. With ears submerged, I drifted in the water and lost myself in the world that existed around me.

My eyes clenched tightly together when I heard muffled rumblings. I was desperate to block out the intrusion. My body swayed, my mind lost in thought as waves surged around me.

"Georgia." Strong arms curled around me and held me so tightly I could hardly breathe. I refused to open my eyes. I wanted to stay in the world I'd found for myself. The world where the pain subsided for just a little while.

"Georgia, thank God."

I nuzzled into the body that held me and took a deep breath.

That scent.

His scent.

Tears jumped to my eyes as I snuggled in desperately. I wrapped my arms round his neck and my fingers curled into his too long hair. The hair that I loved to thread my fingers through and tug gently. The hair I dreamed about, the beautiful golden strands I saw on the kids in my daydreams.

"Tristan," I whispered as he hauled me out of the water. He sat down, his clothes drenched, me in his lap. I curled around his body, locked my ankles behind his back as he held me in an iron grip. He held me forever and he didn't ask any questions. He knew I didn't have the strength for words.

"I came to see you. I wanted to have coffee on the deck. I missed our mornings together. I couldn't stay away anymore." He rocked me back and forth, soothing me against his chest. Our wet clothes plastered to our skin as we sat tangled in each other. I took deep, calming breaths of his intoxicating scent. Stubborn tears trickled down my cheeks.

"I love you," I said so quietly I wasn't sure he'd heard me. I didn't care. I hadn't said it for him. He heaved a big sigh, and I felt his heart hammering in his chest, my own meeting his, beat for beat. His fingers wove into the hair at my nape.

"Georgia," he breathed. He held my head tightly in the crook of his neck.

"Thank you," I murmured.

"For what?" His husky voice breathed in my ear.

"Coming to me," was all I said—all I could say.

TWENTY-SIX

Georgia

TRISTAN STAYED AFTER he found me floating in the ocean. Weeks passed, the waves crashed, the wind blew, the summer slipped by, and all the while, a silent understanding existed between us. We didn't talk about what had happened, what had been said, but we'd been affected. I'd taken off Kyle's ring, but I hadn't told him yet—at least all the things I needed to say. I didn't know if I had the strength to break up with Kyle, but I knew I had to tell him. He deserved honesty, I was sure of that at least. He'd ceased calling every day; he'd apparently grown sick of my one-word responses because we were back to calling and texting a few times a week. I knew he was busy, and it was easier this way. Whenever we spoke on the phone, guilt for cheating on him tightened my chest and choked the words in my throat. It was easier to not talk at all.

The days flew by and Silas and Drew tried to

pull me out of myself. They talked about house renovations and dragged me on outings to pick out paint colors or shop for furniture. I made decisions when necessary, but I didn't feel the excitement I once had. Gavin and Tristan worked each day, and Tristan spent a lot of time on his boat, but every night he came home, and every morning we sat on the porch over coffee. Not much was said and we hadn't slept together again, hadn't even touched. The easy smile I'd fallen so hard for at the beginning of the summer had disappeared from his face. We'd broken each other. I knew I'd done most of the breaking, but regardless, we were both broken. I was living inside my head—working through my life, sifting through the rubble, making sense of what was left.

Soon we found ourselves in the middle of August. We were officially into hurricane season and a storm was predicted in the coming days. Drew had scheduled a construction company to come in and refinish the second story bedrooms, but with the approaching storm, they'd recommended we put the work off until it had passed.

Hurricane Isla was predicted to make landfall up the coast and while we wouldn't take a direct hit, the effects could be severe and damaging nonetheless. Many in the area were boarding up and evacuating. I was determined to stay until I was forced to leave. Over the summer this house had become my home. We were making progress on the remodel, and I was as stubborn as I was smart, so I wasn't willing to pack up the one thing that had become essential to my existence over the past few months.

As the winds picked up and the days grew more overcast, more houses along the beach were shuttered and vacated. Silas was with Justin, the guy he'd been dating on and off all summer. They'd gone inland to weather out the storm at Justin's house, and Gavin and Drew drove back to Jacksonville for a few days. In the end Tristan told Drew that he would stay with me until I left, or until they could make it back. I rolled my eyes at their entire conversation, as if they were talking about a child or someone who was sick; I was neither, I had just succumbed to the pain and the guilt that'd been chasing me. Finally Drew and Gavin had driven off after she'd hugged me tightly and had made me promise a thousand times over to call her if I needed her. She promised she would come rushing back. I knew that she would, and I promised her I would call if I needed her, knowing I wouldn't. She also whispered in my ear to not be afraid to lean on Tristan. I nodded, but I knew I wouldn't do that either. She left with a pained look on her face as they pulled away.

That left Tristan and me alone. He'd refused to leave me by myself, even though I'd insisted I didn't need him to stay with me. Things weren't even awkward between us. Awkward was a feeling, and I'd run out of those.

I made a list of things we'd need for the storm, and Tristan and I drove into town to stock up. Things were picked over, but we managed to get batteries, flashlights, a weather radio, bottled water, and plenty of canned goods. I made breakfast for dinner that night—eggs, bacon, and toast, and we sat quietly in the living room, television turned to The Weather Channel, watching the progress of the storm as we sipped white wine. We didn't talk much, but I was glad to have someone there, another body in the house.

I stood, wrapped an afghan around my shoulders, and stepped out on the deck. I sat on the porch swing and rocked it back and forth with one foot. I sipped my wine and tipped my head up to look at the midnight sky. The waves were rushing the shore in a thunderous, nearly deafening roar. A noise so loud it couldn't be escaped. It left little room for the thoughts to take over my brain.

"Kyle texted." Tristan stepped out on the deck and passed me my phone.

"Thanks." I checked his message. He'd been texting more the last few days, asking me to come home before the worst of the storm hit. When I did answer, it was brief, and I promised I would keep him up to date. I frowned and looked at the most recent message before turning my phone off and setting it next to me on the railing.

"Have you talked to him lately?"

My eyes focused on Tristan's. We didn't talk about Kyle. Not ever. Not since that day on the porch when he'd told me he couldn't stay because I'd destroyed him. "No," I answered.

"He's probably worried." He took a seat next to me and tipped his wine glass to his lips. The distance between us felt like a million miles. Gone were the easy moments we'd shared together in the beginning, replaced with painful silence.

"He is. He wants me to lock up the house and go home," I said.

"I didn't mean about the storm. He's probably worried about you, Georgia," he said sadly. I didn't answer him. "I am too." He finally turned to look at me. I continued to stare out at the huge waves, refusing to allow myself to look at his swirling, deep green eyes. His piercing gaze would splinter my soul if I allowed it to. I pressed my lips together to keep a handle on the emotion straining just beneath the surface.

"You don't have to be," I said finally.

"I can't help but think it's my fault."

"It's not," I answered him.

"Fuck, Georgia." He ran an agitated hand through his hair. "You sound dead."

"I am," I answered before looking into his eyes.

"Georgia." My name escaped his lips on a breath. I frowned at him before looking up in the sky.

"You let it take you—the pain. You're gone.

The girl that I took sailing this summer is gone. The girl that read on the beach with me—she's gone." The pain radiated off him. I only shrugged and continued to focus on the night sky above me. So much for wishing on shooting stars, I thought. I'd been here just a few short months ago, the same swing, with the same person, and wished that I could follow the right path for my life without hurting those I loved in the process. Boy, had that gone spectacularly wrong.

"You should talk to someone, Georgia."

"I have. I've gone to therapists, but the nightmares don't stop. The pain doesn't go away." The numbness was so profound I may as well have been talking about what I'd had for dinner the night before.

"You can talk to me." He placed a comforting hand on my knee.

"I can't." My eyes darted to his hand before looking at the sky. Just a few short weeks ago and his touch would have had my nerves dancing. Now they felt all but dead.

"Can't or won't?" He squeezed my leg.

"Both." I stood and walked back into the house and into my bedroom.

* * *

"GEORGIA, WAKE UP. It's okay, it's just a dream."

I woke up to arms shaking me gently, a firm body wrapped around me. The hollow echo of gun shots ran a constant loop in my brain.

Scream. *Pop.* Scream. *Pop.* Scream. *Pop.*

My skin was damp with sweat. Moonlight streamed in my window. My eyes shot to green ones that were searching mine, a worried frown and clenched jaw watching me.

"It was just a dream, I'm right here. You're okay." He laid me back on my bed. "I heard you from down the hall." The gentle cadence of his voice soothed me. "I'm staying with you tonight. Just go back to sleep," he shushed before wrapping his hand around my waist, throwing a leg over mine, tangling me in him from head to toe. He pressed his chest to my side and I curled up into the crook of his arm and inhaled his comforting, clean scent. I burrowed closer and shut my eyes tightly. These nightmares were going to destroy me. Or at least give me dark circles for the remainder of my time on earth. I gritted my teeth in anger. What they'd taken from me, I couldn't get back. It was out of my reach and I didn't know what that meant. I couldn't fathom a life like this for the next fifty years and I didn't want to. I just didn't know how to fix it.

Tristan started singing in a soft timbre in my ear, the song he'd played for me in the car on the way to the vineyard. *Poison and Wine* by The Civil Wars.

I don't have a choice, but I'd still choose you.

The words drifted through my thoughts, holding so much more meaning now than they had then. I knew the pain in the lyrics. I knew what it felt like to want someone so completely that it broke you inside when you couldn't have them.

He hummed and rocked me gently as I tried to clear my brain and focus only on the sound of the waves crashing and Tristan's deep voice soothing me. I settled into a modicum of comfort and finally fell asleep.

* * *

I WOKE THE next morning to the sound of shrill ringing. My head was foggy. I'd slept like shit all night after the nightmare. Having Tristan nearby helped, but my mind was in such a bad place lately, getting rest was becoming nearly impossible. I jumped out of bed and ran to the kitchen to find Tristan on the house phone. He hung up a few moments later with a frown marring his face.

"The city is warning us to prepare to evacuate. The storm is supposed to make shore in the next twenty-four hours." He sat at the dining table with his laptop open before him.

"I thought the storm was hitting north of us?"

"It is, but they're predicting a lot of damage. Flooding, high winds. Maybe we should board up and head out, Georgia. Get a hotel inland until the storm's passed and then we'll come back—"

"I'm not leaving. You can go, Tristan. I'll be fine. I'll leave if there's a mandatory evacuation, but I'm staying until then." I turned and scooped coffee grounds into a filter.

"You're here, I'm here." He slipped an arm around my waist and pulled me next to his body. I froze at the unexpected contact. He hadn't touched me like this in weeks. Maybe he'd gotten the wrong idea by sleeping in bed with me last night; maybe I shouldn't have let him.

"Tristan, I—"

"I know." He pulled away with a reassuring smile. I nodded while I waited for the coffee to finish brewing. Tristan pulled down two mugs, and I filled them and made my way to the porch. I grabbed a quilt on the way and wrapped myself in it before curling up in a deck chair. Tristan took his place next to me, and we sipped coffee quietly while watching the storm brewing offshore.

"Are you working today?" I asked absentmindedly.

"Nothing that can't be put off for a few days 'til the storm passes." The corner of his mouth lifted in a small smile. I nodded and turned back to the water.

The waves roared and crashed, and the beach looked wild and haunting with an overcast grey sky and wind whipping the dune grass. I timed my breathing with the waves hitting the shore and scanned the horizon. It felt like my head and my heart were a whirl of shifting emotion. One minute I yearned for a future with Tristan—those golden-haired kids haunting my dreams, and the next I wanted to run back into Kyle's arms and never leave.

That's why I held myself at a distance from both of them. I texted Kyle and talked to him a few times, but it wasn't hard avoiding the tough conversations because he was so busy. Tristan on the other hand broke my heart when I had to look into his beautiful, sad eyes and see his weak smile every day.

"Penny for your thoughts?" He crooked a grin at me. I heaved a sigh and looked at him.

A grin crept across my lips as his twinkling eyes gazed back at me. "I don't want to leave here." I looked back out to the clouds speeding across the sky.

"We won't unless it's mandatory."

"No, I don't want to leave ever. Part of me wants to stay through the off season," I said aloud, but more to myself. He remained silent beside me. I finally looked over at him after a few quiet minutes passed. He was gazing down the beach with a thoughtful look on his face.

* * *

"WE JUST GOT another call, Georgia." Tristan ducked his head into my room later that afternoon.

"Mandatory evacuation?" I frowned.

"No, but highly recommended." He stepped in the doorway and crossed his arms, leaning against the doorframe.

"Do you have to do anything with your boat?"

"The marina secures all vessels. But maybe we should think about—"

"I don't want to go yet," I mumbled as I dug through my closet for a sweater.

"I know, Georgia, but—"

"I don't want to go yet." I shot him an angry glance. "We've got everything ready, we're okay still."

"Okay," he said cautiously before turning to leave. Part of me was starting to wish he would have gone back with Drew and Gavin—he was becoming a pain in my ass.

The rain started to pelt the roof and beat on the sand outside. It was an instant downpour and I walked to the doors in my room and watched it coming down. It was oddly therapeutic, strangely exciting. It felt like the future was unknown, and I wondered if it was morbid of me to enjoy the adrenaline high of watching the storm sweep in around us. But I knew I couldn't leave. This felt completely like my home now -- I'd bought it, decorated it. I'd only been here a few short months, but I wasn't ready to surrender it to this big, angry storm.

The winds picked up and the dune grass twisted outside my window. The waves pounded the shore and the sky dimmed to near black. I instantly had the urge to head outside and feel the power of the elements against my skin. I stepped out the doors and walked down the steps.

"What do you need? I'll get it." Tristan bounded out of the French doors off the living room and caught my arm. The wind whipped around my face and snapped my hair against my neck. The rain stung as it pelted my skin and streamed down my body in rivulets.

"I don't need anything." I tugged my arm out of his grip. A confused look crossed his face before I continued down the steps. I couldn't hear him over the howling wind and rain, but I knew he was following me.

I held my hands out, palms upturned, and felt the rain stinging my hands. The cold drops cooled my skin after all the humidity we'd had this summer. The wind whipped and I turned my head to the sky, my eyes squeezed shut. A wide grin spread across my face as I felt the angry drops pounding my body. A banging from behind me caught my attention and I spun to find a shutter had ripped off the house and landed in a corner of the deck.

"Georgia, we should go." Tristan grabbed my hand and tugged.

"No," I hollered over the roaring of the

elements.

"It's dangerous." His eyes pleaded as his hand tugged.

"No, I want to stay." I shook my head stubbornly.

"I'm not letting you go, Georgia. Come on." Fire flashed in his eyes.

"Let go," I screamed and yanked my arm from his grasp.

"Georgia," he growled before lifting me in his arms and hauling me over his shoulder. He stomped toward the house and I beat on his back with closed fists.

"Let me go," I screamed. "I want to be here, this is my home." I wrestled out of his grasp, hit the sand and ran back toward the angry frothing waves. The power of it overwhelmed me, consumed me, made me feel alive. I was sick of being safe. My entire life I'd been safe and only bad things had happened.

Tristan's arms circled my waist and held me tightly.

"Go." I tried wrestling out of his grip before my body finally went slack. "It's not working," I sobbed.

"What?"

"The rain—it's not cleansing. I don't feel it cleansing."

"Georgia. Let me take you in. You're going to get hurt." He spun me in his arms and held my head in both his hands. Just like he'd done every other time he'd kissed me. I shut my eyes tight to block his beautiful face from my line of vision and the sweet memory from my mind.

"I don't care." Tears streamed down my face. "I don't care."

"I do," he hollered back at me. "You may not care, but I fucking do. I love you, Georgia. I fucking love you, and I care."

My eyes flashed open in shock. I opened my mouth to say something but wasn't sure what. "You don't, Tristan," I said.

"I do, Georgia. I care and I love you and I want you safe. I want to take care of you. I don't want you to leave. I don't want to leave." He still held his palms on either side of my face, his thumbs pressed on my cheekbones, his fingers threaded through my long, wet hair. I averted my gaze, refusing to acknowledge what he'd said.

"Turn your emotions back on. You told me you loved me, and yet you've done nothing. You're more broken than ever. Come back, Georgia. You're sinking; the pain is taking you." Tristan dipped his head to make eye contact with me.

"I don't deserve it, Tristan. I don't deserve you. I'm broken." I sobbed and dropped my head in anguish.

"Yes, you do, you deserve it. You deserve everything. I've waited so long to feel anything and you make me feel, so I'm not letting you go without a fight." He tipped my head up to look in his eyes.

"I've broken everything. I'm toxic, everything

I touch—"

"That's not true—"

"It is. It is, Tristan, you have no idea." Hot, wet tears streamed down my face, mingling with the cool raindrops.

"Then tell me. Tell me why you think that." He raised his voice again.

"My parents. It's my fault. It should have been me too, but I was a coward, and I hid, and I'm still hiding," I rambled inconsolably.

"What are you talking about?" Tristan's stormy eyes blazed into me.

"They're dead and I should be too. But I hid under my bed. I fell asleep. There were boots, and voices, and my dad—" I choked on another sob as the painful memory overtook me.

"What the fuck happened? Tell me what happened to you, Georgia." He fingered the strands of my hair soothingly.

"They were murdered. And I hid under my bed the whole time. They were tortured, all night, while I was asleep under my bed."

"God, Georgia." He pressed me to his chest and held me so tightly the breath could hardly escape my lungs.

"My parents were murdered when I was twelve, a break-in, and they didn't even get away with anything valuable. They found some jewelry and a couple hundred dollars. My dad tried to save me and my mom, he tried to fight them, they were angry that they didn't find much, so they tortured them." My heart shattered on the wet sand at my feet. Pain raged inside me, beat through my chest just like the waves on the shore. I was dizzy with suffering and exhaustion and devastation.

"They didn't get much because my parents had a safety deposit box. They left it all to me, everything—an insurance policy, inheritance. That's how I bought the house. I refused to touch the money—blood money—for years, until now, until I finally started to live, so I bought the beach house," I whimpered. I'd had some sad hope that buying the beach house with the blood money would be therapeutic in some way, that it would help me heal from the tragedy of my childhood.

"I'm so sorry. God, I'm so sorry." He rocked me back and forth in his arms as the rain pounded us. We were knit together, his arms encircling me, as we stood in a cocoon of pain and devastation while the storm raged around us.

"That's not the worst part. The part that haunts me—that I dream about," I swallowed the lump in my throat. "I saw them. When the cops found me, they tried to shelter me on the way out of the house, but I looked up and I saw them, I saw their bodies. And every five years it comes back. One of the murderers killed himself, but the other—he's in prison—but every five years he's up for parole. Every five years they send me a letter. Every five years I'm faced with the notion that he might be released." Sobs wracked my entire body and I fell to my knees on the beach. The rain and tears mingled together down my cheeks, and my eyes hurt from the crying, and the lump in my throat wouldn't go away.

"Fuck, Georgia. Please let me take you inside," Tristan whispered in my ear as he slipped his hands under my knees and around my back to carry me through the driving rain and into the house. He laid me on the couch and wrapped his body around mine, holding me so tightly it helped to calm the shaking of my body.

"That's why I can't leave Kyle," I finally whispered once my sobs had subsided.

"Why?" he mumbled in my ear, his breath kissing my wet neck. It chased goosebumps down my skin and I rolled over to face him, tucking my head under his chin. I inhaled the fresh, clean scent that soothed me and pressed my hot cheek to his neck.

"He was the only one… I moved in with my aunt and he lived next door. I didn't talk for months after they were—after what happened. Kyle was the first person I talked to. The only person I talked to for months. He's the first person I ever told, and he didn't care. And by not caring, he cared completely. He didn't ask me about it all the time like other people when they found out. He knew, but it didn't matter to him. He's been my best friend since I was twelve." My lips ghosted against his neck as I spoke. I was glad I could finally tell him why I couldn't leave Kyle. The lump in my throat finally broke up and eased away.

Adriane Leigh

"I understand," he murmured and stroked my hair.

"You do?" I looked into his breathtaking, green eyes.

"Yeah." His eyes shone with emotion. "But don't you think it's unfair to be with someone just because of the past you share with them?"

I stared at him for long moments, our gazes locked as I processed his words. "That's why I took off the ring." I held up my naked ring finger.

"I noticed," he whispered and pressed his warm lips to my hand in a reverent kiss. Then the lights flickered and the house fell under a cloud of black. Minimal light passed through the windows as the storm blazed outside.

"You okay? Want me to get a flashlight?" Tristan asked. I shook my head in response as I curled into his warm body and fell asleep, feeling all cried out and lighter than I had in months.

* * *

"GEORGIA, WAKE UP." Tristan ran his palm over my forehead soothingly. "You had a nightmare," he murmured as my eyes flew open. I searched his face, needing reassurance he was really here, I was really wrapped in his arms. I tucked my head into his chest, nestled my nose into the crook of his neck, and inhaled his familiar, fresh scent

"Wanna talk about it?" He continued to swipe his fingers through the damp hair at my forehead.

"It was about you. I'd lost you. I was so afraid. We were swimming and then you were gone. Just disappeared. You slipped under the water and you were gone and I searched and it was too late. I was too late." Tears leaked down my cheeks. He swiped one away with the pad of his thumb.

"I'm here, Georgia. I'm not going anywhere." He folded me into his arms and rocked me back and forth. He held me in his arms as the nightmare of seeing Tristan slip away from me played on repeat in my mind. Finally the dim morning light shone through the windows. The weather radio crackled to life and a warning went out over the airwaves.

"It's getting worse," Tristan murmured. He hadn't slept after my nightmare either. I sighed deeply. I knew what this meant. "The storm's moving closer, we have to evacuate." Tristan moved from his position behind me on the couch. I finally stopped to listen and heard the wind howling outside, the storm coming through the cracks of the house causing a haunting whistling noise.

"Is it mandatory?" I sat up on the couch and wrapped the blanket around me.

"We have to leave now." he nodded. "Grab a few things and we'll go to a hotel."

"Okay," I whispered, my brain thick with the fog of exhaustion. I'd bared my soul to him and the pain in my heart had fallen at my feet and splintered into a thousand pieces. I felt like I didn't know who I was anymore, the pain I'd worn like a shield for so long was gone. He affected me like no one I'd ever met, no one since Kyle and I had first gotten together when we were teenagers. It terrified me.

"Pack up some things and meet me back here."

"Okay." I plodded to my bedroom and threw a few changes of clothes into my suitcase. I tossed in *Tristan and Isolde* and headed back to the kitchen. Tristan stood jangling my keys off his finger and a small smile lifted his face.

"Ready?"

I nodded in response. I gave the house one last glance before turning and making my way out the front door with Tristan's hand locked with mine.

We drove into Wilmington and every decent-sized town up Interstate 40—"no vacancy" signs at every hotel we passed. We were too late; we'd taken too long to evacuate and it was my fault.

"We're not going to find anything," I frowned.

"We will, we'll just keep moving inland, we'll find something, Georgia." He squeezed my knee through my jeans as he pulled onto the interstate heading further west.

After a few more towns I finally insisted we

turn around.

"I should go back to D.C. We're not going to find anything, Tristan."

"No way, we'll find something, Georgia." He turned to face me.

"We won't. I'll take you back to the house and you can drive Gavin's truck back to Jacksonville."

"You want me to go back to Jacksonville? To leave you?" Tristan's jaw tightened.

"It's the only way." I averted my gaze to the rainy world outside the window.

"That's what you want?" I could feel his eyes blazing into me.

I knew if I told him anything other than yes he wouldn't go, and we'd run out of options. "Yes," I said blankly.

"Fine." Tristan whipped through a service drive and headed back the way we'd came.

"ARE YOU SURE this is what you want to do? 'Cause it's not what I want," he said a while later as we found ourselves back in the kitchen of the beach house, Gavin's keys in his hands, a large duffel bag hanging off his shoulder.

"It's only temporary," I forced a smile. It isn't what I wanted to do either, but we didn't have a choice. "We'll be back when the storm passes. You've got your boat and I have to come back to lock up the house for the season. Got everything?"

"This is it." He lifted the bag on his shoulder.

"Okay." I leaned in and gave him a quick squeeze.

"Georgia, I—"

"No goodbyes, just a few days," I said before lifting to give him a peck on the lips. "Really." I squeezed his forearms and gave him my brightest, most reassuring smile. He sucked his lower lip into his mouth and I watched his eyes—the eyes I'd been lost in all summer—swirl and darken with emotion. I bit the inside of my cheek to stop myself from begging him to stay with me.

"You could go with me," he mumbled, dusting the pad of his thumb along my cheekbone.

I shook my head. "No, I can't. It's only a few days," I said softly. He licked his lips before dropping his head and breaking eye contact with me. My heart thudded in my chest as a stray, golden lock of hair fell over his eyebrow. I brushed it away with my fingertips and stroked the skin along his cheek.

"A few days," I said again as water welled in my eyes.

"I'll call you."

"'Kay."

"Okay." He pulled me into a tight embrace, my feet lifted off the ground, and I wrapped my arms around his neck. "This summer was... perfect," he mumbled in my ear.

"The best," I whispered and squeezed my

eyes tightly to stop the tears from leaking out.

"See you in a few days?" He pulled away from me.

"A few days." I pulled away and stroked his cheek again, memorizing the sharp angle of his jaw, the stubble that swept his golden skin, the line of his nose, the sparkle in his ridiculously green eyes.

His grin tipped sideways, breaking my heart, before he traced my top lip with his thumb. "I'm all bad for you, Georgia, you deserve a man better than me, but I'll make good for you." His forehead grazed mine. "I promise I'll be good enough for you."

"Tristan… You're not bad for me." I croaked through the pain that radiated in my chest.

"Bye," his lips whispered against mine, "Georgia."

CONTINUE READING…

Adriane Leigh

WHISKEY GIRL EXCERPT

copyright 2020 by Adriane Leigh

The first time I met Augusta Belle Branson, she was fixin' on killin' herself.

Said the minute I'd walked up, she was tryin' to decide if jumpin' off the bridge in the center—where the water was deep and the current stronger—would be a swifter end, or if she should jump near the edge, where jagged limestone slabs anchored the slow-moving current.

Certain death for sure.

I replayed the split second when the Indian summer sun burst through the orange oak leaves, a halo of warmth enveloping her.

Like an angel. Stardust sparkling straight from heaven, ploppin' her in my path.

And then she turned, the most startling shade of liquid amber eyes breathing something real and alive, like fire, into my soul.

That same something I'd been runnin' from—

or chasin', dependin' on how you looked at it—just about every day since.

I settled myself on the lone wooden stool that awaited at center stage, my thoughts drawing back to the present. My head swam, but the old familiar chords floated on through the current of whiskey in my blood, and I strummed the first few notes of a song I wrote a lot of nights ago by an act of sheer muscle memory.

Old acoustic guitar resting on my knee, my first and third fingers in position on the strings, the opening chords of "Whiskey Girl" bled from my fingers.

Every chord, another dagger.

Every whispered lyric, my undoing.

I still didn't know what the fuck had overtaken me the night I'd written this song in a fevered rush.

Well, the booze might have played a part, but I happened to think my best shit came out of uninhibited states.

I'd just had a fuckton of uninhibited states recently.

And the harder the liquor, the more she haunted me.

Whiskey Girl.

My poisoned lullaby.

The crowd of a few hundred erupted into a standing ovation when I ended with the final, emotion-charged words.

The irony of this song was it was the one that'd launched my career. The first single to hit radio waves and then the top spot on the Billboard charts, and brought reporters, music executives, long-lost family members I wasn't even really sure I was related to, and too much other scum with an end game that carried dollar signs to my front doorstep.

I'd moved to Nashville a rising star and left two years later, middle finger in the air as I tossed my once-promising music career out with last night's liquor bottles in favor of the open road.

Chasing something.

Not finding the one thing I needed.

Playing local honky-tonks for a fraction of the money I could have made.

But the truth was, the road was the only place I could find my happy.

A familiar ball of pain formed in my throat as I stood, pushing my guitar over one shoulder and bowing deeply. I couldn't see a single face behind the glaring stage lights, but still, some part of me pretended she could be out there, that I was singing to her.

That she would hear her song and find her way back to me.

After hundreds of faceless crowds and too many bottles of Tennessee whiskey to bother counting, I still felt the pull inside me to travel to every town in America if that's what it took to find her.

Hell, maybe she was happily married with a few kids, a dog, and a fucking minivan by now.

I nodded my head, giving one last wave to

the crowd in the dark beyond, then left the stage, taking the steps two at a time and angling past the curtains to head for the tiny-ass dressing room this dive bar provided. Heading for another chug of amber gold before packing my shit into my truck and hitting the road.

I pushed a hand through my hair, thinking maybe a shower would be in order before I bailed, when a curvy little thing backed right up into me.

My palms landed on her shoulders, warm blond waves falling in a cascade over one side. The heady scent of peaches and honey filled my nostrils. My eyes slammed closed and brought me back to summer nights under a giant oak, fireflies melding together with the stars above like a painting.

"Sorry, I just dropped my phone." The sweet-scented creature spun, brilliant smile falling from her face when our eyes made contact for the first time.

Every coldhearted memory slammed into my chest like a pallet of bricks.

I narrowed my eyes, gaze tracing the familiar yet unfamiliar angles of her porcelain face.

She was thinner now, cheeks sharp slashes of bone that highlighted her always-devastating round eyes and full lips. It was her, all right. I'd know this woman anywhere.

"Hi, Fallon." I'd been dreamin' of this moment for the better part of a decade, and still, my heart wasn't prepared for those two words.

My name on her lips left me with a toxic reaction.

My whiskey girl.

My damnation and my salvation.

"I need a fucking minute." I dropped my hands from her shoulders, her skin still haunting my fingertips, and walked straight down the narrow hallway, pushing the rusted back door open so hard the hinges protested.

Warm night air filled my lungs, replacing the empty feeling seeing her again had left.

"Fallon…" Hell, she'd followed me out.

And hell if wanted her to, but I didn't *not* want her to either.

The emotions bombarding my mind were just a-fucking-bout unbearable.

"I said I *need* a fucking minute." The sentence came out as more of a growl than I intended. Before she could reply, I stomped across the potholed parking lot, aiming for my heavy-duty Ford.

I yanked the door open, digging behind the driver's seat for a fresh bottle of my favorite recipe.

I couldn't be bothered to retrieve the half-full bottle I'd left in my dressing room. I had to get as far the fuck away from her just to clear my head and process what her being here even meant.

My hands circled the neck of the bottle, and I opened it in a flash, chugging back the first warm bite of pleasure I'd been craving.

I tossed the cap on my dash and fished the

keys out of my pocket, about to climb into the cab and make hay, when fingertips painted a dark navy filtered into my vision and back out again, my goddamn truck keys hanging from one finger.

"Fuck," I bit out, crawling out of the cab and swiping for the keys.

My reactions were a helluva lot slower than I thought they were. *How much of that bottle had I drunk before the show?* I shook the thought from my head, realizing this was probably about close to my average state of play on any given day. Runnin' away from the life Augusta Belle and I'd had took something out of me. Something only whiskey could fill.

"I don't care what your stupid ass does on your own time, but you're not dying on mine, Fallon Gentry."

My head pounded then. A whole fucking sentence out of her pretty pink lips, and my body's old dependable reaction to her infuriating every cell of me.

I'd never been in control when it came to Augusta. Shouldn't have been surprised it was no different now.

"As irritating as ever, I see," I said, swiping for my keys one more time and missing before I stumbled off around her, whiskey bottle clutched in my hand and hell on my mind.

Augusta was back, and there wasn't enough whiskey in the state of Tennessee to help me deal.

Adriane Leigh

...CONTINUE READING

REBEL PRIEST EXCERPT

copyright 2020 by Adriane Leigh

"The dark night of the soul? Mind telling me what the hell that was about?" The heavy wooden door echoed through the tight chamber when it slammed against the door jamb.

Bastien remained still across the small sacristy, head bowed as he continued to work quietly, deft fingers sliding thin, golden ropes of sacred fabric through his fingers. "I'd rather know what you think."

Frustration thickened my blood. "I'm your dark night of the soul?! I think you went a step too far."

"If that's what you call a step too far I'd hate to hear what you call indecent." His body was against mine in an instant, my breasts heaving with shallow irritation and grazing the fabric of his vestments.

This profoundly infuriating man was under

my skin like no one else had ever been, and just like a bad tattoo, I'd pay a professional to gouge him out of my soul if I could.

"This, for instance," he hissed, "is surely a step too close to your precious comfort zone." His body pressed closer, the deep ridge of his arousal cutting at my hip and causing my throat to crack and turn to dust. "Don't trick yourself into believing that you know *you* more than I do, Tressa."

His dark eyes glinted in the dim light, heartbeat vibrating in my ears the only noise in the room. "What's that supposed to mean?"

I couldn't catch my breath, his fingers crawling their way past my wrists, grazing the underside of my elbows before his thumbs dug in and he was as far deep inside my own heart as he could possibly go.

"You like the dance, sweet dove, but just when things get intimate you pull away."

His scathing truth cut like a hot blade.

"No," I squeaked.

His soft chuckle my only reply, my eyelids already glued shut in opposition of his words.

"You think you only show me the side of you you want me to see," Bastien's thumb danced the arch of my brow, "but I see so much more than that." His eyes flicked down to my lips, hips working softly against mine.

"I'm trained to see the broken parts you've spent a lifetime hiding. I'm trained to be your light in the darkness, Tressa, but all that darkness," his thumbs worked inside my elbows, swaying me against his body as he grit against my neck, "it weighs on me some days. Seminary doesn't teach a flesh and blood man how to channel all that darkness into…" he flexed behind his robes, my body humming with pure desire for anything more he had to give, *"productive activities."*

I didn't have a reply for him, the way he swallowed my space and caused my heart to thrum like a hummingbird was distracting enough, but his skin setting flame to mine was beyond unbearable.

"What about you, then?" I summoned my earlier anger. "You fancy yourself some sort of holier than thou saint? Forgive me Father, but I call *bullshit."*

Bastien's eyes held mine, the amusement chasing through his chocolate irises giving me enough satisfaction to live on for days.

I squared my shoulders. "You're a prisoner to your belief."

His eyebrows rose, shock striking him before his face settled to that same well-orchestrated calm he reserved for his parishioners. "You can bet I'm a prisoner, but not for the reasons you think."

His admission caught me off guard, but not more than the next moment did.

His palms caught my face, thumbs trailing down the warmth of my throat before he smashed our lips together.

His kiss defiled as much as it gave life.

He raped me to the depths of my soul without ever removing a strip of my clothing.

"But that's where my beliefs with the church diverge." He lips teased at the corners of my mouth before his tongue darted out, tasting the bow of my top lip.

Oh sweet fucking heaven.

"I happen to believe it isn't living if you're not breaking a rule every now and again."

He caught the soft whimper on my lips with his, swallowing it instantly before his tongue pushed past the barrier and he was sheathed in me again.

His taste, far deadlier than I'd remembered.

"Despite what my church may believe," Bastien's thumbs hooked at my shirt, the warm pads of his fingertips sliding against my skin and cutting through my nerves like hot butter, "I can't renounce you."

His palms slid up my torso, divesting me of my shirt while one hand cupped a shiny chalice, drips of wine already making their way between my breasts. Staining the satin bra I wore, pooling in my navel, soaking a rebel river of red overtop the elastic of my panties.

"I know the taste of sin, sweet Tressa, I've tasted it every night in my dreams. Craving you is a new and deadlier form of hell than the last I'd overcome." He dropped to his knees, the empty cup slipping to the floor and soaking his white robes in scarlet before his tongue met my flesh in slow swipes, eyes glinting as he held me flush to his mouth.

Soft mewls formed on my lips as my body fell apart in his arms, limbs loose as he worked his way up my body, tongue tasting every inch of the blessed wine from my skin as he went.

"I am very surely a prisoner *to you,* my sweet dove."

READ REBEL PRIEST

Adriane Leigh

MORE FROM ADRIANE LEIGH

or check out my novellas

under the pen name

BAD FOR LOVE

<u>Aria Cole in KU!</u>

Adriane Leigh

Want to learn about the real life TRUE STORY of a rebel and a saint that fell in love and inspired this book?

Check out my new podcast: *The Creative Life Project with Adriane Leigh!*

YOUTUBE:

http://bit.ly/2CoOb0t

APPLE:
https://apple.co/2TEB1Hp

ANCHOR:
https://anchor.fm/adriane-leigh

Coming soon to Spotify, Stitcher, Breaker, and more!

BAD FOR LOVE

Join Adriane's mailing list for **exclusive** material and *free e-books* ➜ https://bit.ly/2WraRWb
Facebook➜ https://bit.ly/2MAoygS
Reading group ➜ https://bit.ly/2LaHJNe
Website ➜ www.adrianeleigh.com
Instagram➜ https://www.instagram.com/adriane.leigh.writer

Adriane Leigh is a USA Today and Amazon Top 20 best-selling author of more than forty-five independent contemporary and new adult romance titles. She was born with a book in her hand and won her first Young Authors Award before the age of ten. She earned a literature degree, founded, hosted, and organized international book conventions, and lives with her husband and daughters on Lake Michigan. She enjoys good wine, bad reality TV, walks in the woods, and travel to dreamy destinations.

★★ Hot Reviews! ★★

"Adriane Leigh delivered a beautiful slow burn second chance romance that truly made us feel with twists that made our hearts plummet and soar." **- TotallyBooked Blog**

Adriane Leigh

"With prose that is beautiful and confident, affecting without being maudlin-Whiskey Girl squeezed my heart while continuously bringing tears of joy to my eyes, and I had to take a very long, deep breath in the end to fully absorb all the emotions it left in me. I was totally captivated from the first page and it left me in absolute awe of this author's talent-every moment between these characters leapt from the page with profound emotion. This was undoubtedly one of the most moving books I've read in a long time." **- Natasha is a Book Junkie**

"Sizzling chemistry, a glamorous world, plot twists...a perfect combination held together with Adriane Leigh's addictive writing. I dove into this world, and didn't want to come up for air. I can't wait for more!" **- Alessandra Torre, Hollywood Dirt**

BAD FOR LOVE

If you or someone you know struggles with mental illness, the Substance Abuse and Mental Health Services Administration (<u>SAMHSA</u>): **(800) 662-4357** *runs a* **24-hour mental health hotline** *that provides education, support, and connections to treatment. It also offers an online <u>Behavioral Health Treatment Locator</u> to help you find suitable behavioral health treatment programs. You are not alone.*